Books by Dick Francis

Published by POCKET BOOKS

Dick Francis
BLOOD SPORT

PUBLISHED BY POCKET BOOKS NEW YORK

POCKET BOOKS, a Simon & Schuster division of
GULF & WESTERN CORPORATION
1230 Avenue of the Americas, New York, N.Y. 10020

Published by arrangement with Harper & Row, Publishers, Inc.
Library of Congress Catalog Card Number: 68-11821

ISBN: 0-671-42277-4

First Pocket Books printing April, 1975

10 9 8 7 6 5 4 3

POCKET and colophon are trademarks of Simon & Schuster.

Printed in the U.S.A.

BLOOD SPORT

Chapter 1

I awoke with foreboding. My hand closed in a reflex on the Luger under the pillow. I listened, acutely attentive. No sound. No quick surreptitious slither, no rub of cloth on cloth, no half-controlled pulse-driven breath. No enemy hovering. Slowly, relaxing, I turned half over and squinted at the room. A quiet, empty, ugly room. One third of what for want of a less cozy word I called home.

Bright sunshine bypassed the thin pink curtains, spilling a gold slash on the faded brown Wilton. I didn't like pink. Also I didn't have the energy it would take to argue the landlord into changing to blue. After eight months I knew he never renewed anything until it had fallen to bits.

In spite of the prevailing calm the feeling of foreboding deepened and then identified itself and dissolved into a less threatening, more general state of gloom. Sunday morning, June 20. The beginning of three weeks' leave.

I rolled back onto my stomach and shut my eyes against the sun, and took my hand six inches from the Luger, which was far enough, and wondered how long a man could sleep if he really put his mind to it. Even a man who never slept soundly to start with. Three weeks, the three obligatory overdue weeks, could be got through more easily asleep.

Three millenniums of sleep lay under the pillow. The nine-millimeter equalizer, my inseparable friend. It went with me everywhere, to beaches, to bathrooms, to other beds than my own. It was there to save my life. Not to take it. I had lived through a lot of temptations, and I lived with that too.

The telephone bell put paid to the three weeks before they had gone half an hour.

"'Lo," I said blearily, balancing the receiver on the pillow.

"Gene?"

"Uh-huh."

"You haven't gone away then." There was relief in the voice, the voice of my boss. I looked at my watch. Ten o'clock.

"No," I said unnecessarily. He knew I wasn't going away. I didn't understand his relief. It was missing when he spoke again.

"How about a day on the river?"

He had a motor cruiser somewhere on the upper Thames. I'd never seen it. Hadn't been asked before.

"Invitation or order?" I said, yawning.

He hesitated. "Whichever you'll accept."

What a man. You did more for him than you believed you would, every time.

"Where do I go, and when?"

"My daughter will fetch you," he said. "She'll be there in about half an hour. Family party. Boating clothes. Come as you are."

"Sure," I said. Complete with stubble, Luger and shorts. A riot. I never wore pajamas. They slowed you up too much.

Boating clothes, I decided, were grayish brown cotton trousers and an olive green nylon jersey shirt. I carried the Luger with me in the left-hand pocket when the doorbell rang. One never really knew. But a look through the wide-angled spyhole showed it was only Keeble's daughter, as arranged. I opened up.

"Mr. Hawkins?" she said hesitantly, looking from me to the dingy brass six screwed onto the solid dark-stained wood.

"That's right." I smiled. "Come in."

She walked past me and I shut the door, interested to notice that four flights of stairs hadn't left her breathless, as they did most visitors. I lived high up for that purpose.

"I was just finishing my coffee," I said. "Would you like some?"

"It's very kind of you, but Daddy said not to waste time, he wants to be off upriver as soon as possible."

Keeble's daughter was just like her photograph on Daddy's desk. Half woman, still at school. Short bouncy dark hair and watchful dark eyes, a rounded body slimming down, a self-possessed touch-me-not expression, and an endearing gaucheness in her present situation.

She looked cautiously round the sitting room which neither she nor I nor anyone else would have classed as elegant living. The landlord's furniture was junk-shop stuff and I had made no effort to improve it. My total contributions to the scene were two rows of books on the shelves and in one corner a tin trunk of oddments which I had never bothered to unpack. A drawn-back curtain revealed the kitchen alcove and its entire contents: cupboard, refrigerator, sink, and stove, all of them showing their age.

One went through the sitting room to the bedroom, through the bedroom to the bathroom, and through the bathroom to the fire escape. The flat had everything but a drawbridge and a moat, and it had taken me weeks to find it. Only the tiny spyhole had been lacking, and the landlord had been furious when he finally noticed I had installed it. It had cost me three months' rent in advance to convince him it wasn't there for the sole purpose of being out when he came.

I watched Keeble's daughter search for something nice to say about my living quarters and give up the struggle with a defeated shake of her young head. I could have told her that I had once had a better flat, a spacious comfortable first-floor front with a balcony overlooking a tree-dotted square. It had proved too accessible to unwanted guests. I had vacated it on a stretcher.

"I'll fetch my jacket," I said, finishing the coffee. "And then we'll go."

She nodded, looking relieved, oppressed already by the emptiness of my home life. Five minutes of it had been enough, for her.

I went into the bedroom, picked the jacket off the bed, and transferred the Luger from my trousers into its built-in underarm holster, fastening it there with a press stud on a strap. Then, coat over arm, I dumped the dirty coffee cup in the sink, pulled the curtain across the kitchen, opened the front door, and let myself and Miss Keeble out.

Four uneventful stories down we emerged into the quiet sunlit Putney street, and she looked back and up at the solid old converted house. It needed paint and oozed respectability, exactly like its row of neighbors.

"I wasn't sure I'd come to the right place. Daddy just said the fourth house along."

"He gives me a lift home, sometimes."

"Yes, he said so." She turned to the white Austin standing at the curb and paused with the key in her hand. "Do you mind if I drive?"

"Of course not."

She smiled for the first time since she'd arrived, a quick flashing affair which verged on friendliness. She unlocked her door, climbed in, and reached over to unlatch the opposite one for me. The first thing I noticed as I bent to get in were the L plates lying on the back seat.

"When did you pass the test?" I said mildly.

"Well . . ." the smile lingered, "as a matter of fact, yesterday."

For all that, she drove very well, careful but confident, quiet with the gears though a bit heavy with the hand signals. She crept somewhat tentatively around the Chiswick circle and up the slope to the M4. The big blue motorway sign said no L drivers and her nose twitched mischievously as we passed it.

"Did you come this way to fetch me?" I asked idly.

She edged into the slow lane and hit forty.

"Er, no. I live in a hostel with about sixty other girls in South Ken. Daddy just rang me and said as I'd got the car up in London this weekend I could collect you and meet him in Henley. Sort of spur-of-the-moment thing."

"I see."

We came to the end of the fifty-mile-an-hour limit and her foot went down with determination.

"Do I scare you?" The needle quivered on sixty-five.

I smiled wryly. "No."

"Actually . . ." Her hands gripped the wheel with the

tension of inexperience. "Actually, you don't look as if you'd scare easily."

I glanced at her in surprise. I look ordinary. Quiet and ordinary. And very useful it is, too.

"Anyway," she went on frankly, "I asked Daddy about coming this way, and he said he guessed your nerves would stand it. He seemed to find it very funny, for some reason or other."

"He has his own brand of humor."

"Mm." She drove for several miles in silence, concentrating on the road. The speed dropped slowly down to fifty again, and I guessed she was finding the motorway not such pure fun as she'd imagined. The usual number of Sunday Jim Clarks were showing off in the fast lane and family outings with Grandma driving from the back seat were bumbling about in the slow. We went down the center and pulled out bravely now and then to pass an airport bus.

Eventually, in thinner traffic after Windsor, she said doubtfully, "You do . . . er . . . work for Daddy?"

"Yes. Why not?"

"Well, no reason why not. I mean," she looked embarrassed, "I mean, I can't remember him ever asking anyone from work . . . Well, he just doesn't usually, that's all." She looked as if she wished she hadn't started.

"A kind thought," I suggested; and wondered what he wanted. Not just to give me a sunny day out. As his daughter said, he didn't do that sort of thing.

We made it to Henley with the paint intact, and she parked neatly in a large graveled enclosure by the railway station. Her hands trembled slightly as she locked the doors, and I realized that it must have been her longest drive, as well as the fastest.

"You drove beautifully," I said sincerely. "Like a veteran."

"Oh." She gave a laugh which was half a cough and looked relieved and pleased. "Well, thank you." She would be more relaxed, I knew, on the way back, and less strung up when she got there. To give and to remove confidence were tools of my trade, and there was no union to say I couldn't use them on Sundays.

"*Flying Linnet*—that's our boat—will be somewhere along the bank," she said. "It isn't." She smiled again and gestured, "That way."

We walked down to the river and along the neatly built broad tarmac towpath, where half the town seemed to be out feeding the ducks. The sun sparkled on the dark-green water and there was a queue at the boatyard for rowing boats and punts. There were gardens and lawns and seats, and a bowling green, and a playground with a slide and swings, all of them sprinkled with sunny Sunday faces and murmuring summer voices. Families and couples and groups: few alone. Three weeks alone, I thought bleakly. I could spend them beside the deep green river feeding ducks, and just jump in when I couldn't stand any more of it.

"There's Daddy," said Keeble's daughter, pointing. The sun lay along her light-brown arm and shifted in burned toffee shadows on the curves of her orange-tan dress. Too young for me, I thought inconsequentially. Or, rather, I was too old. Aeons too old. Forty still lay a couple of years ahead but I could have told Methuselah a thing or two.

Keeble had stepped ashore from one of the boats moored top to tail along the towpath and was walking toward us, hand outstretched, welcoming smile on face. My boss, except for an open-necked shirt, looked his usual weekday self, a short slightly chubby man with a mild manner and a faintly anxious expression. The light blue-gray eyes blinked freely as usual behind the unimpressive spectacles and as usual he had missed a patch while shaving. Premature baldness had made him look fifty at thirty-five but, far from regretting this, he believed it was the cause of his rapid promotion over well-thatched contemporaries. He may have been right. He looked harmless, cautious, unambitious, one of nature's safest plodders. It was eight years since he had inherited me along with the rest of the setup, and to discern the cutting brain behind the waffle had taken me two minutes flat.

"Gene," he said. "Glad you could come." He pumped my hand up and down perfunctorily, the social gesture as meaningless to him as to me, and we exchanged smiles to match. For his daughter the warmth came from the heart. She kissed him affectionately on the cheek and his eyes held a glimmering pride I had never seen in him before.

"Well, Lynnie my love, you got here safely. Or did you let Gene do the driving?"

"Do me a favor," she said. "He didn't even flinch."

Keeble flicked me an amused glance, and I repeated the compliment to her skill, with her father nodding his thanks to me over her head, knowing exactly why I said it.

They turned and began to walk back along the path, gesturing to me to come. Keeble's boat, the one they stopped at, was a graceful neat-looking fiberglass cruiser with a cabin forward and a large open cockpit at the back, the decks spotless and the chromium shining. Sitting casually side by side on the pale-blue plastic upholstery were a man and a woman, both of whom raised smiling faces at our approach and neither of whom got up.

Lynnie jumped down into the boat and kissed the woman, and Keeble stepped carefully after.

"Come aboard," he said to me, and again in his tone there was a choice. An invitation or an order, whichever I would accept. I opted for the invitation, and embarked on more than the *Flying Linnet*.

"My wife Joan," said Keeble, stretching a hand to the seated woman. "Gene Hawkins, honey."

Joan Keeble was a frail birdlike woman with a coyness of manner left over from the time when she was pretty. She twinkled her eyes at me, inviting admiration. I scraped some up, and exchanged the necessary platitudes about weather, boating, and driving daughters. Keeble waded into this with a wave towards the man sitting beside her.

"You two haven't met . . ." He hesitated a fraction. "Dave . . . Gene, this is Dave Teller."

Teller stood up, shook hands economically, and said he

was glad to know me. He wore a sloppy wrinkled pale-blue shirt hanging out over patched cotton trousers, battered plimsolls on his feet, and a dirty old baseball cap on his head. American, well educated, prosperous, assured: the categories clicked over from habit in my assessing mind. Also he was a lean man nearing fifty, with a strong beaky nose, straightforward eyes, and a marvelous dentist.

Keeble offered no information beyond the bald introduction, but bustled about getting his ship ready to put to sea. His yell into the cabin for a certain Peter to come and help produced no results. I stuck my head through the door and saw a boy of about twelve engrossed in fitting a new roll of film into a small simple camera.

"Peter!" his father yelled.

Peter heaved a martyred sigh, scrambled the back of the camera shut, and went out past me with his eyes down and his fingers winding the knob. Sure-footed, he stepped without looking onto the narrow side of the boat and from there to the towpath.

"He'll fall in one day," Lynnie said to the world in general. Her brother didn't even hear. Still concentrating on his camera with one hand he was slowly untying the rope from the mooring ring with the other, crouching down on the tarmac in his clean black jeans and getting up with two large dusty patches on the knees. Pointing his viewfinder at a passing formation of ducks he clicked the shutter and with a serious, absorbed expression wound on the film.

Farther up the path Keeble and Teller were undoing the bow rope, talking amicably in the sun. Lynnie and her mother straightened the cushions and coiled the ropes and fussed around over a lot of nothing, chatting trivialities. I wondered what the hell I was doing there and felt out of contact with everything around me. Not a new feeling, but recurring more often. The two levels of living were growing farther apart. The day-to-day social level had lost all meaning, and underneath, where there should have been rock, had opened a void of shriveling loneliness. It was getting worse. The present was bad enough: the

future an abyss. Only work brought my splintering self
into any sort of whole, and I knew well enough that it was
the work itself which had started the process. That and
Caroline. Or, to be more accurate, Caroline's husband.

"I say, hold this rope, will you?" Peter said. I took the
wet snake he offered. "Hi," he added, seeing me properly
for the first time, "who are you?"

"Anybody's guess," I said with more truth than sense,
and his mother stared at me with astonishment and told
him my name.

Keeble came back on board and started the engine.
Teller stood up on the small forward deck and cast off the
bow rope when Keeble told him, and Peter left it until
almost too late to leap on board with the stern rope. The
camera bounced on the cord round his neck. "Birthday
present from Gran," he said to Lynnie with pride. "Super,
isn't it?"

"You'll drop it in the river, if you aren't careful."

"This is only my second film. I used the first one up on
the boys at school. Do you think those ducks will come
out all right?"

"I expect you had your finger over the shutter."

"I've got a book in there." He nodded toward the cabin,
expertly sifting out the affection behind her sarcasm and
showing no resentment. "It tells you about exposures and
focuses. I think I'll just check what it says about sunny
days. It was cloudy dull all week at school."

I don't belong here, I thought. I wished I was asleep.

The *Flying Linnet* nosed upstream through a scatter of
rowboats, Keeble at the wheel, Teller sitting forward still
on the cabin roof, and Peter trying to get past Lynnie
teasing him in the cabin doorway. Joan Keeble sat down
on the wide seat across the back and patted the place
next to her for me to join her. With an effort I did so, but
after a minute or two, in the middle of apparently idle
hostessy chat, she pulled me back to attention by trying
delicately to find out who I was and why I had been
invited, while not wanting to have me realize that she
didn't know.

I could play that sort of game forever. Inference on

inference. I didn't know the answer to why was I there, but that she needed to ask it, that indeed she had asked it, told me a great deal about noncontact between Keeble and his wife, and opened new doors into Keeble himself. I knew then why he'd never before asked me home. It was one thing to employ a microscope, but another to put oneself under the lens. I thought it all the odder that he'd done it now.

As if he could feel my mind on the back of his neck he turned round and said, "The lock's just ahead." I stood up and joined him, and Peter gave up his struggle and went back to his duty with the stern rope.

"Marsh Lock," Lynnie said, standing beside me and looking forward through the windshield. "Not an easy one, from this side, going upstream."

When we got nearer I saw what she meant. The broad stretch of river narrowed abruptly to the lock gates on the left and the weir on the right, alongside. Baby whirlpools and trails of bubbles met us fifty yards away with larger eddies and convolutions bubbling up as we went on. The boat tended to swing sideways under their power, and Keeble spun the wheel rapidly to keep her straight. Ahead of us water in tons tumbled over the weir, green and brown and splashing white, thundering down in great curving leaps, smelling of mustiness and mud.

A low wooden wall divided the lock approach from the turbulent weir water, and to the calm side of the barrier Keeble neatly steered his boat. Teller standing at the bow threw his rope over the hook on a mooring post there, and Peter slung a loop over a bollard at the stern.

I looked idly over the side of the boat, over the wall, up to the weir. Bouncing, tumbling, foaming, sweeping away back into the width of the river, the rough water looked superb in the sun. I felt the warmth and the fine spray mixed on my face and wondered whether if someone fell in there he would ever come up.

The lock gates opened, the downcoming boats chugged out, and the *Flying Linnet* went in. Teller and Peter did their stuff mooring us to the side and Peter took a photograph of the boat in the lock. Water surged through the sluices in the upper gates, lifting us up, and in ten minutes we were going out of the lock onto another broad calm stretch of river, six feet higher than the one below.

"There are fifty locks on the Thames," Keeble said. "Lechlade is as far up as you can go except in a rowing boat, and that's about 300 feet above sea level."

"Quite a staircase," I commented.

"The Victorians," he nodded, "were a brilliant lot. They built them."

Teller stood on the foredeck holding the coil of rope, the peak of his baseball cap pointing forward like an attentive bird. I watched him, speculating, and Keeble followed the direction of my eyes and gave me only silence to work on.

Less than half a mile upstream from the lock we made an obviously prearranged stop at a riverside pub, Teller jumping ashore with his rope and fending the boat off the concrete edges as we drifted toward it. He and Peter tied expert knots, and everyone followed them ashore.

We drank sitting on a ring of uncomfortable metal chairs round a table with a sun umbrella spiked through its center. Lynnie and Peter had Cokes and without consultation Keeble bought Scotch for the rest of us. Joan sipped hers with a pursed mouth and screwed eyes, as if it were a mite too strong for fragile little her, but I noticed she finished a long way first. Teller left his untouched for several minutes and then tossed it back in king-sized gulps. Keeble drank in pauses, revolving his glass in his hand and squinting through it at the sun. They were talking about the river, and other days on it, and other weather. On either side of us, round more umbrellas, sat more family parties much the same; Sunday morning drinks, Sunday lunch, Sunday snooze, Sunday *Express,* Sunday supper, Sunday Night at the London Palladium . . . ; safe little families in a sheltered routine, well intentioned and more or less content. Even Keeble fitted in. Whereas I . . . was apart.

"Drink," Keeble said. "You're on holiday."

Faced with instant sharp curiosity from the rest of his family I meekly picked up my glass, still full when theirs were empty. It felt wrong to drink in the morning; it raised subconscious bells of alarm. I liked the taste of alcohol all right, but couldn't afford its effects. Alcohol encouraged you to put your trust in luck, and I was better off trusting a clear head. Consequently I sometimes didn't touch the stuff for weeks on end and on that morning had had none for nearly a month.

Keeble watched me swallow, the whiskey as vivid and familiar as a long-lost friend. The extent to which I was ever on holiday lay in the jacket across my knees, a pound of deadly mechanism in an underarm holster; but it did seem most unlikely that I would need it on the Thames. When Teller ordered a refill, I drank that too. And then, since it was my turn, a third.

Peter lasted the course to three Cokes, and then wandered away with his camera poised, looking for excuses to use it. Next door a boatyard, like the one at Henley, was doing a roaring trade in punts. Four of the pub's more enthusiastic customers were having trouble stepping aboard, and Teller said, chuckling, "What's the fine for punting under the influence . . . ?"

"A soaking," Lynnie said. "Silly nits."

The punt pole waved recklessly as they set off but the four men didn't fall in. The punt skidded ten feet up the river and hit the pub's landing stage with a thump that tumbled them into a leg-waving heap. I tried to laugh with everyone else and only succeeded in feeling more remote than ever.

We finished the drinks, re-embarked, and went up through the next lock, Harbour, to an unpopulated green pasture stretch of river, where we moored for lunch. Peter swam, jumping off the boat repeatedly in glittering splashes, and Lynnie helped her mother in the cabin, preparing the food. Teller sprawled lazily on the back seat, and Keeble sat down with a Sunday newspaper and unfolded it, and I wearily began to wonder just when he would come to the point.

The point, however, was the newspaper. We had arrived.

"Read that," he said, tapping a small paragraph on an inside page.

I read it.

There is still no sign of Chrysalis, free in Kentucky, U.S., since Tuesday. Anxiety mounts for the safety of the £500,000 stallion, sire of this year's Derby winner, Moth.

"Is this what you mean?" I asked, puzzled, making sure I'd read the right section. I had. He nodded vigorously.

"Didn't you know about it?" he asked.

"That Chrysalis had got lost? Yes, I suppose so. It was on all the news bulletins on Wednesday."

"And it didn't mean a damn thing to you," Teller said, with a trace of controlled and civilized bitterness under his smile.

"Well . . ."

"I have a share in that horse," Teller said. "A one-eighth share—200,000 dollars' worth."

"Wow," I said blankly. It seemed a lot of money to invest in one eighth of a horse.

"What is more," he said, sighing, "I spent all of last month negotiating the sale, and was lucky to beat out another syndicate that was bidding for him. And now as soon as he gets over there, this has to happen."

"I'm sorry," I said, conventionally polite.

"I can't expect you to understand." He shook his head excusingly. "It isn't the money which matters, it's the horse. He's irreplaceable."

"They'll find him." I had no doubt of it, and I didn't care one way or the other.

"I'm not so sure," he said. "And I would like you to get out there and look for him."

For five seconds no one twitched a muscle, least of all me. Then Teller turned his head to Keeble and smiled his glossy smile. "I wouldn't play poker with him," he said. "O.K., I'll buy what you say about him being all that good."

I glanced at Keeble and he gave me raised eyebrows, a tiny shrug, and a slightly embarrassed expression. I wondered just how complete his testimonial had been.

Teller turned back to me. "Sim here and I, we were in the same business, way back in World War II."

"I see," I said. And I did see. Quite a lot.

"It was just a war job for me, though," he said. "I got out of the Army in '47 and went back home to Pappy, and a couple of years later he died and left me his race horses and a few bucks on the side." The beautiful teeth flashed.

I waited. The story had hardly begun.

After a pause he said, "I'll pay your fare and expenses, of course, and a fee."

"I don't hunt horses," I protested mildly.

"I can guess what you hunt." He glanced again at Keeble. "Sim says you're on vacation."

I didn't need reminding.

"Chrysalis," he said, "is the third stallion of international status to have disappeared in the last ten years."

Chapter 2

THEY tried pretty hard in their subtle way, but it seemed ridiculous to me.

"You know about horses," Keeble said. "Your father trained them for racing."

"There's the police," I pointed out. "Also the insurance company. Also every man, woman and child with an eye for a horse in the state of Kentucky. And I presume there's a reward?"

Teller nodded.

"So why me?"

"No one found the other two."

"There's a lot of land in America," I said. "They're both probably free on a prairie somewhere having a high old time siring herds of wild horses."

Teller said grudgingly, "The first one was found dead in a gully two years after he disappeared."

"That's it, then."

"But the second one . . . I bought that one too. I had a one-tenth share. This is second time around for me."

I stared at him. "Were any of the circumstances the same?"

Reluctantly he shook his head. "No . . . except that they both got free. Allÿx was never found. That's why I want something special done about Chrysalis."

I was silent.

Keeble stirred. "You've got nothing else to do, Gene. Why not take your holiday in the States? What will you do with yourself if you stay in Putney?"

His eyes had stopped blinking, as they always did when he was intent. It was the surest guide I had to the complex calculations which sometimes lay beneath his most casual remarks. He couldn't have guessed, I thought in alarm. He was a manipulator but not clairvoyant. I shrugged and answered him on the surface.

"Walk round Kew Gardens and smell the orchids."

"They have no scent," said Teller, pointing out the obvious.

"He knows that." Keeble nodded, still unblinking. "Any fruitless way of passing the time is what he meant."

"I guess you two operate on your own private wavelength," Teller said with a sigh. "But I'd like you to come back with me, Gene, and at least take a look. What's the harm in that?"

"And what's the good in it? It's not my sort of job." I looked away, down into the green water. "And . . . I'm tired."

They hadn't a quick answer to that. I thought it would have been simple if all that was the matter with me was the straightforward tiredness of overwork, not the deadly fatigue of a struggle I wasn't sure I could win. Chasing some crazy colt over a thousand square miles didn't look like any sort of cure.

Joan came out of the cabin into their defeated silence

with a bowl of salad and a string of bright fussing chatter. A folding table was erected and the dishes put on it, and we sat around in the sun eating cold chicken and hot French bread. There was a pleasant pink wine to drink and strawberries and cream afterwards, and Peter, still in wet bathing trunks despite orders from his mother, took mouthfuls and photographs by turn. Lynnie, sitting beside me, told Dave Teller an amusing story about the finishing school she attended, her warm bare arm brushing unselfconsciously against mine. I should have enjoyed that placid Sunday picnic on the river. I tried to. I smiled and answered when I was spoken to and concentrated carefully on the taste and texture of what I was eating, and all that happened was that the fat black slug of depression flexed its muscles and swelled another notch.

At four o'clock, after dishwashing and dozing, we started back toward Henley. My refusal to go to America hadn't basically disturbed Teller or Keeble an ounce. I concluded that whatever had prompted the suggestion it wasn't a burning conviction that I and only I could find the missing horse. I put the whole thing out of my mind. It wasn't hard.

There was a punt in difficulties at the approach to Harbour Lock. Teller, again standing on the bow with rope at the ready, shouted back to Keeble and pointed ahead. We looked, all of us, following his finger.

Where the river divided, going slowly into the left fork round the bend to the lock and fast on the right straight to the weir, a sturdy square post in midstream bore a large notice, a single word: DANGER.

A girl lying flat half in and half out of the punt with her arms round the post was trying to tie up to it by passing a rope from one hand to the other, and making a poor job of it. On the stern, watching anxiously, punt pole in hand, stood a young man in a red and yellow shirt. He waved his arms when he saw us coming and as Keeble throttled back and drifted near he shouted across the water.

"Could you help us, sir?"

Since the punt was full in the weir stream with only the

girl's slender arms keeping it from floating straight to destruction, he seemed remarkably cool. Keeble cursed about ignorant nitwits and edged nearer with his engine in slow reverse. The *Flying Linnet,* unlike the punt, was too big to go through this particular weir, a long row of separately openable gates: but the summer current was quite strong enough to crash her nastily against the thick concrete supports and pin her there for someone else humiliatingly to rescue.

Keeble shouted to the girl that we would tow them away, and to hand the mooring rope to me or Lynnie, whichever she could reach, as soon as we were nearer. The girl nodded, her arms still stretched forward round the big post, her long fair hair nearly brushing the water, her body quivering with the strain.

"Hold on!" Lynnie shouted urgently. "Oh, do hold on. Just a little longer, that's all." She leaned over the side as if trying to shorten the few yards of water which still lay between, her worry and fright growing as we drew nearer. With the engine doing little more than tick over, the noise of the water on the far side of the weir began to fill our ears with its threat, but Keeble at any rate remained calm and sure of himself, an easy master of his boat and the situation. With six feet still to go the girl took one arm off the post and held out the rope toward Lynnie's groping hand. Then, disastrously, she dropped it. Crying out, beating in big splashes on the water, she struggled to get her arm back round the post. Lynnie yelled to her to get hold of the rope again, it was fastened to the punt under her chest, to get hold of it again and hand it over. But the girl was now far too frightened either to listen or to let go of the post again, and the panic was rising to screams in her voice.

Out of the side of my vision I saw the young man start forward to help her, apparently at last realizing that their position was serious. The punt pole swung awkwardly in his hands, curved through the air in a clumsy arc, and hit Dave Teller on the head. With buckling knees the American fell forward off the bows and straight down into the water.

I was up on the cabin roof, out of my shoes and into the river after him almost before any of the others realized what had happened. I heard Keeble's despairing voice shouting "Gene" in the second before I went under, but I was thinking simply that speed was the only chance of finding Teller, since anything that sank in a river the size of the Thames was instantly out of sight. Algae made the water opaque.

Diving in as near to where he had gone as I could judge, I kicked downward, arms wide. I was going faster than Teller, I had to be. I had a strong impression that the punt pole had knocked him out, that he was on a slow one-way trip to the bottom.

About eight feet down my fingers hooked almost immediately into cloth. Even with my eyes open I could see nothing and with my right hand I felt for his face while I tried to kick us both to the surface. I found his face, clamped his nose between my fingers and the heel of my hand on his mouth, and turned him so that I held his head against my chest. He didn't struggle; couldn't feel.

From that point on the rescue operation failed to go as per schedule. I couldn't get back to the surface. The current underneath was much stronger, very cold, sweeping us downward, clinging round our bodies with irresistible force. I thought, We'll hit the weir and be pinned there down deep, and that will be that. For a treacherous instant I didn't even care. It would solve all my problems. It was what I wanted. But not really with another life in my arms, for which I was literally the only hope.

My chest began hurting with the lack of air. When we hit the weir, I thought, I would climb my way up it. It's face might not be slippery smooth. It had to be possible . . .

There was a sudden tug as if some fisherman had us hooked. I felt us change direction slightly and then a tug again, stronger and continuing and stronger still. No miraculous rescue. The water had us, gripping tighter, sucking us fast, inexorably, into the weir. The sheer overwhelming weight and power of it made nonsense of human strength, reduced my efforts to the fluttering of a moth in a whirlwind. The seizing speed suddenly accelerated further still, and we hit. Or, rather, Teller hit, with a jar that nearly wrenched him away from me. We spun in the current and my shoulder crashed into concrete and we spun again and crashed, and I couldn't get hold of any surface with my free hand. The tumbling and crashing went on, and the pain in my chest went deeper, and I knew I wasn't going to be climbing up any weir, I could only find it when it hit me, and when I reached for it it hit me somewhere else.

The crashing stopped, but the tumbling went on. My ears were roaring to bursting point. There was a sword embedded in my chest. The searing temptation came back more strongly just to open my mouth and be finished with it. But by my own peculiar rules I couldn't do that, not with someone else involved, not when what I was doing was in a way what I'd been trained for. Some other time, I thought lightheartedly, some other time I'd drown myself. This time I'll just wait until my brain packs up from lack of oxygen, which won't be long now, and if I haven't any choice in the matter then I haven't any guilt either.

The tumbling suddenly died away and the clutching current relaxed and loosened and finally unlocked itself. I was only seconds this side of blackout and at first it didn't register: then I gave a feeble kick with legs half entwined round Teller and we shot upward as if on springs. My head broke the surface into the sun and the air went down into the cramp of my lungs like silver fire.

The weir, the killing weir, was fifty yards away. Fifty yards *upstream*. We had come right through it under the water.

I took my freezing stiffened fingers off Teller's face, and held his head up to mine, and blew into his flaccid mouth. The current, gentle again and comparatively warm, carried us slowly along, frothy bubbles bursting with little winks against our necks. I trod water with my legs, and held Teller up, and went on pushing into him all my used-up breath. He showed no response. It would be exceedingly inconsiderate of him, I thought resignedly, if he had died right at the beginning and I had gone to all that trouble for nothing.

There were shouts from the banks suddenly and people pointing, and someone came after us in a dinghy with an outboard motor. It puttered noisily past my ear and hands stretched over the side to grasp.

I shook my head. "A rope," I said, and breathed into Teller. "Give me a rope. And pull slowly."

One of the two men argued, but the other did as I asked. I wound the rope round my arm twice and held it, and when I nodded they let the boat drift away until we were a safe distance from its propeller and slowly began to pull us toward the bank. Teller got ten more of my ex-breaths on the way. They didn't seem to be doing him a bit of good.

The dinghy towed us out of the weir stream side of the river and landed on the same side as the lock. People appeared in a cluster to help, and there was little doubt it was needed, but even so I was loath to part with Teller until one large calm man lay on his stomach on the grass and stretched his arms down under the American's arm-pits.

"Don't worry," he said. "We'll go straight on with the breathing."

I nodded, took my mouth away from Teller's, and transferred his weight into the stranger's arms. He began to pull him out of the water as fast as he could. I put a steadying hand on Teller's chest and felt it heave sudden-ly under the clinging blue shirt. I hadn't enough breath left myself to tell the man who was lifting him, and while I was still trying to, Teller half out, gave a choking cough and opened his eyes. There was some water in his lungs, racking him. The stranger pulled him even more quickly out onto the grass, and as his ankles bumped over the edge his returning consciousness flooded into a stark sort of awareness which had nothing to do with a release from drowning. Somewhere between a cough and a groan he said, "Jesus," and again went completely limp.

Another couple of strong wrists hauled me up onto the bank in his wake, and I knelt there beside him feeling the reassuringly small swelling on the side of his head but anxiously listening to the dragging breath bubbling in his throat.

"Roll him over," I said. "Carefully . . . just so his tongue isn't choking him."

We put him on his side and his breathing eased immediately, but I wouldn't let them pick him up and carry him to the lock. Almost any injury was bound to be made worse by moving, and he'd been moved too much already. The calm man agreed and went briskly off to fetch a doctor.

The lockkeeper arrived along the towpath, followed at a rush by Keeble and all his family. Their faces were all strained with shock, and Lynnie had been crying.

"Thank God," Keeble said, crouching beside me. "You're both all right." His voice held almost more incredulity than relief.

I shook my head. "He's hurt, somewhere."

"Badly?"

"Don't know. . . . He crashed into the weir."

"We didn't see you go over. We were watching . . ."

"They must have gone under," said the lockkeeper. "Through one of the gates. Those gates wind upward, same as a sash window. We've got two of them a couple of feet open at the bottom today, with the river a bit full after all that rain."

I nodded. "Under."

Dave Teller choked and woke up again, coughing uncontrollably through the puddle in his lungs, every cough jerking him visibly into agony. From his fluttering gesture it was clear where the trouble lay.

"His leg," Keeble said. "He's not bleeding . . . could he have broken it?"

The jar when he hit the weir had been enough. I said so. "We can't do anything for him," said Keeble, watching him helplessly.

The crowd around us waited, murmuring in sympathy but enjoying the disaster, listening to Teller coughing, watching him clutch handfuls of grass in rigid fingers. Not a scrap of use begging them to go away.

"What happened to the punt?" I asked Keeble.

"We towed it ashore. Lynnie got hold of the rope. Those kids were terribly shocked." He looked round for them vaguely, but they weren't in the crowd. "I suppose they've stayed back at the lock. The girl was nearly hysterical when you and Dave didn't come up." A remembering bleakness came into his face. "We towed them into the lock cut and moored there. Then we ran along to the lock to get the lockkeeper . . . and he was already down here." He looked up across the river to the pretty weir. "How long were you under the water?"

"A couple of centuries."

"Seriously."

"Can't tell. Maybe three minutes."

"Long enough."

"Mm."

He looked me over objectively, boss to employee. One shoulder of my green jersey shirt was ripped in a jagged tear.

"Bruised," he said matter-of-factly.

"The weir," I agreed, "has knobs on."

"It's like a flight of steps under there," said the lock-keeper solemnly. "Going down from the top level to this one, you see. The current would have rolled you right down those steps, I reckon. In fact it's a bleeding miracle you ever came up, if you ask me. There's some every year fall in this river and never get seen again. Current takes them along the bottom all the way to the sea."

"Charming," Keeble said under his breath.

Dave Teller stopped coughing, rolled slightly onto his back and put his wrist in his mouth. His strong beaky nose stuck uncompromisingly up to the sky, and the wetness on his face wasn't from the Thames. After a while he moved his hand and asked Keeble what had happened. Keeble briefly explained, and the screwed-up eyes slid round to me.

"Lucky you were with us," he said weakly, the smile in his voice making no progress on his face. He moved his hand apprehensively behind his ear, and winced when it reached the bump. "I don't remember a thing."

"Do you remember asking me to look for your horse?"

He nodded a fraction, slowly. "Yuh. You said no."

"I've changed my mind," I said. "I'll go."

In the cabin of the *Flying Linnet* Keeble watched me slowly strip off my sodden clothes. I had never, as far as I remembered, felt so weak. I'd left half my muscles under the weir. Buttons would no longer come out of their holes.

"You heard what the man said," Keeble remarked. "It was lucky you were with ùs."

I didn't answer.

"Make a note of it," Keeble said. "Stick around. You never know when you'll be needed."

"Sure," I said, refusing to acknowledge that I understood what he was talking about.

He wouldn't be deterred. "You're like Dave's horse. Irreplaceable."

My lips twitched. That was the crunch, all right. His job would be a little harder if he lost his head cook and bottlewasher. Personal regard didn't come into it.

I struggled out of my jersey. He handed me a towel, glancing noncommittally at the marks of this and previous campaigns.

"I'm serious, Gene."

"Yeah." I sighed. "Well . . . I'm still here."

It was too much of an admission, but at least it seemed to reassure him enough to change the subject.

"Why are you going to the States?"

"Maybe I owe it to him."

"Who? Dave?"

I nodded.

"I don't follow," he said frowning. "Surely he owes you? If anyone owes anything."

"No. If I'd been quicker, he wouldn't have gone in, wouldn't now have a smashed thigh. Too much whiskey and wine and sleeping in the sun. I was much too slow. Abysmally, shamefully slow."

He made a gesture of impatience. "Don't be ridiculous,

Gene. No speed on earth could have prevented an accident like that."

I put the towel round my neck and started to take off my trousers.

"That accident," I said briefly, "was attempted murder."

He gazed at me, eyes blinking slowly behind the mild spectacles. Then he turned, opened the cabin door, and stepped up into the cockpit. I heard him shouting to Peter.

"Get out of that punt at once, there's a good chap. And don't let anyone else get in it. It's important."

"Not even Lynnie?"

"Not even Lynnie."

"I don't want to," said Lynnie's voice in a wail from the cockpit. "I never want to go in a punt again."

She wasn't much her father's daughter. His mind was as tough as old boots. The chubby body which contained it came back into the cabin and shut the door.

"Convince me," he said.

"The boy and girl have scarpered."

He raised his eyebrows and protested. "They were frightened."

"They didn't stop to answer questions. They may quite possibly think Dave and I are dead, because they didn't even wait to make sure. I should say they never even intended to appear at any inquest."

He was silent, thinking about it. The boy and girl had gone from the lock when we had eventually returned to it: gone unnoticed, leaving the punt behind. No one had given them a thought until after the doctor had splinted Teller's leg and seen him carried on a stretcher a hundred yards to an ambulance. When the doctor asked how the accident had happened, the causes of it weren't around.

"We don't know," Keeble said. "They may very likely have come down the towpath and seen you were all right, and they might have dozens of personal reasons for not wanting to stay."

I finished kicking my legs out of the clammy cotton trousers and peeled off my socks.

"The boy stood on the stern too long. He should have been helping with the rope."

Keeble frowned. "Certainly he seemed unconcerned, but I don't think he realized quite what a jam they were in. Not like the girl did."

"The first time he moved, he hit Dave straight on the head."

"Punt poles are clumsy if you aren't careful . . . and he couldn't have counted on Dave standing in so vulnerable a spot."

"He'd been standing there most of the way, seeing to the bow rope."

"The boy and girl couldn't know that."

"He was certainly standing there when we approached the punt."

"And," Keeble said in a demolishing voice, "no one would deliberately put himself into so much danger just to bait a trap."

I dried my legs and wondered what to do about my underpants.

Keeble sighed down his nose and fluttered his fingers. "No one except you."

He reached into a locker and produced a bundle of clothes.

"Emergency falling-in kit," he explained, giving them to me. "I don't suppose anything will fit."

As there was a mixture of his own cast-offs, which were too wide, and Lynnie's, which were too narrow, he was right. Everything, besides, was too short.

"In addition," he went on, "how did the boy and girl know we were on the river at all and would be coming down through Harbour Lock? How long did you expect them to wait there clinging to the post? How did they know exactly which boat to hail, and how did they avoid being rescued by any other boat?"

"The best accidents always look as if they couldn't possibly be anything else."

"I grant you that," he said, nodding. "I just think that this one literally couldn't be set up."

"Yes, it could. With a safe get-out, in that if it didn't

work according to plan, if for instance Peter had been on the bows instead of Dave, they had no need to go into the act of yelling for help, because of course they waited to make sure it was us before they started."

"They were in danger," Keeble protested.

"Maybe. I'd like to take a close look at that post."

"And there might have been other boats around, helping. Or watching."

"If Dave never came within range of the punt pole, they lost nothing but an opportunity. If other boats had been watching, there would simply have been more people to cry accident. The girl was screaming and splashing and dramatically dropping her rope when the boy hit Dave. We were all watching her, not him. Any sized audience would have been doing the same."

"And how could boy and girl have known where Dave would be this Sunday, in the first place? And why on God's earth should anyone want to kill him?"

I stepped into some aged trousers of Keeble's and found them a foot too generous round the waist. My boss wordlessly held out a short striped elastic schoolboy belt, which took care of the problem by gripping like a tourniquet.

"It was a simple accident, Gene. It had to be."

The trousers ended four inches above my ankles, and the socks I slowly fumbled my way into made no effort to bridge the gap.

"Gene!" said Keeble, exasperated.

I sighed. "You'll agree I'm a sort of specialist in arranging accidents?"

"Not usually fatal ones," he protested.

"Not often." And no more, if I could wriggle out of it. "Just a general stage-managing of events, so that the victim believes that what has happened to him is the merest mischance."

Keeble smiled. "You've sprung more hares that way . . ."

"So," I said reasonably. "I'm apt to spot a rig-up when I see one."

The smile half faded and changed into speculation.

"And no," I said, "I was not concussed in the recent boating party and I haven't got water on the brain."

"Keep your telepathy to yourself," he said uncomfortably. "I just think you are mistaken."

"O.K., then I'll spend my holiday in Putney."

He said, "No," so vehemently, so explosively, that there was no subtlety left in the situation. From his naked alarm I saw unmistakably how much he understood of my depressed mental state and how convinced he was that I wouldn't survive three weeks of my own company. Shocked, I realized that his relief when I answered his telephone call had not been at finding me at home, but at finding me alive. He had dug me out onto the river to keep an eye on me and was prepared to send me off on any old wild-goose chase so long as it kept me occupied. Then maybe, I supposed, he thought I would snap out of it.

"The blues," I said gently, "have been with me for a long time."

"Not like this."

I had no answer.

After a pause he said persuasively, "Three world-class stallions disappearing . . . isn't that also the sort of accident you don't believe in?"

"Yes, it is. Especially when someone tries to get rid of the man who bought two of them."

He opened his mouth and shut it again. I almost smiled.

"It was a craftsman's accident," I said. "It could hardly have been done better. All they didn't bargain for was interference from someone like me."

He still didn't believe it, but as he was now happy that I should, since it meant that I would go to the States, he raised no more objections. With a shrug and a rueful smile he tossed me a darned brown sweater, which hung round me like a tent; and I picked up my own wet clothes and followed him out into the sunshine.

Peter and Lynnie both giggled at my baggy appearance, the nervous shock still sharp in their voices, especially Lynnie's. I grinned at her and ruffled her hair, and made as if to kick Peter overboard, and some of the tension loosened in their eyes. In another half hour they would have reached the compulsive talking stage and an hour after that they would be back to normal. Nice ordinary kids, with nice ordinary reactions.

I climbed wearily up onto the cabin roof and spread out my clothes to dry. My shoes were still there where I had stepped out of them, and absentmindedly I put them on. Then, standing up, I looked across to the weir, and back to the hefty post with its notice DANGER, and at the innocent empty punt tied up behind the *Flying Linnet*: and I found myself thinking about the legend of the Sirens, the sea nymphs who sat on a rock near a whirlpool and with their pretty voices drew passing sailors toward them, to lure them to their death.

Chapter 3

THE punt had the name of the owner screwed onto the stern on a small metal plate. The lockkeeper, consulted, said that it came from a boatyard about a mile down the river, next to a pub; you couldn't miss it.

"That," I murmured to Keeble, "is where we had our drinks this morning."

His eyelids flickered. He said to the lockkeeper, "I suppose a lot of punts from there come up through your lock?"

"They sure do, on a fine Sunday like this," he agreed.

"Did you happen to notice this one, with a girl and a young man in it? The girl had long fair hair, white trousers, and a pink shirt, and the boy was wearing tight pale-blue jeans and a red and yellow check shirt."

"I should say they came up before my dinner break. I can't remember anyone like that this afternoon."

The lockkeeper eased the white-topped hat back on his head and eyed the boats lining up to go into the lock. He was a youngish man with an air of long-suffering patience, the occupational result, no doubt, of a life spent watching an endless procession of incompetence. People, he had said matter-of-factly, fell into his lock every day of the week. Near-drownings, however, were of no special interest to him: he too often had to deal with the unsaved.

"Would you know them again?" Keeble asked.

The lockkeeper shook his head decisively. "Not a chance. And if I don't get back to my lock there'll be a lot of bad tempers coming through the gates and as like as not we'll be fishing out another one."

He gave me a sketchy farewell salute as one of the few who had gone down his weir and walked away, and strolled unhurriedly back to deal with his Sunday going-home traffic problem.

"We may as well tow the punt back to the boatyard," Keeble said thoughtfully. "We've got to go down past there anyway, and they won't be able to spare anyone to come and fetch it on a busy day like this. And maybe they'll know where the boy and girl came from."

And maybe they wouldn't, I thought: but even the most hopeless questions have to be asked.

"I'd like to look at the post," I said.

Keeble was agreeable, but Lynnie and Peter and their mother were horrified when they found where we were proposing to go, and said they would wait on the bank. In a row, with anxious faces, they stood guard over the punt, while Keeble neatly maneuvered the *Flying Linnet* upstream a little way through the downcoming cruisers and then drifted gently across toward the post. I, standing on the stern seat, caught hold of the crossbar with its emphatic warning and clung to it while Keeble put the boat into reverse against the drag of the weir stream.

Once the engine was thrusting hard enough to hold its own, so that the tension on my arms slackened, I knelt down on the seat and tried to do what the girl had been doing, to pass a rope around the post from one hand to the other. The tendency of the two-ton *Flying Linnet* to drift away couldn't have been much less to deal with than the weight of the punt, but even allowing almost for the fact that my arms were longer and stronger, it was easy. I secured the rope and gave a thumbs-up to Keeble, who stopped the engine. Then with one toe wedged and the narrow side of the boat under my pelvis, I shoved up the sleeves of the brown sweater and leaned down and over to inspect the scenery.

"For God's sake be careful," Keeble said, his voice sharp over the noise of the weir.

I turned my head and laughed at him.

"We haven't any more dry clothes," he pointed out, scowling. "None that you can get into. If you fall in again you'll have to go home wet."

Smiling, I turned back to the post. But feel and look how I might, there was nothing out of the ordinary about the square sturdy white-painted balk of timber set rock-like up on end in the Thames bed.

Keeble shrugged and said, "I told you so," and steered his boat back to the bank.

"How about fingerprinting the punt?" I said.

"You never let up."

"You should be glad of it."

The long line of past occasions when not letting up had led to a useful harvest rose up between us, and I saw his conviction waver.

"All right, Gene, if you're sure."

"Get Raben to do it. He's the best."

"All right. Tomorrow."

"How about the police?"

He pursed his lips. "It's not our usual territory. More theirs, I agree. But they're not likely to take your theory seriously, or to act on it, unless we tell them what your job is . . . and impress them with it. No, I'm not in favor of that. We could just go along with this quietly on our own for a little while, I think."

"So that if nothing turns up, we won't have made bloody fools of ourselves?"

All his facial muscles contracted for a second. "You are not paid to turn your perceptions on your boss."

"I probably am."

"That's a point."

The boat grounded gently against the bank, and I helped Joan and Lynnie back on board. Peter, on his father's directions, stepped into the punt and handed him up the mooring rope, which Keeble fastened to the cleat on the *Flying Linnet*'s stern. Then, towing the punt, we took our turn into the lock, explained what we were doing to the lockkeeper, and cruised downstream to the pub and its next-door boatyard.

A flustered middle-aged boatman there was trying to cope with returning family picnic parties and a bunch of youths and girls who wanted to fill in the half hour before the pub opened at seven o'clock. The late afternoon sun shone redly on his big sweating face and his freckled bald head, and we had to wait while he juggled his customers precariously in and out of skiffs and punts and took their money and warned the young couples that it was an offense to be on the river without lights after dark and that the boatyard closed at nine-thirty anyway.

When Keeble at last had a chance he asked the boatman if he had seen the girl with fair hair and the boy in a red and yellow check shirt who had hired a punt that morning.

"Seen 'em? I suppose so, I've been here all day."

"I mean, do you remember them," Keeble said patiently.

"Where are they then?" The boatman looked round suspiciously.

"They've gone," Keeble began.

"Then who's going to settle up?" said the boatman belligerently, this last problem looking to be just one too many for his temper.

"Oh, I will," said Keeble soothingly. He took his wallet out of his back pocket and unfolded it to show the usual thickish wad. Keeble didn't have to live on Her Majesty's pay and worked from conviction, not need; his beer money represented a week's wage to me and his boat a year's.

"How much do they owe you?" He handed over what the boatman asked and offered a fiver on top. "I'd like to hire this punt for this evening and tomorrow," he said. "Is that all right?"

The boatman took the money without hesitation and made a few halfhearted efforts to appear cautious.

"Where'll you be taking it?"

"Henley," Keeble said.

"You won't leave the cushions out if it rains?" Keeble shook his head.

"All right then." The boatman had already tucked the notes away. "And you'll bring it back tomorrow?"

"Tomorrow afternoon," Keeble agreed. "Now, about those young people who took it this morning . . ."

Unexpectedly the boatman suddenly leered. "I remember 'em," he said, "come to think of it, they was the two who had no business to be out together."

"What do you mean?" Keeble asked.

"Well, see, this girl, she said, like, what if her old man had put detectives on her, what would they say if she went off all day with him in a punt, and how she'd said she'd only come out as long as it was nothing anyone could use in a divorce. And the fellow in the check shirt turned round and said old moneybags, meaning her old man, see, would never find out where they'd been, he was in France on business wasn't he, or some such, and then they took note that I was standing there hearing and they sort of nudged each other and shut up. But I reckon as they were off for a bit on the side, see, and didn't want no one to catch 'em."

"Exactly," said Keeble to me with another touch of I-told-you-so.

"And very nicely done," I agreed. "Artistic."

"You haven't seen them since then, since this morning, I suppose?" Keeble said to the boatman. "Do you happen to know how they got here?"

"Car," said the boatman, waving an arm. "They came from the car park back there."

"Which car, do you know?"

He gave Keeble a pitying stare. "Look, there's cars in and out all day, what with the pub and us. And I'm looking at the river, see, with my hands full an' all, and I couldn't tell you no one who's come and gone nor what they came in, but they must have come in a car, because they come in the morning, and there's no buses along here on Sundays before half-past two in the afternoon."

"Thank you anyway," said Keeble, sighing. "You've been very helpful." He added another pound to his over-payment and the boatman's eyes swiveled rapidly from the pub to the clock over the boathouse door. Still ten minutes until the bar opened. I proceeded to fill them.

"Did the young man, or the girl, or both of them, speak with any special type of accent?" I asked.

Since he spoke broad Berkshire himself, the boatman's hesitation was understandable. "They talked," he said, considering, "like they do on the telly."

"Not much help," Keeble commented.

"How do you lash the end of your punts' mooring ropes?" I asked.

"Eh?" said the boatman, puzzled.

"Do you lash the end of the ropes to stop them unraveling?"

"Oh, I get you. No, we splice 'em. Turn the ends back and sort of weave them in. Lashing's no good as it comes undone too easily."

I unwound the punt's mooring rope from the *Flying Linnet*'s stern cleat. "This one is coming undone, though."

"Let's see that," he said suspiciously, and I gave it to him. He twisted the frayed unraveling strands in his strong dirty fingers and hovered in what I guessed to be a fairly usual mixture of fury and resignation.

"These bleeding vandals . . . excuse me, ma'am," he apologized to Joan, "these so-and-sos, they tie up to a tree, see, or something, and come they want to push on, they can't undo the knots if the rope's wet, and they just don't bother, they cut through the rope and off they go."

"Does that often happen?"

"Every summer we has this trouble now and then." He pulled the rope up straight, measuring its length with his eye. "There's a good four or five feet gone off this one, I shouldn't wonder. We've been talking of switching to chains, but they can get into holy terrors of knots, chains can. Here," he added to Keeble, "you'd better have another punt, one with a better rope."

"This one will be fine," Keeble said, fastening it on again. "We'll see you tomorrow."

He towed the punt down to Henley and right into the garage-like boathouse which kept the English summer off the *Flying Linnet*. The punt was secured alongside by Peter and his father and everyone disembarked along a narrow boardwalk carrying things like the remains from lunch, newspapers, bathing towels, and in my case wet clothes and a loaded jacket, out through the boathouse and into Keeble's Rover, which was parked on a neat square of grass at the back.

Peter's main care was for his precious camera, again hanging round his neck on its cord.

"I suppose," I said idly, "you didn't happen to take a photograph up there by the weir? You didn't happen to get a shot of those people in the punt?"

He shook his head, blinking like his father.

"Gosh, no, I didn't. I don't suppose actually I would have thought of taking one, not when everything was happening, do you think? I mean, it would have looked a bit off if you and Mr. Teller had been drowning and I was just standing there taking pictures and so on."

"You'll never be a newspaperman," I said, grinning at him.

"Wouldn't you have minded, then?"

"I don't think so."

"But anyway," he said mournfully, "I couldn't, you see, because I finished the film at lunchtime and I didn't have another one, so even if there had been a fire or something I couldn't have taken it." He looked at his camera thoughtfully. "I won't finish up any more films in the middle of the day, just in case."

"A fire," I agreed seriously, "would anyway make a much better picture than just people drowning, which they mostly do out of sight."

Peter nodded, considering me. "You know, you're quite sensible, aren't you?"

"Peter!" exclaimed his mother in unnecessary apology. "That's not the way to talk." And she wasn't much pleased when I said that as far as I was concerned he could say what he liked.

Keeble drove round to the station car park, where Lynnie and I transferred to the Austin.

"I'll ring in the morning," Keeble said, standing half out of his respectable car.

"Right."

"Take care of Lynnie."

"I'll do that."

Lynnie kissed her parents good-by, but her father more warmly, and made a face at Peter as the Rover rolled away out of the gate. Then she climbed into the Austin, waited until I was sitting beside her, and stretched out her hand to the ignition.

She was trembling again.

"Shall I drive?" I said mildly, making it absolutely her own choice.

She put both her hands in her lap and looked straight out through the windshield. Her face was pale above the orange dress.

"I thought you were both dead."

"I know."

"I still feel churned up. It's silly."

"It's not silly. And I expect you're fond of Dave Teller."

"He's sent us presents and things since we were little."

"A nice man."

"Yes." She sighed deeply and after a pause said calmly, "I think it would be better, if you really don't mind, if you drive back."

"Of course I will."

We changed places, and went back to London with more cars passing us than we passed. At the Chiswick circle I said I would drive her to her flat and go on home by taxi, but with a sideways laughing glance she said no taxi would stop for me in her father's clothes, and that she was feeling better and could quite easily do the last lap herself: so I rolled round the few corners to Putney and stopped outside my own front door.

Summer dusk filled the quiet street. No one about. Lynnie looked out of her window upwards at the tall house, and shivered.

"You're cold," I said, concerned for her bare arms.

"No . . . I have a cardigan in the back. I was just thinking about your flat."

"What about it?"

"It's so . . . empty." She gave a half-laugh, shrugging it off. "Well, I hope you won't have nightmares, after to-day."

"No . . ." I collected my things and got out of the car, and she moved over into the driver's seat.

"Will they have saved any dinner for you at the hostel?" I asked.

"Not a hope," she said cheerfully. "But I expect there'll be some cake and milk about, there usually is."

"Would you care to eat with me? Not up there," I added hastily, seeing the beginnings of well-brought-up suspicion. "In a restaurant, I mean."

"I've my mother to thank for my beastly mind," she said unexpectedly. "I really am rather hungry, and I don't see at all why I shouldn't have supper in your flat, if you've got any food." And without more ado she got out of the car and locked it, and stood expectantly beside me on the pavement.

"There are some tins," I said, reflecting. "Wait here just a second, would you? I just want to have a look round the back."

"Round the back?"

"For burglars," I said sardonically. But I went to look, as usual, at the powder-coated bottom flight of the fire escape. No one had been up or down all day.

Lynnie climbed the stairs to the fourth floor as easily as before, and having checked via a well-placed paper clip that my door hadn't been opened since I had shut it that morning, I put the key in the lock and let us in.

The green plastic lampshade in my sitting room scattered its uncozy glare over the tidy room, switching the soft gray light outside into sudden black and evoking the forlornness of institution buildings on winter afternoons. It wouldn't be much trouble, I thought, to go out and buy myself a red shade in the morning, and see if it propagated rosy thoughts instead.

"Sit down," I suggested. "Are you warm enough? Switch the electric fire on if you'd like it. I think I'll go and change, and then we can decide about going out."

Lynnie nodded, but took things into her own hands. When I came out of the bedroom she had already investigated my meager cupboard and had lined up a packet of soup, some eggs, and a tin of anchovies.

"Soup, and anchovies on scrambled egg," she said.

"If you'd really like that," I said doubtfully.

"I can't cook much else."

I laughed. "All right. I'll do the coffee."

There were burnt specks in the eggs when she had finished, which harmonized nicely with the scraped-off overdone toast and the brown anchovy strips, and there had been a slight overemphasis on pepper.

"No one," she sighed, "is going to marry me for my cordon bleu."

There were plenty of other reasons why she'd be fending off suitors knee-deep in a year or two: a curvy figure, delicate neck, baby skin; the touch-me-not expression, the awakening social courage, the quick compassion. No one was going to care if she couldn't cook. But she wasn't secure enough to be told so at that moment.

"When were you seventeen?" I asked.

"The week before last."

"You didn't waste much time passing the driving test."

"I've been able to drive since I was twelve. Peter can, too." She finished her eggs and stirred two heaped teaspoonfuls of sugar into her coffee. "I was hungry. Funny, that."

"It's a long time since lunch."

"A terribly long time . . ." She suddenly looked me

straight in the face, which she had mostly been avoiding, and with devastating innocence said, "I'm so glad you're alive."

I turned a hopeless wince into a laugh. "I'm so glad Dave Teller is."

"Both of you," she said. "It was the worst thing in my whole life when you didn't come up."

A child untouched by tragedy, I thought. A pity the world was such a rough place, would catch her by her pretty neck one day and tear her guts apart. No one ever escaped. To have got to seventeen unlacerated was merely a matter of luck.

When we had finished the coffee she insisted on doing the dishes, but when she hung up the tea towel I saw all her mother's warnings pour back, and she glanced at me and quickly away, and stood stiffly in the center of the room, looking nervous and embarrassed.

"Why don't you have any pictures on your walls?" she said jerkily.

I gestured to the trunk in the corner. "There are some in there, but I don't like them very much. Not enough to bother with hanging them up. . . . Do you know it's after ten? I'd better take you home or the hostel will shut you out."

"Oh, yes," she said in great relief, and then hearing her own voice, added in confusion: "I mean . . . I didn't know if you would think me very rude, dashing off as soon as we'd finished eating."

"Your mother is quite right to tell you to be cautious," I said lightly. "Little Red Riding Hood couldn't tell a wolf from her grandmother . . . and you can never rely on a woodcutter turning up in the nick of time."

The rigidity dissolved like mist. "You do say some extraordinary things," she said. "As if you could read my mind."

"I could." I smiled. "You'd better put that cardigan on. It will be cold outside."

"O.K." She pulled a dark-brown jersey out of her bucket-shaped tote bag and put it on. I bent to pick up a clean

folded handkerchief which had fallen out with it, and
when she was ready, handed it to her.

"Thanks," she said, looking at it casually. "That's the
one Peter found in the punt."

"In the punt?"

"Yes, down a crack between two of the cushions. He
gave it to me because it was too small for him, he said.
Too sissy."

"Did he find anything else?"

"I don't think so. I mean it isn't stealing or anything, is
it, to keep her handkerchief? I'll give it to her of course if
she comes back, but by the time Peter was sitting in the
punt, they had been gone already for ages."

"No, it's not stealing," I reassured her, though technically it was doubtful. "But may I have a look at it?"

"Of course."

She gave it back and I unfolded it: a white square of
thin gauzy material. In one corner a stylized bear in a flat
straw hat.

"Is that out of Walt Disney?" I asked.

She shook her head and said with surprise at my ignorance, "Yogi Bear."

"Who is Yogi Bear?"

"I can't believe it! Well, he's a character in a lot of
cartoon films. Like Top Cat and Atom Ant and the
Flintstones."

"I've seen the Flintstones," I agreed.

"Like them, then. The same people make Yogi
Bear."

"Do you mind if I keep it for a day or two?"

"Of course, if you really want to," she said, puzzled.
"But it surely hasn't any value."

Down in the street I said I might as well finish the job
and drive her to her hostel.

"I'm really all right now," she protested. "You don't
need to come."

"Yes, I do. Your father said to look after you, and I'm
seeing you safe to your door."

She raised her eyebrows and gave me a comical look,
but compliantly went round to the passenger seat. I

started the car, switched on the lights, and started toward Kensington.

"Do you always do what Daddy tells you?" she asked, smiling.

She was feeling much surer of herself, I thought.

"Yes, when I want to."

"That's a contradiction in terms."

"So it is."

"Well, what do you actually *do?* What does *anyone* do in the Civil Service?"

"I interview people."

"What sort of people?"

"People who want jobs in government departments."

"Oh!" She laughed. "A sort of Personnel Officer?"

"Sort of."

"It sounds a bit drizz."

"The sun shines occasionally."

"You're pretty quick. We only made up drizz yesterday."

"A very useful word."

"Yes, we thought so too. Covers a lot of things nicely."

"Like wet boyfriends?"

She laughed. "Actually, it's pretty drizz to *have* a wet boyfriend." She pointed. "The hostel's down there, but we have to drive around and find somewhere to park the car all night. One or two squares down here don't have meters yet."

The nearest empty space was a good quarter of a mile from the hostel, so I walked her back.

"You don't need to . . ." she began. "Well, don't say it. Daddy said."

"Right," I agreed.

She sniffed resignedly and walked beside me out of step, the leather bag swinging and her flat shoes silent on the pavement. At the hostel's glossy black well-lit front door she came to a stop and hovered on one foot, her half-anxious uncertain expression saying clearer than words that she wasn't sure how to part from me. I wasn't old enough for uncle terms or young enough for a casual contemporary brush-off. I worked for her father, but wasn't his servant. Lived alone, looked respectable, asked nothing: I didn't fit into any of the categories she had yet learned how to deal with. I put out my hand and smiled.

"Good night, Lynnie."

Her clasp was brief, warm, relieved.

"Good night . . ." There was a pause while she made up her mind to it; and even then it was little more than a breath. "Gene."

"I wish you," I said, "blind traffic wardens and foam rubber bumpers."

"Good night." The chuckle rolled spontaneously in her throat. "Good night." She turned on one toe and jumped the two steps up to the door, then looked over her shoulder and waved as she went inside.

Little Lynnie, I thought, whistling to a passing taxi, little Lynnie, right at the beginning of it. Flying half consciously, half unconsciously, the notice-me flags of the pretty young female; and it was no use pretending that she didn't make me hungry; that she wasn't absolutely what I would have liked as an oasis in my too continent life. But if I had learned anything in thirty-eight years it was who not to go to bed with.

And, more drearily, how not to.

Chapter 4

THE Buttress Life offices on Thirty-third Street were high on customer appeal on the sixth floor. On the fifth and seventh they tucked the computers and electric typewriters into functional plasterboard cubicles. I sat three inches deep in black leather and considered that of all American craftsmen I admired the chair designers most: in no other country in the world could one sit on the same seat for several hours without protest from the sacroiliac.

I had waited forty pleasantly cool minutes already.

Long enough to discover that the rows of potted plants along the low wall dividing the 40-foot square hall into five smaller bays were made of plastic. Long enough to admire the pinewood walls, the ankle-deep carpet, the carefully lowered ceiling with its inset lights. In each bay there was a large desk, with one large chair behind it, one at the side, one in front. Nearly all occupied. Dividing each bay neatly in two stood a second, smaller desk; for the secretary-receptionist with his back discreetly to his boss. In front of him, in each bay, the long black leather bench for waiting on.

I waited. There was still someone for the big man to see before me. Very sorry, said the secretary apologetically, but the schedule had been crowded even before Mr. Teller's cable arrived. Could I possibly wait?

So why not? I had three weeks to spare.

The light was dim and piped music poured over everything like syrup. That and the built-in deadness of the acoustics made the earnest consultations going on at the five big desks completely inaudible to the waiting benches, while at the same time giving the customers a comforting illusion that they weren't alone in their troubles. Everyone, at the core of things, was alone. Just some more than others.

I hadn't slept all night after leaving Lynnie; but not her fault. It had been one long stupid struggle between a craving for oblivion and conviction that appeasing it wasn't so much morally wrong as a thoroughgoing defeat. I had never learned to accept defeat. Obstinacy had given me what success I had had in my job, and it alone seemed to be keeping me alive, since all other props were as much use as toothpicks in an avalanche. Enthusiasm for finding Dave Teller's horse burned in me as brightly as wet coal dust: and the nation would hardly collapse if I left its employ.

Caroline had crowded like a flood tide through my head and down my body. Caroline . . . whom I would have married had it not been for the husband who would not divorce her.

Caroline had left him to live with me, and had felt

guilty about it. A mess. An ordinary, everyday mess. Her fine passion had fretted away over six frustrating years of will-he won't-he?—and to the end he wouldn't. Not that he'd ever got her back. In the year since she had left me she had returned to nursing and was working in a Nairobi hospital, impervious to come-back letters from either of us.

The sharp pain of her departure had dulled to the extent that I no longer felt it through every waking minute: it came stabbing back at longer and longer intervals. But when it did, I remembered her as she'd been at the beginning, and the hunger was pretty well unbearable. It was easy enough to find different girls to talk to, to work with, to take to bed: hard to find a match on all levels: and Caroline had been a match. In the past year, instead of receding, the loneliness had closed in. My work, of its nature, set me apart. And I had no one to go home to, to share with, to care for. The futility and emptiness had gone down to my roots, and nothing seemed to lie ahead but years and years more of what I was already finding intolerable.

The clients at the big desk stood up, shook hands, and left. The secretary ushered the man with the earlier appointment into the presence. I went on waiting, without impatience. I was accustomed to it.

The punt, investigated in Henley that morning, had produced nothing but ten different sets of smudged fingerprints, of which the topmost and stickiest were Peter's. The Yogi Bear handkerchief was on its way round the manufacturers, in the distant hope that someone could tell where it had been sold. Dave Teller, briefly visited, had said wanly to charge everything to him. The super VC 10 which lifted off at 3 P.M. British summertime from Heathrow had landed at Kennedy at 3:10. Buttress Life closed its doors at six, which gave it still a half hour to go. And outside in the canyon streets the 100-degree heat wave crept up a notch to 101.

My turn came for the big desk. The big man, on his feet behind it, held out a large dry flabby hand and produced the sincere smile of the professional insurance man. Having settled me into the large comfortable chair alongside, he sat down himself and picked up the cable discreetly placed to hand by the secretary. A polished chunk of wood sat on the desk between us. On it, neat gold letters facing me said helpfully: PAUL M. ZEISSEN.

"We received this cable from Mr. Teller," he said. A slight, very slight, undertone of disapproval.

I nodded. I had sent it myself.

"Our own investigators are experts." He didn't like me coming: but he wouldn't want to lose the Teller policies. His politeness had effort behind it.

I soothed him down, more from habit than anything else.

"Of course. Please think of me simply as an auxiliary. Mr. Teller persuaded me to come over because he has unfortunately broken a leg in England and will be immobilized in hospital for a few weeks. He sent me very much on impulse, as a personal friend, to kind of represent him. To see if there was anything I could do. There was no suggestion that he wasn't satisfied with your firm." I paused delicately. "If he criticized anyone, it was the police."

Paul M. Zeissen's smile warmed up a fraction from within: but he hadn't risen to high executive status in his tough profession without disbelieving half that everyone said. That was all right with me. Half of what I'd said was true. Or half-true, anyway.

"Mr. Teller understands of course," he said, "that it is for our own sakes that we are looking for the horse?"

"Naturally," I agreed. "Mr. Teller is also most anxious that you should succeed, as the horse is irreplaceable. He would infinitely prefer his return to any amount of insurance money."

"A million and a half," said Zeissen reverently.

"Worth more on the hoof," I said.

He glanced at me with a first gleam of real welcome. Once he'd swallowed the firm's affronted pride, it was quite clear that they'd nothing to lose by letting me in.

"One of our best men, Walt Prensela, is in charge of the Chrysalis case," he said. "He'll give you the picture.

He knows you're coming, I sent him a memo with a copy of the cable." He pressed the switch on his desk intercom.

"Walt? We have Mr. Hawkins from England here. Shall I have him come up to you now?"

The polite question was, as so often in American affairs, an equally polite order. The affirmative duly came. Zeissen flipped the switch and stood up.

"Walt's office is one floor up, number four-seven. Anyone will direct you. Would you like to go up now?"

I would; and I went.

I'd expected to have to deal with the same ruffled feathers in 47, but I didn't, because Walt had done his homework though I wasn't sure of that at first. He greeted me with businesslike casualness, shook hands, waved me to the spare chair, and sat down himself, all in five smooth seconds. Much my age, I judged, but shorter and a good deal thicker. His hands were square and powerful with nails so brief that the fingertip pads seemed to be boiling over backwards. There were middle European origins in the bone structure of the skull, topped by roughly cropped wiry gray-brown hair, and his deep-socketed brown eyes were set permanently into the I-don't-believe-a-word-of-it expression of his boss downstairs, only more so.

"So, Gene," he said, neither with nor without much friendliness, "you've come a long way."

"Dave Teller's idea, Walt," I said mildly.

"Looking for horses. . . . Do you do much of that?" His voice was flat, uninformative.

"Practically none. How about you?"

His nostrils twitched. "If you mean, was it I who didn't find the other two, then, no, it wasn't."

I tried a smile: didn't get one back.

He said: "Buttress Life had to pay up for Allyx three years ago. One million six hundred and forty-three thousand seven hundred and twenty-nine dollars, give or take a nickel. Showman, the first one, was insured with another company."

"Accident?" I murmured. "Or design."

He rubbed his left thumb over the top of the round-ended fingers, the first of a hundred times I saw that gesture.

"Now that you've come, design. Before, I wasn't sure."

"I'm officially on holiday," I protested. "I came only because Teller asked me. You should read no meaning into it."

He gave me a level, half-sardonic stare.

"I checked you out," he said, flicking at the copy of the cable, which lay on his desk. "I wanted to know just what sort of limey busybody was being wished onto me."

I didn't say anything, and he made a clicking noise at the side of his mouth, expressive of understanding, resignation and acceptance, all in one.

"A screener," he said. "How come Teller found you?"

"How come you found me?" I asked instead.

"I mentioned your name in two places," he said complacently. "The FBI, and the CIA. And got a positive reaction from both. A couple of useful pals there filled me in. It seems you're a major stumbling block in the way of the planting of spies in certain government departments and places like biological warfare research laboratories; and you've passed on some useful warning on that subject to our people at Fort Detrick. They say the other side have tried to deter you, a little roughly, once or twice." He sighed. "You have a clean bill with our boys. And how."

"And with you?"

"They said you didn't like limelight."

"It's all yours."

"Just so as I stand in right with Buttress."

My decisive nod satisfied him. If we found the horse, he was welcome to the handshakes.

"Fill me in, then," I said. "How did Chrysalis get lost?"

Walt glanced at his watch and checked it against the electric clock on the wall. The little boxlike office had no windows, as the single glass panel faced out onto the corridor; and although it was cool and comfortable enough, it was no place to talk if one didn't have to.

"Five after six," Walt said. "Do you have any other engagements?"

"Know any good bars?" I suggested.

"A mind reader." He raised eyes to heaven. "There's Delaney's a block up Broadway."

We stepped out of the air conditioning into the sweltering street, up 30 degrees in two paces. With the humidity running also at 98 percent, walking as little as a hundred yards left one damp to the skin. I never minded it: New York in a heat wave was always preferable to New York in a snowstorm, or anywhere hot to anywhere cold, for that matter. Cold seeped farther than into the bones, numbed the mind, drained the will. If the depression deepened toward winter, defeat would come with the snow.

Delaney's was spilling out onto the pavement with a business convention let out of school. An oblong name tab sat on each neat seersucker lapel, a confident smile hid the anxiety behind every face; they stretched from the substantial group outside into the deep cool gloom of the bar. Pushing through them looked a problem; conversation in their company an impossibility.

"How about your hotel? Where are you staying?" Walt said.

"The Gotham."

Walt's eyebrows rose two clear inches.

"Teller's paying," I said. "He has an account there."

"What did you do then? Save his life?"

"Six times," I agreed, matching his sarcasm.

"He must really think," Walt said reflectively, "that you might get his horse back."

"We," I said.

"Nope. You. There's no trail. I've looked."

A colored cab driver in rolled-up shirt sleeves took us to the hotel, hot air blowing in gusts through the open window each time he accelerated. The city moved sluggishly under the brazen sun and there was more rubbish than usual littering the streets.

"This is a filthy town," said Walt, seeing it through my eyes. "Give me Chicago."

"Too cold," I said automatically. "Beautiful, but too cold. That freezing wind off the lake . . ."

"Are you guys from Chicago?" said the cab driver. "I was born there, in the Loop."

Walt talked to him about that. I drifted away into the disoriented state of not caring a jot about the cab driver, or Walt, or Dave Teller, or Caroline, or anyone on earth. We went up to my hotel room and I dragged through the host motions of ringing down for a bottle of Scotch and ice and seeing to temperature, light and ashtrays. Walt loosened his tie and took a first appreciative swallow.

"You look pooped," he said.

"Natural state."

"I guess it's midnight already, to you."

"I guess."

There was a considerable drinking pause. Then he said, shifting his sturdy body in the leather chair, "Well, do you want to know about this horse, or don't you?"

"Sure." The boredom in my answer came over shockingly strong, even to me. He looked faintly startled and then speculative, but when he spoke it was strictly business.

"They were taking him in a horse van from Kennedy airport to Lexington, Kentucky. He'd spent the compulsory twenty-four hours' immigration quarantine in the airport stable, along with six other horses which came over on the same flight. All normal at that time. They loaded Chrysalis and four others into the van, and drove westward from New York on the Pennsylvania Turnpike."

"Time?" I asked.

"Left Kennedy 4 P.M. Monday. Last Monday, that is. A week today. Estimated Lexington midday Tuesday. Seven hundred miles."

"Stops?"

"Yeah," Walt said. "Stops. That's where the trouble started." He swirled the clinking ice round in his glass. "They took their first meal stop at a diner near Allentown, ninety-three miles from New York. There were four men in the van, two drivers and two grooms. Drivers in the cab, grooms in back with the cargo. At the first stop they took turns to eat, drivers first, grooms after. The drivers chivvied the grooms, and gave them too short a time to eat a good meal. There was an unfriendly argument."

"They all say so?"

"Yeah. I've talked to all four, one at a time. They're all trying their hardest to pin the blame on the others. They left the diner and went about two hundred miles to their next stop at Bedford. That was no better. Far from cooling off, they had begun to scuffle.

"They turned off the turnpike onto the interstate highway—70—south of Pittsburgh, and left that again at Zanesville, taking the southwest fork to Cincinnati. About fifty miles farther on they turned due south to cross the Ohio River into Kentucky, and go on through Paris and down the Paris Pike to Lexington."

"I'll need to see it on a map," I said.

He nodded. "From Zanesville to Paris they took secondary routes, though all paved roads, of course. Right? Now, it was in Ohio that the van was hijacked, and it was over the state border in Kentucky when it was found, which has caused a couple of arguments here and there."

"Hijacked! That's the first I've heard of that."

"It was hijacked all right."

"How did it happen?"

"By that time, Tuesday morning, the drivers and the grooms were all eating at the same time, though at each end of the lunch counter. They left the horses unguarded for a full quarter hour, and during that time someone simply drove off with the whole works."

"Surely the drivers locked up, and took the keys, at least?"

"Oh, sure. It was a good job though. A direct wire contact from the battery terminals to the starter motor."

"So then what?"

"When they found the van gone the drivers called the police, but it wasn't until Wednesday morning that the van was found off the road and out of sight around a hill in Kentucky. But—no horses. The ramps were down, and all the horses had been let loose."

"Deliberately."

"Sure. United. All the halters were still in the van. Those race horses were all free with no bridle or anything to catch them by. The Kentucky boys reckon the horses were let out to create a diversion, to get the cops off the tails of the hijackers by making them chase horses all over."

"And it worked."

"Yeah," said Walt gloomily. "The owners kicked up stink. All the horses were valuable, not only Chrysalis. But only Chrysalis was insured with Buttress."

"Did they get all the others back?"

"Yeah. But Chrysalis has as good as disappeared off the face of the earth."

"Fingerprints?"

"Gloves."

Walt had talked himself dry. I refueled his glass and felt like sleep.

"What do you think?" he said.

I shrugged. "It was Chrysalis they really wanted."

"But why? Why should anyone want to steal a stallion? That's what's got us all floored. I don't know much about horses, I'm a false claims man really. I just got pitched into this between cripple cases, if you get me. But even I know that it's the stallion's name that brings in the stud fee. Say someone's stolen Chrysalis, what's the point? They can't advertise him for stud, so he isn't worth a dime. We figured someone might be nutty enough to want him all to themselves, like some world famous painting, but you can hide a painting quietly in a cellar, which you can't do with a horse. The whole thing doesn't make sense."

I had my own views on that, but I said only, "What happened to Allyx?"

"I only know about that from the files. I got the case out and looked it up this morning. Allyx was a French horse, apparently one of the best young sires in Europe.

He was nine when he came over here, and already his get had won a list of races as long as your arm. Dave Teller was head of the syndicate which bought him; that's why he was insured with us, as we do all the Teller estate work. Allyx was delivered safely to the Teller stud farm. No trouble in transit that time. But he was there only four days. Then there was a fire in the stables one night and they took all the horses out of the barn and turned them loose into a small corral."

"And when they came to fetch them—no horses?"

He nodded. "There was a broken rail over the far side, which no one knew about. All the horses had got through it, including Allyx. They caught all the others, though some were free for days. No sign ever of Allyx. The company had to face that he probably got into the foothills of the Appalachian Mountains and maybe broke his neck, and in the end they had to pay up."

"What about the fire?"

"There was apparently nothing suspicious about it at the time. One of our very best men found no evidence of fire being set. Still, stable fires can be started so easily . . . a cigarette butt in a pile of straw leaves no trace. This one didn't do much damage before they put it out. No question of kerosene, for instance. The whole chain of events was agreed to be accidental."

I smiled thinly.

"What about Showman?"

Walt shook his head. "I don't know how he got loose. But they found him. Dead, of course. He'd been dead some time, I think."

"Where?"

"Oh, in the Appalachians. He came from that area, same as the others. But then Lexington has more stud farms than anywhere else in the States, so there's no significance in that really."

"You went down to Lexington last week?"

He nodded. "Flew there Wednesday, when Mrs. Teller called us."

"Mrs. Dave Teller?"

"Uh-huh." Something moved obscurely in Walt's face.

Dave's wife had made an impression. "She's English, like you."

"I'll go down there tomorrow," I said. I watched him waver and decide not to tell me about her. Instead, he looked at his watch, put down his glass firmly, and stood up.

"Must be off," he said. "It's our anniversary, and my wife's fixed something special."

"Give her my apologies for keeping you."

"That's all right. It fitted in fine. I go home from Grand Central, not far. Walk it fast. Twenty minutes to traintime."

I walked him to the door.

"Walt, would you be free to come down to Lexington in the morning?" As he hesitated, I added, "There's no point in my covering all the ground twice. I'd appreciate having you along."

"Be glad to, Gene," he said too politely, and I thought to hell with you, Walt, to hell with everything on earth, including me, but I'm stuck with this horse nonsense for the next three weeks, and if I say go to Lexington, you go. I hid the violent moment of irritation in turning from him to open the door, and I understood his reluctance anyway, as who likes to be dragged down to do the same piece of work twice, especially under the critical eye of an imported limey busybody?

He shook my hand. "I'll call you in the morning," he said, his feelings under better control than mine.

"Seven-thirty?"

"All right." He loosened his jaw muscles into what looked like going to be a smile but didn't quite make it, sketched a salute with the thick-topped fingers, and ambled unhurriedly away down the passage.

I had dinner in the hotel restaurant. A steak. Never eat steak west of Nebraska, they used to say. The beef was bred on the prairie and walked eastward to the markets: when it got to eastern Nebraska it hit the corn belt and only after that was it fat enough to kill. New York steaks were mostly superb, but I didn't suppose they'd walked in through the New Jersey Tunnel. Long-distance haulage took care of that . . . and whoever had removed Allyx and Chrysalis had had a haulage problem too. You couldn't ride a stallion along state highways. For one thing, they no longer took kindly to a saddle after years at stud, even if they had been reasonable to handle in the first place.

Nightclubs attract me like wet Mondays in Manchester, and apathy kept me from even reading the list of shows. I went straight upstairs after dinner to catch up on a lot of lost sleep and woke again infuriatingly at two, dead tired and with a restless brain.

From habit, the Luger lay under my pillow.

It was another long night.

Chapter 5

WE flew down in the morning, Walt's puffed eyes showing that the anniversary had been duly celebrated and mine feeling as if they'd been rolled in grit.

The two drivers, reached by telephone, met us by appointment in the entrance hall of a motel near the center of Lexington, where Walt had stayed on his previous trip. He booked rooms for us both, and we took the drivers up to his, which proved a mile short of Gotham standards but hot on cleanliness and Kleenex.

Walt switched on the air conditioning, shuffled chairs around, and promised beer later. The drivers, very much on the defensive, went sullenly through the disastrous tale again, aware beyond any doubt that they should never have left the horses unwatched and were more than likely to lose their jobs. Nothing they said added much to what Walt had already told me.

"Do you know each other well?" I asked.

The thin birdlike one said they did.

"And the grooms. Do you know them? And do they know each other?"

"Seen them around," said the heavy one. "The lazy so-and-sos."

The thin one said, "One of them came from the Midway Farm."

That was Dave Teller's. "He came specially for Chrysalis. It's him ought to be blamed for the whole thing."

"Did the boys know each other before the trip?"

"Sure," said the heavy one. "Way they talked they both been in the horse game all their lives."

Walt sniffed and nodded. He'd checked all this, his resigned face said. Routine.

To the drivers I said, "I want you to think back and make a list of all the cars and trucks you can remember seeing on the road, all the way from Kennedy to the place you lost the horses."

They looked aghast and as if I were crazy.

"Look," I said, "on those turnpikes you sometimes see the same cars over and over. The ones going your way, that is. You see them at the rest stops, and maybe you start off first, and then they pass you, and then you see them again maybe stopped at another diner while you go on to the next one, and then they came past you again. Right?"

They nodded.

"So maybe you still remember some of the cars and trucks you saw on that trip? Especially any you saw on both days."

They stared at me. The heavy one said, "It's impossible. It was a week ago."

"I know. Try, anyway. Think it over. See if you can remember any at all, between you. Then write them down and leave the list here for us, sometime this evening."

I took out my wallet and tried twenty dollars each for size. It went down well enough. They said they would try.

"Don't invent anything," I said. "I'd rather pay for nothing than a lot of hogwash."

They nodded and went, with the beer postponed to their return.

"What are you looking for?" Walt asked curiously.

"Another horse van, I suppose."

He thought it over. "They could just have planned to rendezvous where the empty van was found. They didn't need to be seen on the road."

"I don't think they can have been sure when they would be able to do the hijacking. They wouldn't know where the drivers would stop for meals. No good fixing a rendezvous in Kentucky if the opportunity came earlier, up near Wheeling."

"They wouldn't want to drive too far with a hot truck," Walt agreed. "In fact, it was twenty-five miles, mostly back roads. They made straight for the hills, where it would take longest to round up loose horses."

"Any tracks?"

"No tire tracks of any use. The nearest road was gravel, dry and dusty this time of year. There were the tracks of the van going off the road round behind a hillock, but on the road itself they were just a jumble. Every car which passed raised a cloud of dust and wiped out all tracks which were there before."

I grunted. "Hoof prints?"

"Dozens of those. In all directions."

"Back onto the gravel road?"

He shook his head resignedly. "Impossible to tell. None on top of the van's tire tracks, anyway. But we took a lot of soil samples, on the outside chance something would turn up later."

"You did it pretty thoroughly."

The smile almost came. "A million and a half," he said briefly, "is a lot of insurance."

Midway Fam had prosperity printed on its gateposts, and I went through them alone, as Walt had said he felt the onset of a migraine headache.

A middle-aged Hungarian woman opened the door to me and in halting English asked me my business. Diagnosing her accent from long practice, I replied in her own language, as it was simpler, and presently, having consulted in the drawing room, she showed me in there.

Dave's wife stood in the center of a quarter acre of

deep green carpet, surrounded by deep green walls, white paint, and tomato-red upholstery. She flicked my card with one thumb and said, "You're the man who fished Dave out of the river."

"Yes," I said, surprised.

"He telephoned to me yesterday," she explained. "He says I am to trust you entirely."

She was a slim small-boned creature with the rounded tight little bottom which comes from riding horses a great deal in early girlhood. Her jawline was delicately square, nose narrow, eyes wide and bright. Gray speckled the mouse-brown springy hair, and if she was wearing cosmetics one would have needed to be nearer that I was to be certain of it. Decisive assurance showed from every crisp gesture, and from her tone I gathered that taking her husband's word for things was not her habit.

"Sit down," she said, pointing to a tomato chair. "Drink?" It was two o'clock on a hot afternoon. "Scotch," she said without waiting for an answer, making it a statement, not a choice.

I watched her splash the pale golden liquid onto ice cubes in two tall glasses, and add a token drop of water. She came across and held out one of them with a graceful sun-tanned arm. A heavy gold chain bracelet loaded with fobs and charms clinked from her wrist, and into my nostrils floated a trace of Joy.

I tasted the whiskey. Hedges and Butler's Royal, I thought. Too fine and light for anything else. The flavor from one sip lasted a long time on my tongue.

"Eva says you speak Hungarian," she said, moving away, picking up her own glass, and taking an adult swallow.

"Mm, yes."

"She was most impressed."

"I came about Chrysalis," I began.

"Do you speak any other languages?" Her voice veered more to American than English and had the abrupt, inconsequential lurch of two drinks too many; but it didn't show in her face.

"German," I said, raising a dutiful social smile.

The way I'd been taught languages, it took a week for a smattering, three months for fluency, and two years to bring one to the point of reorganizing typical speech and thought patterns when one heard them translated back into perfect English. In one period of seven years, in my twenties, I'd been crammed with German, Hungarian, and five Slavonic languages, from Russian and Czech to Serbo-Croat. None of them was likely to come in handy for finding stallions, and in any case they were almost out of date. The new boys were learning Swahili, Arabic and Chinese.

"And French, I suppose?" she said.

"A little," I agreed.

"Enough for the necessities of life, I expect." Her expression and emphasis gave the word "necessities" a precise meaning, which wasn't food and drink.

"Absolutely," I agreed, acknowledging her definition. She laughed. Nothing frail or fine-boned about that.

"Chrysalis," she said, "is a right bloody nuisance. He wouldn't have been my choice in the first place; that Purple Emperor strain is as soft as an old man's pencil and he's passing it on, they always do. Moth won the Derby in a shockingly bad year and if anything had given him half a race he'd have folded like a wet sheet." She took a deep swallow. "Do you know the first bloody thing about horses?"

"What *is* the first bloody thing about horses?"

She gave me a startled stare which turned into an incredulous laugh. "The first bloody thing about horses is that they make bloody fools of men."

I smiled back spontaneously, amused by the contrast between her robustness of thought and language and her delicacy of frame.

"I'm going for a swim," she said. "Bring your drink."

She mixed herself a new one in passing, and without looking back crossed the green carpet, pulled open a sliding glass door, pushed through the screen outside it, and walked with rocklike steadiness across a paved terrace and onto a deep green lawn. Sighing, I got to my feet and followed her. The grass was thick and resilient, a different species altogether from English turf, and a sprinkler on one side threw out diamond sprays.

She stopped on another paved area around a kidney-shaped pool and unfastened some clips on her yellow dress, which came off in one piece and left two more in view underneath. Her body was slender and well cared for, but not at all a young girl's. Middle to late forties, I thought: and the sort of woman who would have been uninteresting under thirty.

She slipped into the water and floated and I watched the sun make watered-silk ripples over her brown stomach.

"Come on in," she said. "There are plenty of swimsuits in the hut."

I smiled and shook my head, and sat down on one of the soft plastic poolside chairs. She took her time, humming and splashing gently with her hands. The sun was hot, but not like in the city. I took my jacket off and felt heat baking into my skin through the white cotton shirt. Peacefulness gradually seeped in too. I was in no hurry for her to rejoin me, which she presently did, the water drops shining singly on her oiled skin.

"You've hardly touched your drink," she observed accusingly. "Surely you're not one of those soft buggers who can't hold their liquor?" She picked up her own glass and went on proving that she, at any rate, wasn't.

"Chrysalis . . ." I began.

She interrupted immediately. "Do you ride?"

"I can," I said, "but I don't."

"Why not?"

"I haven't a horse. Nor a kingdom to give for one."

"Drink your whiskey," she said, smiling.

"In a while."

"Then strip off and get in the pool."

I shook my head.

"Why not?"

"I like it as I am." And I had too many bruises from the weir.

She shrugged, half annoyed. "Don't you do any bloody thing?"

"How many people knew at what hour Chrysalis would leave Kennedy Airport?"

"God," she said, "you're a bloody bore."

"Don't you want the horse back?"

"No," she said vehemently. "As far as I'm concerned, we'd be far better off with the insurance."

"Two hundred thousand dollars," I agreed, "is a heck of a gamble. Supposing he never sired another like Moth?"

"There's no stopping Dave when he's set his mind on something." She sat on the edge of a full-length chair and smoothed cream onto her face from a dusky pink tube. "And he had meant to sell off a bit of that, when he got back. God knows what will happen now he's strung up on those goddam pulleys."

"He'll be home in about four weeks."

"Yes. So he said." She lay down flat and closed her eyes. "I told him to take his time. It's too bloody expensive being ill over here."

Five quiet minutes passed. A single jet plane flew across, a silver streak so high up one couldn't hear it until it had gone. The air was still. The oiled brown body in the yellow bikini took in a hefty dose of ultraviolet and the ice cubes melted in the drinks.

"Take your clothes off, for God's sake," she said, without opening her eyes. "Or are you ashamed of that pink-white slug of a body the English usually bring over here?"

"I'd better be going."

"Do what you damn well like." She fluttered a lax wrist in a double gesture which said equally well, stay or good-by.

I stood up and walked over to the hut, a large beautifully made pinewood structure with a protruding front roof, for shade. Inside were a bathroom and two changing rooms, and in the tiny lobby some shelves in a cupboard held bright-colored towels and swimsuits. I took a pair of blue shorts and put them on. The bruises on my legs very nearly matched. I left my shirt on, picked up a towel for a pillow, and went back and lay down on the next chair to hers.

She merely grunted with her eyes still shut, but after another minute she said, "If you want to know about the timetable for Chrysalis, you'd better ask Sam Hengelman in Lexington. He fixed the van. He runs a private service from here. Dave called me and told me the date the horse was being shipped over, and I called Sam Hengelman. And he took it from there."

"Who else did you tell the shipping date to?"

"It wasn't any goddam secret, for God's sake. I called six or seven of the syndicate to let them know. Dave asked me to. Half Kentucky knew about it, I guess."

She suddenly sat up straight and opened her eyes.

"Why the hell does it matter how many people knew when Chrysalis was coming? How do you know it was him the hijackers wanted?"

"Supposing they got just what they wanted?"

"Were you born yesterday? The bloodline is what breeders pay stud fees for. Chrysalis isn't worth a sou to anyone if they can't use his pedigree. No one's going to even send a decent mare to a stallion someone just happens to have handy, which has no name in the studbook, no history, and no papers; let alone pay fifteen thousand dollars for the privilege."

"Buttress Life have been looking for an insurance swindle."

"They can look till they're blue in the face." She picked up her glass, swallowed, and grimaced. "This drink's as warm as that pool and just as sodden. Mix me another, will you?" She held out the glass and I unwound myself and took it and my own back into the house. I mixed her the same size dose as before, concocted a different one for myself, and took them both back, the ice clinking coolly as I walked.

"Thanks." She drank almost half. "That's better."

I stood beside the pool and put one toe in the water. It was blood warm, or more.

"What's the matter with your legs?" she said.

"The same as your husband's, only mine didn't break."

"What's under the shirt?"

"The sun's too hot. I can do without a sunburn."

"Yes." She lay flat again. "Pink-white slug."

Smiling, I sat down on the edge of the pool with my back toward her and dangled my feet in the water. I ought, I supposed, to go away and do something more useful, like interviewing Sam Hengelman. But Walt would no doubt have thought of that, and done it, since his threatening migraine would only have lasted until the car we had rented had taken me out of sight. Walt and Dave's wife hadn't exactly clicked.

"Mr. Hawkins," she said from behind me.

"Mm?"

"What do you do for a living?"

"I'm a civil servant."

"With this?"

There was a sharp metallic click, the one sound guaranteed to raise the hairs on my neck as if I'd never left the jungle.

"Do you know what you're doing with that thing?" I asked, as conversationally as I could.

"Yes."

"Then put the safety on."

She didn't answer, and I stood up and turned round, and looked straight into the barrel of my own gun.

I deserve it, I thought. Slow, careless and stupid, I was anything one cared to mention.

She was sitting with her legs curled underneath her, the Luger lodged unwaveringly in her fist. The gap between us, five yards at least, was too great for anything constructive in the way of action, so I simply stood still.

"You're a cool bastard, I'll say that for you."

"You won't shoot me," I said, smiling.

"Why not?"

"I'm not insured for a million and a half."

Her eyes widened. "Does that mean that you think that I . . . I . . . *shot Chrysalis?*"

"It's possible."

She stared. "You're a goddam fool."

"So are you, if I may say so. That gun goes off very easily."

She looked down at it vaguely and before I could stop her she threw it away from her onto the paving stones. The jar as it hit the ground inevitably fired it. Flame streaked out of the barrel, and the bullet smashed through the whiskey glass which stood on the ground beside her long chair, nine inches from her body.

It took her a second to realize what had happened, then she shuddered heavily and put her hands over her face. I walked across to fetch the gun, and put the safety on, and then perched on the chair facing her.

"Games," she said in a shattered voice. "What do I have but games? Bridge and golf. All games."

"This too?" I put the Luger back in the underarm niche and buttoned the strap.

"I just thought I'd make you sweat."

"Why?"

"That's a bloody good question. A bloody good question. All games. Life is all bloody games."

"And we're all poor bloody losers," I agreed sardonically.

She put her hands down and looked at me. Her eyes were dry, but half her assurance had drained away.

"It was only a game. I didn't mean you any harm."

She thought she was telling the truth, but I'd met too many of the tricks the unconscious mind gets up to. Perhaps because I'd saved her husband, or was looking for his horse, or merely represented some obscure form of male challenge, she'd had an undoubted urge to destroy me. And she was a very troubled lady in far more obvious ways than that.

"Give me your drink," she said abruptly.

"I'll get you some more whiskey," I said.

"Yours will do," she insisted.

I gave her the glass, but one sip was enough. Dry ginger ale. On the rocks.

"Do you cheat all along the line?"

"Whenever it's kinder, or safer, or gets better results."

I walked away across the lawn and brought her back another glass. She took a moderate pull and put it down amid the ruins of the first one.

"Stay to dinner," she said. She made it a casual suggestion rather than a warm invitation, and I answered her need, not her tone.

"All right."

She nodded briefly and flattened herself face down, to roast her back. I lay with one arm over my eyes to shield them from the direct sun, and thought about all the things she hadn't asked, like how was Dave when I saw him and how bad was the broken thigh.

After a while she went back to floating.

"Come on in," she called.

I shook my head.

"Don't be so prissy," she said. "I'm not a swooning virgin. If your legs are like that, the rest of you must be the same. Take that bloody shirt off and give yourself a break."

It was indeed very hot, and the clear blue water looked good. I sighed, stood up, took the shirt off, and slid down into the pool. Its lukewarm antigravitational gentleness unlocked knots and tensions in my nerves and muscles that I hadn't even realized were there, and I swam and floated tranquilly for nearly an hour. When finally I hauled myself out over the edge she was smoothing on another coating of oil. Her glass was empty.

"Is Dave in that state too?" she asked, eying me.

"Pretty much."

She grimaced slightly and said nothing when I put my shirt back on.

The sun had begun to lose its height in the sky and shadows were fanning out from the trees. A golden sheen lay on the big cream colonial-type house across the green lawn. The pool water stilled, and the quietness of the place crept subtly into all the senses.

"It's so beautiful here," I said. A banal enough phrase for the promise of peace.

She looked round casually. "I suppose it is. But we're moving, of course."

"Moving?"

"Yes. To California."

"Moving the stud? Horses, and everything?"

"That's right. Dave's just bought a farm down near Santa Barbara, and we're moving over there in the fall."

"I would have thought you were settled here for life. Wasn't this Dave's father's place?"

"Oh, no. We moved here about ten years ago. The old farm was on the other side of Lexington, out on the Versailles Road."

"California is a long way," I commented. But she didn't respond with a reason for the move, and after a pause I said, "If it wouldn't be much trouble to you, I'd like very much to see the horses and stables you have here."

She narrowed her eyes. "Business or pleasure?"

"Both," I smiled.

She shrugged. "Help yourself. But get me another drink first."

A poolside icebox, I reflected, would save a lot of walking: but maybe she still needed the illusion that she didn't drink in the afternoon. I fetched her a refill, changed into my clothes, and found her still face down in the bikini.

"Say I sent you," she said.

Before I could move, however, Dave rang from England, and Eva brought a portable telephone out and plugged the long cord into a socket in the hut. Dave's wife made three or four unanxious inquiries about her husband's condition, and then said, "Yes, he's here right now." She held out the receiver to me. "He wants to talk to you."

"Gene?" His voice was as clear as if he'd been in Lexington, and much stronger than it had been the previous morning.

"Hi," I said.

"Look, fella, Sim and I want you back here for a conference. Can you get a plane tomorrow?"

"But the fare . . ." I protested mildly.

"To hell with the fare. You've got a return ticket."

"All right."

"You haven't found the horse yet?"

"No."

"Do you think you will?"

"I don't know yet."

He sighed. "See you Thursday, then," and the line went dead.

The stables lay some distance away on the far side of the house. I walked round there and was shortly talking to the stud groom, Chub Lodovski, a large good-natured man with slow speech, a bird head, and great hamlike hands. He showed me round the whole setup with unlimited patience and an obvious pride in his job. The state of the place was his testimonial. The mares and foals ate peacefully in neatly railed paddocks reached by impeccable narrow drives with sharply cut grass edges. The stallions lived in a short row of six large airy box stalls in a spacious barn, with a wooden railed exercise paddock in front, flanked by two high-walled mating compounds.

Only five of these stalls were occupied. The vacancy was for Chrysalis.

"Is this where you kept Allyx?" I asked.

"That's right. Second stall from the end. He was only in it four days."

"And where was the fire?"

He frowned. "It started in some straw one night, just about here." We were fairly central. "It wasn't much. Mostly smoke."

"And you turned the horses out into the exercise paddock in front here?"

"That's right. Just as a precaution. But one of those doggone animals got scared and broke a rail on the far side, and the whole bunch got out across that stretch of grass onto that dirt road over there. We never did find Allyx. There hasn't been sight nor sound of him since."

We talked for a while about the search they'd made

next morning, but, Lodovski said, the whole of Kentucky was plastered with horses, and no one thought much about it if they saw one loose, and although a reward had been offered, and the insurance people had swarmed around like bloodhounds, they'd never found him.

"And now Chrysalis." I sighed sympathetically.

"Sure. And they say lightning never strikes the same place twice!"

He was moderately upset that the stud looked like losing another major attraction, but it wasn't his money that was involved, and besides that he was proud enough of the stallions remaining in residence. I asked him if he'd ever been to California.

"The farm's moving out there, did you know?" he said.

"Are you going, yourself?"

"Mebbe, mebbe not. Depends on the missus, and she can't make up her mind." He grinned comfortably and accepted the note I gave him with dignity.

When I got back to the pool Dave's wife had got her dress on again and Eva was brushing the splinters of glass into a dustpan, which she carried carefully away across the lawn.

"Well, what did you think of the place?"

"The horses all looked very well. The stallions especially."

"So would you, if all you had to do was——" she began, and then stopped and shrugged. "So would you."

Apart from an occasional "bloody" which crept in from habit, that was the last of her verbal squibs for the day. But my lack of scandalized reaction didn't have the same effect on her drinking, and she kept up a slow but steady intake right through dusk and dinner. Her mental brakes remained half on, half off, as before.

Over thick slices of rare beef she said, "Are you married?"

"No." I shook my head.

"Divorced?"

"No," I said. "I've never been married at all."

"Are you queer?" she asked, as simply as if she'd said "Are you comfortable?"

I smiled slightly. "No."

"Then why aren't you married?"

"I haven't found anyone who will marry me."

"Don't be ridiculous. You must have women lying down for you in droves."

"It's not the same thing."

She looked at me broodingly over the rim of her glass. "So you live all alone?"

"That's right."

"No parents?"

"They're both dead," I said. "And I've no brothers, no sisters, no uncles, aunts or cousins." I smiled. "Anything else?"

"Stay the night."

She said it abruptly, as if it came from a deeper level than her fairly harmless interrogation, and there was an element of surprise and alarm on her face afterwards.

"I'm sorry," I said matter-of-factly, "but I can't."

She looked at me without expression for about ten seconds.

"I have a mother," she said. "And sisters, and brothers, and dozens of relations. And a husband, and a son, and all this." She waved a hand around the millionaire-bracket walls. "I have everything." Her eyes filled with tears, but she went on looking straight across the table, without blinking.

"I have ... bloody ... everything."

Chapter 6

THERE was an envelope from Walt in my room at the motel containing a short note and a list.

Gene,

This is all the drivers came up with. I think it's

safe to bet that they actually did see these vehicles. The top three, they both remembered. The others, only one of them remembered. No horse vans, though.

Walt

The list read:

Impala, lilac, 2 years old, California number plates. Passengers included a fat child who made faces out of the rear window. Both days.

Gray station wagon trailing a load of furniture. Both days.

Dark green Ford Mustang, Nevada plates. Young couple, no description. The horse van drivers remember this one because they were discussing whether the Mustang was a good car or not. Second day only.

White convertible: young woman with blonde hair wound on rollers. Second day only.

Army green pickup truck with white lettering on the doors. Second day only.

The pickup, one of the drivers thinks, was probably on Interstate 70, after Zanesville and before they turned off south. He doesn't remember clearly.

I read the list through three times while I undressed. The load of furniture looked the most promising, but none of it exactly inspired.

Walt, driving to the airport in the morning, damped even the furniture.

"It was only one of those Snail Express trailers."

"Like the U-Haul," I said.

"That's right. 'Carry your house on your back, but let us take the weight,' " he said, quoting the Snail Express advertising slogan. "The drivers said it wasn't big enough to put a horse in."

"How about the pickup?" I asked.

"Much too small for a horse," Walt said gloomily.

He came back with me to New York and rubbed his

thumb continuously over the finger pads while I went through the file we had made on the case.

There was a batch of photographs of the missing horse, mostly taken from studbook advertisements by the look of them. Not a very remarkable creature on paper, I thought.

Sam Hengelman had sent his two most careful drivers to fetch Chrysalis. He had had a call from Mrs. Teller informing him of the date fixed for the horse to fly over, and also a cable from England when he was on his way. Hengelman had telephoned Kennedy Airport and been told the horses would be through the 24-hour immigration regulations at noon on Monday. He had sent the van as soon as he got the cable, on Sunday. There was, he agreed, a system like the U-Haul in operation among horse vans, to avoid the need for long empty journeys, but some folks liked personal service, and Mr. Teller was one of them.

The Buttress Life insurance covered transport. Sam Hengelman had not had to take out a policy for the trip, and stood neither to lose nor to gain from the hijacking.

Both drivers had clean records going far back.

Both grooms had been in their present jobs for more than three years. One of them came from Midway Farm; the other from another farm which had a horse coming in on the same trip.

An interview with Mrs. Eunice Teller had produced no helpful information.

I shut the folder with a smile and gave it back to Walt.

"How about checking with Snail Express, on the off chance?"

He looked skeptical. "The drivers said the trailer wasn't high enough."

"They're used to thinking in terms of ordinary horse vans. And they were looking down from their cab. You could squeeze a racehorse into a box about seven feet by four, by six feet high, if you were ruthless enough. Find out how many trailers that size or larger Snail Express had out last Monday or Tuesday, which might conceivably have been on the turnpike."

"All right," he said expressionlessly. "If you say so."

With the time lag working in reverse it was 3 A.M. Thursday morning when I landed at Heathrow, and noon before I walked into Dave Teller's room in a Reading hospital. Flaming June had come and gone: it was raining again.

If one discounted the ropes, pulleys, slings and plaster suspending his leg in mid-air, the patient looked healthy enough. He greeted me without fuss, the direct eyes steady and bright.

"Tiring trip?"

"So-so."

"You've eaten?" He waved vaguely at a collection of chocolates and grapes.

"I had breakfast over Ireland, at two o'clock."

He laughed, eased himself on the pillows, and stretched out a hand for a cigarette.

"How's my wife?"

"Very well."

He lit his cigarette and flicked shut the lighter.

"What was she doing when you called?" His apprehension was pretty well concealed.

"Sunbathing. Swimming. There's a heat wave coast to coast."

A couple of muscles relaxed in his forearm and he inhaled deeply. "She gave you a drink . . . I hope?"

"Sure. And a swim. And I stayed to dinner."

He looked at me directly for some time without speaking. Then he said merely, "A good one?"

"Very, thank you. And I saw your horses. Chub Lodovski showed me round."

He talked much more naturally about the horses: no problems there.

"I hear you're moving to California," I said after a while.

The tenseness instantly came back; the small give-away tightening of eye, neck and respiratory muscles that I looked for every day in my job and couldn't be blind to in my friends.

"Yes," he said, tapping off ash. "Eunice loves the ocean, and in Kentucky we're as far from it as can be . . . and of course, the horse-breeding business in California is every bit as profitable. We will do very well out there, I've no doubt."

Eunice would take her problems right along with her, I thought: though with a bit of luck they would recede for a year or two. Perhaps Teller considered the upheaval worth it.

"What's the new place like?" I asked.

"It's good land, pretty well irrigated. And the stable and general layout are as good as Midway. Better even in some respects. It's David L. Davis's old place."

I looked blank, and he explained. "Made his money out of roadside hamburger stands. Well, he died early this year, and last month they held a dispersal sale of his brood mares and stallions, to divide up his estate for inheritance. I put in a bid for the farm to his executors before I came over here this time, and they wrote me a week or so back to say they're accepting it. The contracts are in hand right now, but I don't foresee any difficulties. I'm sure glad to have got it settled at last."

"At last?"

"Been looking for a farm in southern California for over a year now, but there were too many snags to most of them. Eunice and I took a trip over in March of this year, and we saw the Davis farm then, and liked it. So . . ." He waggled his fingers to finish the sentence.

The door opened and Keeble came in, mild spectacles reflecting the pallid light from the window, eyes blinking rapidly, and the usual patch of bristle growing gray where he had short-sightedly missed with the razor. He said hellos all round and settled himself comfortably into the spare armchair.

"Well, how's it with the States?" he said, and I told them everything Walt had told me. They thought it over for a while in silence.

"So what do you think now?" Keble said.

I glanced doubtfully at Teller, but he tapped ash off his cigarette and remarked simply, "Sim says you were convinced I was pushed into the river on purpose. I guess what he's asking you is, have you changed your mind?"

"No, I haven't."

Keeble and Teller looked at each other. Then Teller said, sighing, "We've come up with one or two things which makes it almost certain you are right."

Keeble nodded. "I went to Dave's hotel in London to collect his luggage and pay his bill, and explained where he was if anyone wanted him. The young man at the reception desk asked me if the lady journalist from *Stud and Stable* had found Dave all right on Saturday. She had, he said, been most insistent, owing to a deadline on the magazine, and he had given her my address and telephone number, which Dave had left with him in case he was wanted hurriedly in connection with Chrysalis."

"And that," I remarked, "is how boy and girl knew where to find you."

"Quite," Keeble agreed. "From the house to the river was no doubt a simple piece of following. Incidentally, I checked with *Stud and Stable*. They didn't want Dave, and their deadline is the first of each month."

"Nice," I said.

Keeble took an envelope from his pocket and fished out some three-by-three-inch black and white photographs. "These are Peter's snaps," he said. "Take a look."

I took them from him and looked. The ducks had come out splendidly; better than one of Lynnie, who had been moving. The picnic lunch was there, and the *Flying Linnet* in Marsh Lock, and one of Dave Teller standing on the bows, and a rather grim one of myself staring down into the water. There was one of the four men fallen in a heap in the punt at the pub where we'd had our morning drinks, and another, taken with the photographer's back to the river, of Keeble, Joan, Dave, Lynnie and myself sitting round the little table under the sun umbrella, with glasses in our hands.

Keeble waited without blinking. With this in mind I started through the pile again, and found what he had seen. I looked up at him. He nodded, and from an inside pocket produced a magnifying lens, which he threw over to me. With the help of that, the two figures were clear. A girl with long hair and white trousers, a young man with pale trousers and a checked shirt, standing side by side in the background of the photograph of us all drinking at the pub.

"It's them," I nodded.

"Yes," Keeble agreed. "They were there in the morning. So I'll grant you they could have followed us by car from Henley—you can see the river from several places along that road—and also that they saw Dave standing on the bows when we left Henley and when we left the pub. And possibly also when we arrived at the pub, and at Marsh Lock. They would know there was a good chance of him being there again when we came back through Harbour."

I smiled. "And the five feet which was missing from the punt's mooring rope had been used to tie it securely to the danger post while they waited for us."

"I agree," Keeble said. "We took that punt right out of the water after you'd gone on Monday, and we found that the cleat for the stern rope had been unscrewed from the stern, and screwed on again under the waterline at the bow end."

"So both mooring points were at one end," Teller said. "The safe rope was underwater all the time, hidden by the punt itself and the girl's body and arms. And, of course, we weren't looking for anything like that at the time, so we'd never have seen it."

Keeble finished it. "Once they'd got the visible rope safely in Joan's hands, and we were all looking anxiously for you and Dave to surface, the girl had only to pull some sort of quick release knot, and the punt was free. So I'll agree, Gene, that that was an accident which could be staged, and was staged, and you were right and I was wrong. Which, I seem to remember vaguely, has happened once or twice before."

He smiled at me with irony, and I reflected that there

were few superior officers who would say that sort of thing so utterly ungrudgingly.

A nurse clattered in with Teller's lunch, which proved to be chicken salad and tinned mandarin oranges. The patient poured the oranges onto the salad and ate the combined course with resignation.

"The food is lousy," he said mildly. "I've forgotten what a good steak looks like."

We watched him eat without envy, and I asked Keeble if he'd had any results with the handkerchief.

"Only negative ones. None of the Yogi Bear concessionists in this country imported it. They say, from the material and the sort of paint used for the bear, that it was probably made in Japan. And some of them had doubts it was done by the Hanna-Barbera artists. Not well enough drawn, they said."

"I'll take it back to the States and try there," I said. "After all, the boy and girl were very possibly American."

Teller raised his eyebrows with his mouth full.

"The boy shouted 'Can you help us, sir?' and that 'sir' comes a great deal more commonly from Americans than from the English. Also, the boatman said their accent was 'same as on the telly' and there's as much American as English on our television."

"The same argument might apply to public school boys," Keeble said casually. "But they might well be Americans, I agree."

"So all we need to know now, apart from who were they," I said to Teller, "is why they wanted you dead."

No one had any constructive ideas on that point. Teller drank his coffee and a maid in a green uniform came to take the tray.

"You're guarding against them having another go?" I said to Keeble, watching the maid's back disappear through the door.

Keeble followed my eyes. "All precautions," he nodded. "The works. I got the Radnor-Halley Agency. Only the best for Dave!"

"They won't let me open any packages," Teller complained. "I think they take them outside, dunk them in a bucket, and wait for the ticking to start. And the only chocolates I have were bought by Sim personally. You'd never believe the half of what goes on in here."

I laughed. "It's when you get out of here you'll notice it."

"He'll stay here till you've wrapped it up," remarked Keeble; and he wasn't joking.

I stared. "I'm in anti-infiltration, remember? Not the C.I.D."

"Oh, sure. But the same motivation, I imagine. Just let your hunter instincts loose . . . and tell us what you plan to do next."

I stood up restlessly and went to the window. Still raining. Two nurses ran from one buliding to another, clutching capes around them and spattering mud up the backs of their stockings. Useful people, nurses. Needed people. Constructive, compassionate, tough people . . .

"Well?" said Keeble, behind me.

I turned and leaned against the wall. "How's the ex-chequer?"

Teller answered. "Look, Gene, I've enough to launch a minor space program. And, as I said before, if it weren't for you I wouldn't be here at all. So spend what you need to, and I'll pick up the bills."

"Right. Then I think it would be best to let the Radnor-Halley Agency deal with anything that crops up here. . . . I suppose they did the handkerchief inquiry?"

Keeble nodded.

"And I'll go back to the States tomorrow. I can't believe the attempted murder isn't tied in with the horse theft, so the springboard for everything must be in America. Unless some Irish fanatic disapproves of you skinning off the cream of British bloodstock!"

"Is Chrysalis Irish then?" Keeble asked seriously.

"Irish bred dam," I said. "That's all. His sire was Purple Emperor, in the Read Stud at Newmarket."

"How do you know?" Teller asked, surprised.

"I looked it up," I said briefly. "Also his markings. And that is important." I paused. "Whoever took Allyx and Chrysalis knew a lot about horses. Allyx was one of six stallions loose in a paddock at night. Chrysalis was one of five horses in a horse box. Yet each time the right horse was singled out for removal. We have to believe it was the right horse, not just chance, because each time it was by far the most valuable one of the collection which disappeared. Well, Chrysalis is a dark bay with no distinguishing marks. No socks, no blaze, no star. One color all over. And Allyx was exactly the same. There are literally thousands of horses like that."

The two men didn't stir.

I went on. "This means that if we ever do find Chrysalis, there will be an enormous problem of identification. English horses have no tattooed numbers, like American."

"Christ," Teller said.

"I wouldn't know him if he came up and ate sugar out of my hand. Would you?" He shook his head. I went on: "The only people at all likely to be able to pick him out for us with any certainty are those who handled him in England. And that's where we hit a very big snag. The stud groom at Read's died of a heart attack two months ago and the new man couldn't be sure of knowing Chrysalis again. Read himself is too shortsighted, apparently, to be of any help. This means we have to go back nearly five years, to the season when Chrysalis last raced. To his owner at that time, and his trainer. Though the only one I'd pin any faith on would be the lad who looked after him. And it's the lad, I think, who we'll need to take to the States if we find a horse which might be Chrysalis."

"We could easily find out who the lad is," Keeble nodded, "and shunt him over."

"His name is Sam Kitchens, and he'll be at Ascot at this moment, as one of his horses is running in the four-thirty. It's Gold Cup Day today." I smiled faintly. "I thought I might just drift along to the races when I leave here."

"Just tell me," Teller said in a small voice, "how and when you found out all this?" He spread his fingers. "I only ask."

"I spent an hour this morning at the British Bloodstock

Agency. I was practically camped on their doorstep at
nine o'clock. And then I did some telephoning. That's
all."

"When do you sleep, fella?"

"Between meals. Very bad for the appetite."

"He's mad," Teller said to Keeble.

"You get used to it," Keeble assured him. "The first
eight years are the worst."

"And this is the guy you'd trust your daughter to?"

"Hm," said Keeble. "We haven't mentioned that."

"What?" I said suspiciously.

"We'd . . . er . . . like you to take Lynnie back with
you to the States," Teller said. "She's going to visit with
Eunice for a while."

I glanced at Keeble and saw that he knew what I was
inevitably thinking: that Eunice's special need for company was more compelling than the rest of Lynnie's finishing
school term.

"I'd be glad to," I said to them both with formali-
ty. "On a slow boat via New Zealand, if you like."

"She's too young for you," said Keeble without anxiety.

"She is indeed." I pushed myself away from the wall
and stood upright. "Where will I collect her?"

Keeble handed me an envelope. "Air tickets for you
both. She'll be at the Victoria Air Terminal at eight-
thirty tomorrow morning. Is that all right?"

I took the tickets and nodded. "Can I have the handkerchief?"

He obligingly produced it, in another envelope. I put
that and the air tickets away, and picked up Peter's
snaps. Holding the negatives up to the light I singled out
the drinking group and put it in my wallet.

"I'll get it blown up tomorrow in New York," I said.
"Then it'll only be a matter of sifting through two hundred million inhabitants."

Drizzle was wilting the fluffy hats when I got to Ascot,
but the turf looked greener for it and the horses glossier. I
spotted the trainer I wanted and walked across to where

he was talking to a large woman in a creased pink dress under a dripping pink umbrella. He caught sight of me over her shoulder, and I watched the initial memory job pass through mind search to recognition. He smiled warmly at his success.

"Gene Hawkins!"

The large woman turned round, saw she didn't know me, decided she didn't want to, and departed.

"Mr. Arkwright." We shook hands, and I thought how little age had changed him. Still the upright, brisk, gray-headed neighbor from my father's days in Yorkshire.

"Come and have a drink," he said, "and let's get out of this rain." There were misty beads of water fuzzing his tall gray hat. "Though it's much better than it was an hour ago, isn't it?"

"I've only just come."

He led the way up the staircase into the Balcony Bar and ordered vodka and tonic. I asked if I could have the tonic without the vodka and he remarked that my father, an enthusiastic alcoholic, would have turned in his grave.

"What are you doing now, then?" he said, sipping the clear mixture. "Still in the Civil Service?"

"Yes." I nodded. "But I'm on leave at present."

"It always seemed rum to me, you doing something so . . . so tame," he said. "Considering the sort of boy you were." He shrugged. "Never would have thought it. Your old father always thought you'd do something in racing, you know. You rode well enough, you knew your way around. Can't understand it." He looked at me accusingly. "Those two years in the Army did you no good."

I smiled. "It was while I was in the Army that they offered me this job."

"Safe, I suppose," he said, making allowances. "Prospects, pension, and all that."

"Mm," I said noncommittally. "Actually, I really came here today to see you, to ask you about Chrysalis."

"Have they found him, do you know?" he said.

"Not yet, no. The American who bought him is a friend

of my boss, and they've asked me, as I know you, to see if you would do them a favor."

"If I can," he said promptly. "If I can."

"Their problem is," I explained, "that if and when a loose horse is found, especially if he's some distance from where he was lost, how are they to be sure it is Chrysalis."

He looked startled and then amused. "That certainly is a problem. But Chrysalis hasn't been in my yard since . . . let's see . . . four years last October. I don't know whether I'd be certain of him, not absolutely certain, if I saw him, for instance, among twenty others rather like him. And you'd want it to be more positive than that."

"Yes," I agreed. "Actually I rang your home this morning and your secretary said I'd find you here. And he also said Chrysalis' old lad would be here. Sam Kitchens. Would you mind if I had a word with him?"

"That's right, he came with Milkmaid for the four-thirty. No, I don't mind, you ask him what you like."

"Mr. Dave Teller, who bought Chrysalis, wonders whether you would let Sam Kitchens go over to the States for a few days, if and when the horse turns up, to identify him. Mr. Teller will pay his fare and expenses."

Arkwright laughed. "Sam will like that. He's not a bad chap. Pretty reliable."

"Then if he's needed, you'll get a cable saying which flight he's to go on, and so on. Will that be all right?"

He nodded. "You tell the American I'll let him go."

I thanked him. "They'll be very grateful." I bought him another vodka and tonic and we talked about horses.

Sam Kitchens walked his fair young Milkmaid around the parade ring and I risked ten bob on her, but she turned out to be a cow. I joined Arkwright while he ran his hand down the filly's legs and listened to the jockey explaining forcefully that it wasn't down there that the trouble lay, but up in her pea-sized brain.

Lads usually resent criticism of their charges, but from his expression Kitchens, a short stocky man of about thirty, held much the same view. I asked him, after introductions from Arkwright, whether he would know Chrysalis again with enough certainty to testify if necessary in a court of law.

"Sure," he said without hesitation. "I'd know the boy. I had him three years. Sure I'd know him. Maybe I couldn't pick him out of a herd, now, but I'd know him close to. The way his hide grows, and little nicks in his skin, I wouldn't have forgotten those."

"That's fine," I said, nodding. "Was there . . . is there . . . anything special about him which might help someone who'd never seen him before to recognize him?"

He thought it over for several minutes. "It's four years. More, nearly five, see. The only thing I remember is, we had trouble with his off hind hoof. It was thin, used to crack at the same place every time. But the stud he went to might have cured it, as he wasn't racing any more. Or he might just have grown out of it, being older now." He paused. "Tell you something, he liked sardines. He's the only horse I know of who had a taste for sardines."

I smiled. "That's pretty odd. How did you find out?"

"Took my tea into his box once. Sardines on toast. I put it down for a minute on the window sill, and when I looked round he'd scoffed the lot. It tickled me, it did. I used to share a tinful with him sometimes after that. He always liked them."

I stayed for the last race and picked another loser. I would have made a lousy trainer, anyway.

Chapter 7

I reached the air terminal at 8:15, but Lynnie was there first.

"I couldn't sleep much," she said. "I've never been to America before."

I'd been to America a dozen times. I hadn't slept much either.

Lynnie's clothes, a deep pink shiny PVC raincoat

over the orange-tan dress, were having an antisoporific effect on everyone in sight. Resisting an urge to grope for dark glasses I felt an uncommon lift to the spirits, which lasted to mid-Atlantic. There Lynnie went to sleep and a strong wave of nonenthusiasm for finding Chrysalis invaded my mind like one enormous yawn. I wouldn't mind, I thought idly, I really wouldn't mind lazing around that swimming pool with Eunice and Lynnie, doing nothing at all but drink in sunshine, peace, Scotch, and an uninterrupted view of two well-shaped females in bikinis. Peace most of all. Lie like a log, and not think, not feel. And sleep. Sleep for sixteen hours a day and mindlessly laze away the other eight: a program as near to death as dammit. A very small step from there to eternity, to make the peace permanent. . . .

"What are you thinking about?" Lynnie said.

She had opened her eyes and was watching my face.

"Heaven," I said.

She shook her head slightly. "Hell, more like." She sat up briskly. "How long before we land?"

"About an hour."

"Will I like Mrs. Teller?"

"Haven't you met her before?" I asked.

"Once, when I was little. I don't remember her."

I smiled. "She isn't easy to forget."

"Exactly," Lynnie said. "There's something odd about me going to stay with her. Of course I said I'd love to, and who wouldn't go off on any trip to get away from school, let alone a super one like this, but I distinctly think that Daddy and Mr. Teller have an ulterior motive and I want to know what it is."

"They want her to have company, to stop her drinking too much alone."

"Wow!" She looked surprised. "You're not serious?"

"They didn't say so. I'm only guessing."

"But I can't stop her drinking," she protested.

"Don't try. She doesn't get drunk. And you'll like her all right, as long as your ears don't fall off."

She laughed. "My mother wouldn't approve of her?"

"Quite rightly not."

"I expect that's why I've only met her once." She grinned at me mischievously without a shred of self-consciousness, Joan's influence waning visibly with every hundred miles.

It was late morning, local time, when we checked in at the Gotham. From there Lynnie departed on foot for a private tour of New York, and I cabbed down to Buttress Life. The heat wave was still in position, the air still saturated. Lethargy and haze hung over the city, and buildings shivered like mirages through the blue exhausts of the cars. Once over the Buttress building's threshold the temperate zone took over: I rode up to the seventh floor with the humidity in my clothes condensing into water, and sagged damply into Walt's spare chair in 47.

"Good trip?" he said. "You look . . ." he hesitated.

"Yeah," I said. "Pooped."

He smiled. It was worth waiting for. There's a load to be read in a smile, and Walt's was a good one.

"How's it with the Snail Express?" I asked.

He picked a list off his desk. "They were very cooperative. Only trouble is, they had about thirty-five trailers out on those dates which just might have been going west on the turnpike." He handed me the paper sympathetically. "It was a pretty long shot, of course."

"Hm." I looked at the list of names and addresses, and at my watch. "I think we'd better check them."

"I had a feeling you'd say that." A touch of gloom.

I smiled at him. "I'll start it, if you like. Do you know where we can get good enlargements of a snapshot done quickly?" He nodded and mentioned a name, and I gave him the negative. "The top left-hand corner. A couple. Man and girl." He nodded again. "And there's this hand-kerchief." I produced it. "Would you mind making a tour of all the offices on this floor, and perhaps the fifth as well, and finding out what everyone associates with it?"

Walt took the small white square curiously."

"Yogi Bear," he said. "What's the point?"

"It belonged to a girl who may know more than she ought about Chrysalis. The girl on the negative."

"Find her, find the horse?" He was half incredulous, a fraction excited.

"Maybe."

"Right, then," he said at the door. "See you."

I studied the list. Snail Express had done their best. Most names had two addresses, the old and the new. All were followed by a place and a date, the depot where the trailer had been checked in after its trip. There were several telephone numbers for the Eastern addresses, few for the West.

Working stolidly down the list, with long pauses while new inhabitants went to find the new telephone numbers of the old, I said I was calling from Snail Express, wanting to know that the service had been satisfactory, or if the customers had any suggestions or complaints. I listened to more praise than criticism, and eventually checked off twenty-seven genuine hirings.

Walt came back while I was biting the end of one of his pencils and wondering what to do next. It was three o'clock. He'd added lunch to his itinerary but he carried a large white package, which he opened carefully. Six enlargements of the corner of Peter's negative. Various sizes, from postcard to 9 by 7. The faces were clearest on the smallest print, too fuzzy on the largest.

"He says he'll run off as many as you want by this evening, if you let him know at once."

"Ask him for six, then. Postcard size."

"O.K." He picked up the receiver, pressed the buttons, and asked.

The boy and girl stood side by side, their heads turned slightly to the left, toward where we had sat under the sun umbrella. Their faces were calm, good-looking, and somewhat alike. The boy's hair was darker. They were of almost the same height. The checks of the boy's shirt stood out clearly, and one of its buttons was either undone or missing. The girl had a watch with an extra-wide strap on her left wrist. She hadn't been wearing it while she hung onto the post.

"All-American kids," Walt commented. "So what?"

"So how did you get on with the handkerchief?"

Walt produced it. A little limper, a little grubbier than before.

"Fifteen Yogi Bears, ten don't-bother-me nows, six lewd suggestions, and one Yellowstone Park."

"One where?"

"Yellowstone Park."

"Why Yellowstone Park?"

"That's where Yogi Bear lives. At least, it's called Jellystone in the cartoons, but it's Yellowstone really."

"Real live bears still in Yellowstone?"

"Oh, sure."

"A natural beauty spot . . . holiday place, isn't it?" I remembered vaguely.

Walt nodded.

"With souvenirs?" I suggested.

"Great lot of help that would be to us."

I agreed. It would only narrow the field down to one of the thousands who'd been to Yellowstone sometime, or one of the other thousands who knew someone who'd been to Yellowstone sometime. But I remembered a Jamaican would-be assistant to the Biological Warfare Defense Laboratory at Porton who'd been turned down because of a Russian-made bust of Castro in his bedroom. Souvenirs sometimes had their uses.

"The handkerchief probably came from Japan. Do you have a leg man who can check who imported it, and where it was sold over here?"

"Leg man?" Walt echoed dismally. "That's me." He put the handkerchief away in its envelope, chased up a few answers on the telephone, and heaved himself reluctantly to his feet. "I may as well go see a man about a Yogi, then. How're the trailers?"

"Twenty-seven are O.K. Of the other eight, five don't answer, and three have no telephone."

I tried two of the nonanswerers yet again. Still no reply. Walt looked through the shorter list I'd made of the unchecked.

"They sure went all over, didn't they?" he said. "Nebraska, Kentucky, New Mexico, California, Wyoming, Colorado, Texas and Montana. Just don't ask me to leg

it around all those places!" He drifted out and his solid
footsteps diminuendoed down the hall.

I went on trying the numbers now and then. After two
hours I had crossed Texas off the list, bitten the end right
off Walt's pencil, and started on it an inch farther down,
decided I couldn't work many days in his rabbit hutch of
an office, and wondered how Eunice was making out
beside her pool.

The telephone buzzed.

"Are you staying at the Gotham again?" Walt said.

"Yes."

"Meet me in the bar there?" he suggested. "I'm nearer
there than to you."

"Sure," I said. "I'm on my way."

Lynnie wasn't back. I left a message at the desk for her
and joined Walt. His pale-blue suit looked as if it had just
come out of a spin dryer and there was a damp translu-
cent look to his skin. Repentant, I bought him a large
Scotch on the rocks and waited until he had it where it
would do the most good. He sighed, rubbed the back of
one wrist across his eyes, fished a crumpled piece of paper
out of his pocket, and spread it open on the bar.

"To start with," he said disgustedly, "it's not Yogi
Bear."

I waited in sympathetic silence and beckoned to the
barman for a refill. On the paper a list of about eight
souvenir manufacturers and distributors had been crossed
out, a single line through each. The top lines were neat
and straight, the last three a great wild slash across the
paper. Walt had had a very bad day.

"The handkerchief came from Japan, like you said."
He took a swallow of his second drink and began to
revive. "Several of the firms phoned their West Coast
offices for me. No dice. It seems as if at least half the
souvenirs sold in the West are made in Japan, but all
these Yogi Bear concessionists say that this isn't Yogi
Bear at all, it's the wrong-shaped head."

He pulled out of the by now battered envelope a very
bedraggled-looking handkerchief and looked at it with
loathing.

"If it was sold at or near Yellowstone Park, it could have come from any two-bit import business. As it's not Yogi Bear, no one will have had to pay a commission to use the picture, and there isn't any way that I know of finding who brought it into the country and who sold it to where."

After ten seconds I suggested diffidently, "We could start from the other end."

He glared at me incredulously. "Are you plumb nuts? You can't mean what I think you mean."

The rocks in my drink had melted to pebbles. I tasted the drowned whiskey and put the glass back on the bar.

I said, "One of the Snail Express trailers was checked in at Rock Springs, Wyoming. It's still there: They haven't had another customer for it yet. I've asked them to hold it until I've had a look at it."

"Why that one? Why that one particularly?" Walt asked. Irritation only half repressed sharpened his voice.

"Because it's one of the three with no phone number. Because it's in the same state as Yellowstone. And because it gives me an itch."

"Yellowstone is all the way north from Rock Springs," he said. "Must be four hundred miles."

"Three hundred. I looked at a map."

He drank and rubbed his thumb over his fingers much faster than usual. Tired lines had appeared around his eyes.

"I think it's a futile waste of time," he said abruptly.

"I've no time to waste."

"And I haven't."

He put his glass down with a thump, reached into an inner pocket and brought out another white package which he tossed down in front of me.

"These are your photographs."

"Thanks."

The look he gave me was a long way from the smile of that morning. I wondered whether I would have let him go looking for answers if I'd known he was short on stamina, and decided I probably would. He hadn't given up halfway: only at the end.

Lynnie appeared in the bar doorway and the tired-looking men straightened their spines in a hurry. She wouldn't come in. I eased Walt with me across the heavy carpet and introduced him to her in the hall outside. He made only a few perfunctory remarks and left in a short time with a glowering face and solid back.

"Whatever's bitten him?" said Lynnie, looking after him.

"He's had a tiring day and he's going home to his wife."

She looked at me quickly, half laughing. "Do you always know what you're saying?"

"Frequently."

She chuckled. "Anyway, you look a lot tireder than he does." We started to walk over to the desk to collect our keys.

"That's most encouraging."

"What shall we do this evening? Or do you want to sleep?" She was unselfish enough to keep anxiety entirely out of her voice, but when I said we'd go wherever she wanted there was an extra bounce in her stride. She decided on a two-hour taxi ride to everywhere in the city she'd ever heard of that she hadn't managed to see that afternoon, followed by dinner in a second-floor glass-walled restaurant, looking down and across the lights of Broadway and Times Square. At eleven-thirty, when we got back to the Gotham, she was still wide awake.

"What a fabulous, fantastic day," she said in the lift.

"Good."

"I'll remember it as long as I live."

I smiled at her enthusiasm. It was a thousand years since I'd been as happy as that, but sometimes I could still imagine how it felt. That evening it had been quite easy.

"You are far from drizz," she said, contentedly grinning.

"You'd be no great drag to be stuck in a lift with, yourself."

But the car stopped unimaginatively at the eighth floor as scheduled and we walked along to our rooms. Her door opposite mine.

I kissed her cheek. "Good night, little Lynnie."

Her brown eyes smiled serenely back. "Good night, Gene. Sleep well."

"You too," I said. "Kentucky first stop in the morning." ....

It took four more days to find the girl in the photograph, though maybe I could have done it in two if it hadn't been for Lynnie. Privately aware that it wasn't necessary for me to do the job myself, I dredged up a cast-iron-sounding reason for having to accompany her to Lexington, and we flew down via Washington, which involved another quick taxi tour instead of a lengthy wait at the airport. Lynnie didn't intend to miss a thing.

Eunice met us at the Lexington airfield and drove us to Midway, and after a prawn and avocado lunch lent me her car to go on my errand. I greased Chrysalis' ex-groom into going with me with twenty dollars of his employer's money, and took him off to Sam Hengelman's. The horse van, Sam said out of the corner of his mouth as he watched an old movie on a color set, was still in care of the police department. If I wanted to look at it, go talk to them.

At the police department a state trooper listened to what I had to say, said, "Yeah," several times, consulted higher authority, and sorted out some keys. Higher authority turned out to be a good-looking detective in his twenties, and we all four repaired to the parking lot behind the police building, where the horse van stood in one corner.

Chrysalis' lad pointed out the stall the stallion had inhabited, and the state trooper came up with a successful conclusion to the expedition: four long shining bay hairs.

"From his mane," said the groom authoritatively.

The detective kept two for the state and sent off the

other two special delivery to Walt at Buttress Life, and the groom and I drove back to Midway.

Eunice and Lynnie were both in the pool, and the rest of that day and night came close enough to my daydream on the plane, except that the sixteen hours' sleep shrank to six, but even that was spectacular by recent standards.

When Lynnie said over large cups of breakfast coffee the next morning that she wished I wasn't going, I very nearly didn't. If I'd stayed, Buttress Life would have paid the insurance and a load of grief would never have happened. Yet if I could go back to that crossroads moment again I know I would inevitably make the same decision. Once a hunter always a hunter: the inner compulsion hadn't loosened its grip: the quality they'd hauled me out of the Army for was too basic in my nature, and being what I was, what I am, slopping out of the chase was impossible. Keeble had known, I admitted wryly, that he had only to get me hooked.

"I must go," I said, "if I'm to find the horse."

"Damn the horse," Lynnie said.

I laughed at her. "You've learned quickly."

"I like Eunice," she said defensively. "She doesn't shock me."

I gathered from that that she certainly did, but that Lynnie would never admit it.

"But you will come back here? Before you go home, I mean."

"I expect so," I said.

She fiddled with her coffee cup, looking down. "It's only a week since I picked you up at your flat, last Sunday."

"And you've aged a year."

She looked up quickly, startled. "Why did you say that?"

"It was what you were thinking."

"I know," she said, puzzled, "but I don't know how you do."

"Crystal set in the attic. Intermittent though, unfortunately."

"Just as well, if you ask me." There was a healthy

mockery on her laughing face. "How would you like to be tuned in permanently to Eunice?"

Eunice herself trailed through the doorway at that moment wearing an electric-blue wrapper and a manageable hangover. With both still in place, after two cups of coffee and a cigarette, she trundled Lynnie and me to the airport. ....

"Good-by, you son of a bitch," she said to me, as I stood beside her window. "I guess you can come back any time you want to."

Lynnie glanced at her sharply, with sudden speculation: growing up in front of one's eyes. I smiled good-by to them both and walked into the airport. From there I bus-stopped twelve hundred miles to Denver, and chartered a twin-engine Piper from a local firm for the last three hundred to Rock Springs. The pilot chewed his nails savagely beside me all the way as if he were a dedicated autocannibal, and I arrived feeling sick.

On the hot late Sunday afternoon the little desert town looked lifeless. Shimmering air rose endlessly over the dump of abandoned rusting motorcars, a Greyhound bus rolled past with passengers staring like fish through its green glass windows, and sprinklers on the richer front lawns kept the parching heat at bay. At the bus station I learned that old man Hagstrom's boy was the agent for Snail Express, but when I found old man Hagstrom, fanning himself in a rocker on the front porch of his small frame house, he said that his boy was out calling.

Hagstrom himself seemed to be glad to have company and told me to go inside and bring two beers out of the icebox. The icebox was in the living room, just through the screen door. It was a shambles of a room with sagging broken-spring chairs, dirty worn-out rag rugs, a scattered assortment of cups, glasses and bottles, all unwashed, and a vast new television set. I took the beer out to the porch, sat on the top step, and drank from the bottle, like my host.

The old man rocked, scratched himself, drank, and said vaguely that his boy would be right along, I could bet on it. I looked up and down the hot empty street. There were other shapes rocking gently in the shade of the porches, half-invisible because many had screens round the outside rails. From behind them they watched the world go by: Only thing was, the world rolled past in automobiles and didn't stop to talk.

Two beers later, while old man Hagstrom was telling me how he personally would deal with the Saigon situation, his boy rolled up in a pockmarked Chrysler. His boy was literally a boy, not more than eighteen: old man Hagstrom's grandson. He rubbed his hands down his grease-marked T shirt and jeans, and held one out to me with as easygoing a welcome as his grandfather's. I explained what I wanted.

"Sure you can look at the trailer," he said amiably. "Now?"

"If you don't mind."

"You're welcome."

He waved me into his baking car and whirled it casually around a few corners, drawing up with a jerk outside a rickety-looking gate set in a head-high wall. Through the gate, in a dusty area, stood four Snail Express trailers, all different sizes.

"That one," I said, pointing to the largest.

"Came in last Saturday, I think. I'll look it up." He unlocked a small brick office on one side, and I followed him in. Hot enough in there to please Satan.

"That's right. Saturday," he said, consulting the ledger. "Came from New York State, renting charge paid in advance for one week. The week wasn't up until Monday."

"Do you remember who brought it here?"

"Uh, let's see. Oh, yes. An old guy. Can't remember much about him. He had white hair, I guess."

"What sort of car did he have, to pull the trailer?"

"I helped him unhitch . . . a station wagon, I think. Gray, mebbe."

"It wasn't these two?" I showed him the photograph.

"Nope." He was definite. As far as he knew, he'd never seen them. Had I asked his grandfather? I had.

He said he'd swept out the trailer, but I could look inside if I wanted to.

"Why did you sweep it?" I asked.

"Usually do. It was pretty clean already, though."

I looked anyway. There were no bay hairs. Nothing at all to suggest that Chrysalis had ever been squeezed into it. The only suggestive thing about it was the way it was built: the roof opened outward right along the center line, to make the loading of tall objects easier. It had been worrying me that Chrysalis would not have walked into a tiny dark trailer: but one open to the sky was a different matter.

Old man Hagstrom's boy obligingly dug out the Hertz agent, who rented me an air-conditioned black Chevrolet with only 5,000 miles on the clock. Overnight I added 334 more, and drove into Gardiner for breakfast.

The road there had led through Yellowstone Park itself, where the dawn had crept in mistily between the pine trees, and glimpses of lakes had looked like flat puddles of quicksilver. I had seen an ugly great moose, but no bears. Yogi was asleep.

I spent all morning walking round the town. None of the shops were selling the handkerchief, or had ever stocked any like it. The photograph produced no reactions at all. After a toasted bacon, tomato and lettuce sandwich at a lunch counter I left Gardiner and went about fifty-four miles to West Yellowstone.

The afternoon's trudge produced exactly the same absence of results. Hot, tired, and frustrated, I sat in the Chevrolet and wondered what to do next. No trace of Chrysalis in the trailer, even though it seemed likely it was the one the drivers had seen. No matching handkerchiefs at Yellowstone Park. Walt had been right. The trip was one pointless waste of time.

I thought of the long forest drive back through the park, the canyon gradients at midway, and the final hundred miles of desert to Rock Springs, and decided to put it off until the next day. Sighing, I found the best-looking motel and booked the best room they had, stood under the shower until the day's aches had run down the drain with the dust, and stretched out for a couple of hours on the king-sized Slumberland.

The waitress who brought my steak at dinner was large, loosely upholstered, kind-natured, and with an obvious conviction that a man alone liked a bit of gossip. I wanted her to go away and let me eat in peace, but business was slack and I learnt more than I cared about her complicated home life. In the end, simply to stop the flow, I pulled out the crumpled handkerchief and asked if she knew where I could get a new one like it.

She thought "the girls" might know, and went off to ask them. Relieved, I finished my steak. Then she came back and doubtfully put the white square down beside me on the tablecloth.

"They say you might get one in Jackson. They do have bears on ashtrays and things down there. Down in the Tetons. Just over a hundred sixty miles. It's a holiday town, Jackson."

I'd driven straight through Jackson the night before on the way up from Rock Springs, and seen only a small Western town fast asleep. When I went back on Tuesday morning it was buzzing with holidaymakers and local inhabitants, dressed all alike in cowboy clothes. Dude ranch country, I learned. The main street was lined with souvenir shops, and the first one I went into had a whole pile of small white handkerchiefs with bears on them.

Chapter 8

THE girl in the punt opened the ranch house door, walked halfway to meet me from the car, and greeted me with professional instant welcome.

"Mr. Hochner? How nice to have you with us."

"I'm glad you could take me at such short notice, with the Fourth coming up next weekend." I shook her hand, putting a slight touch of German accent into my voice because it was easier for me than American if I had to keep it up for any length of time. It didn't seem altogether wise to be English. Also, I was wearing thick-rimmed, slightly smoky sunglasses I didn't really need.

"We're seldom full this early in the season." She smiled as far up her face as her cheek bones while her eyes skimmed my clothes, car and luggage. Only a hotelkeeper's checkup: it hadn't occurred to her that she'd seen me before; the accent and the sunglasses helped, too.

"I'll show you straight to your cabin, if you like? Then you can freshen up and come along here to the ranch house for dinner later on. There will be a bell, to let you know when."

I parked the car, and carrying my two suitcases, the old one and the new one from Jackson, followed her along a grassy woodland track toward one of several small log cabins scattered among the trees.

She was tall and strong, and older than she had seemed on the river: twenty-six or twenty-seven, I guessed. The fair hair no longer hung childishly loose, but was combed up into a round topknot, leaving her neck cool and un-cluttered. She wore dark-blue Levi's instead of the white trousers, but the pink shirt on top looked identical. One of the storekeepers in Jackson, the fifth I tried, had known her immediately when I had artistically let the photograph drop face up in front of him as I took money for a local map out of my wallet.

"Yola Clive," he said casually, picking it up. "And Matt. Friends of yours?"

"I'd thought of looking them up," I agreed, sorting out bills. "How do I get there, do you know? I haven't been to their place before."

He obligingly gave me clear directions for a 15-mile drive, finishing, "and the High Zee Ranch is the only place along there, so you can't miss it. But if you're planning on staying, I'd give them a call and make a reservation. It's a mighty popular place they run."

"I sure will," I said: and I did. I also bought some Levi's and shirts and a pair of riding boots, and the suitcase to put them in. In cowboy country guns passed without comment: I added a heavy black tooled leather belt with a silver buckle, and the clerk didn't show any surprise at my wanting to make sure that the small-of-the-back holster I sometimes used would slot onto it.

Jackson preserved its own Wild Western flavor to the extent of a small authentic stagecoach waiting in front of the drugstore: but the sleepy disillusioned horses between the shafts looked a poor prospect against galloping redskins. Broad raised boardwalks edged with hitching rails ran along in front of the stores in the short main street, though the mud they had been built to avoid had long been paved over. Motels with signs saying "air-conditioning and central heating" were called Covered Wagon and Rustlers' Hideout. Jackson was an uneasy mixture of evolution and make-believe, and clearly a success.

I sat in the sun on a hitching rail most of the afternoon: did a bit of thinking, and made two calls to Walt at Buttress Life.

Yola Clive led me round a neat stack of sawn logs, up two steps, across a minimal porch and through a screen door and a wooden door into the cabin.

"Bathroom through there," she said, pointing. "And you'll probably need to light the stove in the evenings. The snows only melted here two or three weeks ago, and the nights are cold." She smiled briefly and indicated a small tubful of a crumbly mixture which stood beside the squat black stove. "Light the logs with two or three handfuls of that."

"What is it?" I asked.

"Pep," she said. "A mixture of diesel oil and sawdust." Her eyes glanced professionally round the room, checking that everything was in order. "There's an ice machine out back of the kitchen, if you want to make drinks. Most guests bring their own liquor. We don't sell it ourselves. I expect you'll want to go riding tomorrow. We usually fix that up over dinner." The half-smile came and went, and Yola walked quietly away along the track.

Sighing, I investigated my quarters. There had been a reasonable compromise between age-old materials and modern construction, resulting in a sturdy two-roomed cabin with a pitched roof and varnished tree trunk walls. Two single beds stood on the polished wood floor in the main room, covered with patchwork quilts. A curtain across a half-shelved recess acted as closet, and the two upright chairs and the table were all home built. So too, I discovered, were the towel rail, stool and shelf in the bathroom. But the backwoods stopped short of the plumbing: and the lighting was ranch-generated electric.

I unpacked onto the shelves and hangers, and changed from town clothes into Levi's and a blue-and-white-checked shirt. The complete vacationer, I thought sourly: and buckled the gun belt round my waist.

After that for an hour I sat on the porch and looked at the view, which was good enough for a chocolate box. The Teton Range of the Rocky Mountains stretched north and south, with dark-green pine forests washing up from the valley to meet spotless snow-capped peaks. Along the bottom ran a sparkling thread of blue and silver, a tributary to the upper reaches of the thousand-mile Snake River: and between the river and the woods on whose edge my cabin stood, a wide stretch of sagebrush and scrub was dotted with yellow weedlike flowers.

The woods around the cabin stood on the lower slopes of another ridge of peaks which rose sharp and high behind the ranch, shutting it in, close and private. The stream ran right along, in and out, but the only road into the narrow valley stopped dead in the parking area of the High Zee.

A bell clanged loudly up at the ranch house. I went back into the cabin and put on a sloppy black sweater which hid the Luger and looked reasonable at 9,200 feet above sea level, though the still-persisting heat wave was doing a good job in the mountains too. Walking slowly along the dusty grass track I wondered if Matt Clive would know me. The accent and the glasses were aids, and I certainly had no clear memory of his face on the punt, though I now knew it well from the photograph. It was unlikely, since his full attention must have been concentrated on Dave Teller, that he had taken much notice of me; but he might possibly have a sharper impression than Yola, as I had been close to him when I went in after Dave. I needn't have wondered. He wasn't there.

Yola sat at one end of a long golden wood table flanked by chattering well-dug-in ranch guests. Family groups, mostly, and three married couples. No singles except me. A bright well-coiffured mother invited me to sit beside her, and her hearty husband opposite asked if I'd had a long drive. On the other side of me a small boy told his parents loudly that he didn't like stuffed pancakes, and every face round the table looked sunburned, vital and overflowing with holiday spirits. I battened down a fierce urge to get up and go out, to get away from all that jollity. I didn't see how I was ever going to make the effort to look as if I were enjoying myself.

By the end of the meal it felt as if my smile were set in plaster, rigid and mechanical to the extent that my face ached with producing it. But the hearty man opposite, Quintus L. Wilkerson III, "Call me Wilkie," seemed pleased to have a practically nonspeaking audience, and made the most of it. I endured a splash-by-splash account of his day's fishing. His wife Betty-Ann had ridden to the lake with him, and then gone on into the hills in a party containing her two children, Samantha and Mickey. I heard about that too, from all three of them. They asked me to ride with their party the next day, and I wrenched my tongue into saying I'd be glad to.

I lasted out the coffee. The Wilkersons promised to see me at breakfast, and Yola asked if I was comfortable in the cabin.

"Thank you, yes." Remember the German accent. Smile.

"That's fine," she said brightly, her eyes sliding past. "Ask if there's anything you need."

I walked stiffly out of the ranch house and along the dark track to the empty cabin; leaned wearily against one of the posts holding up the porch roof and looked at the row of peaks glimmering palely in shifting moonlight, with streaky clouds across the sky. My head ached with a feeling of compression, as if my brain wanted to expand and fill up with air.

How can I go on like this? I thought. Dinner had been about as much as I could manage. I didn't know what to do about it. No use praying: no faith. If I went to a doctor I'd get a bottle of tonic and a homily about pulling myself together. There was absolutely nothing to be done but endure it, and go on with that until it got better. If I could only convince myself that it would in the end get better, at least I would have something to cling to.

Somewhere in the valley a stallion shrieked.

Maybe it was Chrysalis. If he wasn't actually on the High Zee Ranch, I thought the chances very high that he was somewhere near. Maybe Keeble did know what he was doing sending me to find him, because it was evident that I could still function normally on the work level: concentration acted like a switch which cut out the personal chaos. If I concentrated twenty-four hours a day, life would be simple.

One trouble with that. It was impossible.

The ranch held upward of a hundred and twenty horses. About forty of them were penned in a big corral near the main ranch house, saddle horses for the ranch guests to ride.

Breakfast had been early, but the fitting of guests to horses took some time, even though everyone except me had been there two or three days and knew which animal they wanted. The head wrangler asked me if I could ride, and if so, how well.

"I haven't been on a horse for nine or ten years," I said.

He gave me a dead quiet one with U-shaped hocks. The western saddle seemed like an armchair after the postage stamp I'd been teethed on; and there were no newfangled things like buckles for raising and lowering stirrups. The head wrangler unlaced the thong holding the three-inch-wide leathers to the saddle, slid them down two or three holes, and laced them up again. Good soft leather, which could go all day and not rub the horse.

Over to one side of the ranch house, past its green watered lawn, there was a smallish sturdily railed paddock of not more than an acre. I'd spent all breakfast looking out the window at the seven horses in it. Three mares, two small foals, two stallions. Both the stallions were bays, but one had a white blaze and was no thoroughbred.

"What are those horses over there?" I asked the wrangler, pointing.

He paused a second while he worked out how to put it delicately to an ignorant dude, and a foreigner into the bargain, and then said, "We breed most of the horses, on this ranch."

"Oh, I see," I said. "Do you have many stallions?"

"Three or four. Most of these," he glanced round the patiently waiting mounts, "are geldings."

"That's a nice-looking bay," I commented.

He followed my direction over to the small paddock again. "He's new," he said. "A half-bred Matt bought in Laramie two or three weeks back." There was disapproval in his tone.

"You don't like him?" I said.

"Not enough bone for these hills," he said briefly, finishing the second stirrup. "Now, is that comfortable?"

"Fine," I said. "Thank you."

He nodded with casual friendliness and went to see to someone else. The wranglers differed from the dudes only in the matter of age and dress. They were all boys or young men between eighteen and thirty, several of them college boys working their vacation. The dudes were either parents or children; scarcely one in the twenties. No one, Betty-Ann Wilkerson told me knowledgeably, called cowboys cowboys anywhere except in films. Cowhand was possible, but the right word was wrangler. There were no cattle on the High Zee. The wranglers herded the horses, and the horses were there for the dudes to ride.

In the matter of clothes the wranglers were less flamboyant, less well pressed, altogether dustier. They had been up since 5:30 and other people's holidays were their hard work.

"They turn the horses out on the hills every night," Wilkie explained, "and go up and herd them down in the morning."

We set off from the ranch in two parties, about twelve guests and two wranglers in each. Down over a flat wooden bridge across the narrow river, and up into the main Teton Range opposite. Wilkie rode in front of me and Betty-Ann behind as we wound upward through the woods in single file; and neither of them tired of talking.

"They turn the horses out on the hills over here because there isn't enough pasture in the valley to feed them." Wilkie turned half around in his saddle to make sure I could hear. "They go miles away, most nights. The wranglers fix a bell onto some of them, like cowbells in Switzerland, so that they can find them in the morning. The ones they put bells on are the sort of natural leaders, the horses other horses like to be with." He smiled heartily. "It's sure difficult to see them sometimes, with the sun shining through the trees and making shadows."

What he said was true because we passed a group of three in a hollow later on, and I didn't see them until one moved his head and clinked his bell.

"They only bring in the number they need," Betty-Ann filled in. "They just leave the rest out, and maybe bring some of them in tomorrow, if they come across them first."

"So sometimes a horse could be out for a week at a time?" I suggested.

"I guess so," Wilkie said vaguely. He didn't really know. "Of course, if they want one particular horse, the wranglers will go right up the mountain to find him, I do know that."

"Anyone who can ride well enough can go up with the

wranglers in the morning," Betty-Ann said. "But they *canter* up and down here instead of walk."

The path was steep and also rocky.

"These horses are born to it, honey," said Wilkie kindly. "Not like the riding school horses back home."

At 11,000 feet the path leveled out onto a small tree-shaded plateau overlooking a breath-taking pine-wooded valley with a big brilliant blue lake in its depths. The cameras came out and clicked excitedly. The chattering voices exclaimed over an order of beauty that demanded silence. And eventually we rode down again.

Yola asked me at lunch if I had enjoyed my morning, and I said without difficulty that I had. The Wilkerson children were calling me Hans and asked me to swim in the stream with them in the afternoon. Wilkie clapped me heartily on the shoulder and told me I was a good guy, and Betty-Ann had irritatingly begun looking at me in a way which would change her husband's mind about that instantly if he noticed.

I left the lunch table last and whisked away a large slice of bread in a paper napkin. Alone in my cabin I unpacked some specially acquired groceries, filled one pocket with sugar cubes, and onto the bread scooped out a whole tin of sardines. With the bread held still in the napkin I walked down through the sagebrush and along to the mares' and foals' paddock, reaching it on the far side from the ranch house.

There I offered sugar in one hand and sardines in the other. The mares came and sniffed, and all chose sugar. The foals chose sugar. The bay with the white blaze chose sugar. The dusty half-bred that Matt had bought two three weeks ago in Laramie came last, less curious than the rest.

He sniffed at the sardines and raised his head with his ears pricked, staring across at the high Tetons as if hearing some far-off sound, smelling some distant scent. His nostrils quivered gently. I looked at the splendid lines of bone in the skull, the gracefully slanted eye, the perfect angle of head on neck. He had the crest of a thoroughbred stallion, and the hocks of a race horse. He bent his head down to the sardines and ate the lot.

Yola and Matt Clive lived in a cabin of their own, separate from the main ranch house, which contained only the dining room, kitchens, sitting room, and wet-day games room for the guests.

Yola backed an olive-drab pickup with small white lettering on its doors out of a shady carport beside her cabin, and drove away down the dusty road. I stared after her, half amazed, half smiling. Full marks to the horse van drivers, I thought. They'd seen both the Snail Express van and the pickup. They must have seen them both several times, but even so, they'd remembered.

Guests were allowed to use the one telephone, which was located in the Clives' cabin. I strolled over there, knocked on the door, and found the place empty. Not locked, though in this case there was a key. There were no locks on any of the guest cabin doors: one could only bolt them on the inside, with a simple wooden wedge slotted into the latch.

A quick tour of the Clives' cabin revealed two separate single bedrooms, living room, kitchen, bathroom and office. I planted three hypersensitive listening devices as invisibly as possible, and unhurriedly left.

After that I climbed into the Chevrolet and drove myself back to Jackson, where the telephone was more private. My call to Buttress Life lasted a long time, and Walt's contribution to the second part of the conversation consisted of gasps and protests of "You can't."

"Listen, Walt," I said in the end. "We're not policemen. I imagine your company would settle for the property back and no questions asked? And my brief is to restore Chrysalis to Dave Teller. Just that. Nothing more. If we start things the way you want, we'll end up with a lot of smart lawyers and most probably a dead horse."

There was a long pause. "All right," he said slowly. "O.K. You win."

He wrote down a long list of instructions. "This is

Wednesday," I said, thinking aloud. "Sunday morning. That gives you three clear days. Should be enough."

"Only just."

"Never mind," I said soothingly. "You can do most of it sitting down."

Walt wasn't amused. "And you, what exactly will you be doing?" he asked sarcastically.

"On a dude ranch," I said reasonably, "one dudes."

At the post office I mailed off to him by express delivery six hairs from the mane of the sardine horse, and motored back to the grim business of acting the holiday I'd feared from the start.

The three days seemed eternal. Riding took up the mornings and most afternoons and that was the best of it. Meals continued to be a desperate trial. The nights were long. I wished that Lynnie could have come with me, because in her company the depression seemed to retreat, but she was Eunice's crutch, not mine. And her father, trust me as he might, would have found it hard to believe I would only ask for her daytime closeness. And maybe I couldn't have done it. So no props. No props at all.

Yola ran the ranch with a sort of superefficiency which looked easy, juggling staff and guests into harmony without a single wrinkle of anxiety and without any show of aggression. The fair hair continued to be worn tidily on top. Her clothes were jeans and shirt and soft flat shoes. No boots: no masculinity. She radiated friendliness and confidence, and her smile never once reached her eyes.

She didn't go riding with her guests, and I never sat next to her at meals because most of the husbands and many of the wives conducted a dignified scramble for her favors; but on Thursday evening, when with several others I was drinking after-dinner coffee out in the open on the long porch, she dropped gracefully down into the empty chair beside me and asked if I was enjoying my holiday and was finding my cabin comfortable.

I answered with half-true platitudes, to which she half listened.

"You are young," I said next, with great politeness, "to own so beautiful a place."

She replied to this small probe with frank ease. "It belonged to my grandfather and then to my mother. She died a year or two back."

"Has it always been a dude ranch? I mean, it seems a bit hilly for cattle . . ."

"Always a dude ranch," she agreed. "My grandfather built it about forty years ago. How did you hear of us?"

I glanced at her unhurriedly, but she was merely curious, not suspicious.

"I asked in Jackson for somewhere good and fairly quiet, out in the mountains."

"Who recommended us?"

"Just a man in the street."

She nodded, satisfied.

"What do you do in the winter?" I asked.

There was a flicker in the eyes and a quick private smile on the mouth: whatever she did in the winter pleased her more than hotelkeeping.

"We move down south. Snow completely blocks this valley from November through March. Most years it's May before we come back. . . . We usually open the ranch the second week in June, but the canyons are often impassable then."

"What do you do with the horses?"

"Oh, they go down to the plain, on a friend's ranch."

Her voice was as strong and capable as the rest of her. I watched her eyes slide round toward the paddock with the mares and foals, and pause there calmly, and return to me. Expressionless.

I smiled her a force five version of an adults-only smile, and asked if she ever found it lonely, so far out in the wilds. To this mild but unmistakable come-on there was no reaction beyond a crisp shake of the head. I was the only man there not guarded by a watchful wife: Yola wasn't in the least bit interested.

I complimented her on the ranch food, and on the helpfulness of the wranglers. She said she was glad I was pleased. I yawned and apologized, and said it must be all the fresh air . . . she'd heard it all dozens of times a year, said everything she'd said so often that she no longer had to think. No use on this occasion using any jolting technique to force out an unguarded phrase: jolting her was roughly the last thing I wanted to do.

After a while I stood up lazily and said I would turn in, and she gave me the usual meaningless half-way-up smile. She hadn't really seen me at all: wouldn't remember me in another month. Unless I inadvertently gave her cause.

The three bugs in her cabin worked on the audio-switch principle: any noise, and speech especially, which they picked up automatically started the recording machine which occupied the back half of the ordinary-looking transistor radio standing beside my bed. But there was little to overhear. Yola slept alone, and apart from one evening when she invited four of the guests in for a drink, the only conversations were telephone calls.

In my cabin each evening, warmed by the squat black stove, I played back the day's "take." Nearly all the calls were to do with business: grocery orders, laundry, blacksmith's supplies, and future bookings. But one call, on Friday evening, was worth all the trouble.

"Uncle Bark?" Yola's voice said, low and clear. One of the bugs was behind a picture of drooping roses on the wall over the telephone table.

". . . honey." The occasional word escaped from the receiver in return, but Yola must have been holding it close to her ear.

"Sure. Everything's just fine here," she said. "Absolutely no kind of trouble."

". . . Matt? . . ."

"That's what I called about, Uncle Bark. Matt wrote me he's having to give up in Europe. He says he can't get near to you-know-who, they've got him holed up as tight as Fort Knox. So I guess we'll just have to keep everything under wraps for a while longer."

". . . ."

"It sure is a nuisance, yeah. But as long as we get him to you before the snows come again . . ."

". . . ."

"How can we? You know it isn't built for that."

"... stay ..."

"We certainly can't send him down to Clint's with the others. We'd waste a whole year and he might break a leg or something."

"... desert."

"We don't want him at Pitts, it isn't built for it, but there's a good long time for Matt to arrange something."

"... hadn't started."

"Yeah, I'm sure you would. But it's too late now. How were we to know that something so goddam stupid would happen? Matt will probably be home sometime tomorrow. I'll have him call you."

She put down the receiver soon after that: and I wound back the tape and played the conversation over again. Two unsubstantial points emerged. If Dave Teller had been too obviously guarded, Matt would have realized that the punt episode was not considered to be an accident. And the something "goddam stupid" which had somewhere or other upset the Clives' original plans might be that I'd been there to fish Dave out of the river, or might be something else quite different; something which had made the removal of Dave necessary in the first place. The horse had been stolen on June 15, Tuesday, and Yola had asked the London hotel for Dave's weekend address on June 19, Saturday. So what, if anything, had happened in the four days between? Something goddam stupid ...

I told Yola after breakfast on Saturday morning that I had enjoyed my stay immensely and would be leaving the following day. She smiled the regulation smile without clearly focusing, and thanked me for letting her know.

"So if I could have my bill at breakfast tomorrow?" I suggested.

"Sure," she said. "But you can't stay over Monday for the Fourth?"

"I'm afraid not."

She nodded, not caring one way or the other. "I'll get it ready for you then."

The Wilkersons exclaimed over my going. "You'll miss

the barbecue," Samantha said. "And the float trip down the river."

A local man took parties down the fast-flowing Snake on black inflated rubber raft dinghies: one of the area's attractions, like the rodeo and the ski lift. The Wilkersons had asked me to join them. "Maybe I'll come back next year," I said. And maybe I wouldn't.

I looked after the children that afternoon while Betty-Ann went to the hairdresser and Wilkie drove to a distant lake for the fishing. They swam in the stream, where I refused to join them in case my head in the water jogged Yola's sleeping memory, and we fed sugar and handfuls of grass through the rails to the leggy foals in the little paddock. The rails were solid young tree trunks dovetailed and nailed into even sturdier posts, and the gate was just as substantial. Its hinges were bolted through the gatepost, and a heavy padlock fastened it through two strong hasps. None of this strength was new.

Samantha and Mickey didn't think much of the sardine bay.

"Too spindly," Mickey said. "His legs would snap if he went up the mountain." I looked across at the Teton Range, the tops shining white in the hot sun. The sure-footed born-to-it ranch horses picked their way easily up and down the steep rocky paths over there, through the woods growing with flat huckleberry leaves, across the screes left from landslips, and onto the bare stony patches above the snowline.

"Why don't you stay till Monday night?" asked Mickey. "If you go tomorrow, you'll miss the fireworks."

Chapter 9

AT one o'clock, early Sunday morning, I stood on the porch of my cabin, my glasses in my pocket this time, waiting for my eyes to dilate and listening to the night.

A slight wind, riffling the trees. A car horn, very distant. The faint hum of the electric generator in its special house. No sound from Yola's cabin. None all evening. Matt hadn't yet come home.

With some misgivings I had left my riding boots in the cabin, and wore only thin rubber-soled plimsolls, with a pair of socks over them. I walked quietly through the sagebrush on the long way around to the little paddock, the spicy fragrance rising into my nose as I disturbed the silver-gray leaves. The half-moonlight was enough to see by without a flashlight and streaky clouds made shifting shadows across the ground: it couldn't have been better if I'd sent in an order.

The padlock's strength was illusory. It had a simple lever movement inside which took me less than five minutes to fiddle open. No one could have heard the click of success. Nor the tiny squeak of the gate opening. I slipped through and distributed sugar to the mares and foals. The bay with the white blaze greeted this with a trumpeting whinny; but no lights went on in Yola's cabin or the wranglers' bunkhouse.

The sardine horse flared his nostrils at me but ate the sugar and let me slip over his head the simple rope halter I had come armed with. I spent some time rubbing his nose and patting his neck, and when I walked toward the gate he came with me docilely enough. I opened the gate and led him through, and the mares and foals quietly followed, their unshod hoofs making dull little clops on the loamy ground.

The gentle procession went slowly across toward the river, over the flat bridge with hollow thuds, and up into the darkness of the pine woods. The mares soon stopped to graze, and the foals with them, but the bay stallion with the blaze suddenly realized he was free again, and crashed past me at high speed, squealing and cantering up the path and making as much noise as a trainload of football fans. Anxious, heart-quickened moments passed: but still no reaction from below.

The sardine bay tugged hard to follow. I soothed him and steadied him, and we presently walked on. He picked his way too cautiously over the stones and corners of rocks sticking up in the narrow path, but I couldn't hurry him without risk; my neck prickled at the thought of being slung into a Wyoming jail for horse stealing; but it was nothing to the fear I had that Mickey might be right about those spindly legs.

In places all the way up the width of the path dwindled to two feet, with a wall of rock on one side and a steep slope on the other. Riding along them by day one simply had to trust that one's horse wouldn't tumble over the edge, as nothing could then have stopped a rock-strewn rolling descent of two or three hundred feet. At these points there wasn't room to walk side by side with a horse one was leading: I inched up the path ahead of him, and slowly, cautiously, he put his feet delicately down between the bigger stones, and scrunched after me.

Two or three times we passed small groups of horses from the ranch, the cowbell clanking gently round the neck of the leader and betraying their presence. Their dark shapes melted into the jumbled background of woods and rocks, and the moonlight picked out only an eye, a rump, a swishing tail. The wranglers found them each morning by tracking, as the bells were audible for only a furlong. I'd had a long talk with one of the boys about tracking, and he'd shown me how they did it. They were going to be able to follow my way up the mountain as clearly as if I'd given them directions, and to tell the time I went by the amount of dew which formed in the hoofprints. The boy had shown me hoofprints, told me how many horses had gone by and when, and all I had seen were some scattered dusty marks. They read the ground like a book. If I tried to obliterate the sardine horse's hoof prints, I obliterated also any chance of the Clives believing he had wandered off by accident. The fuzzy outline of plimsolls under socks was, I hoped, going to pass unnoticed: nothing less was worth the discomfort of wearing them on such jagged going.

It took two hours to reach 12,000 feet and to come to the end of the tracks I'd learned in the past four days. From there it was a case of trusting my own nose. The drifting streaks of cloud made black shadows like pits across the rocks and several times I stood still and felt ahead with one toe to make sure that the ground was in fact still there and I was not stepping straight off a precipice. The moon itself, and the cold mountain air moving against my right cheek, kept me going in the right general direction, but the dotted-line trail I had studied on the map proved more optimistic than actual.

The horse's legs stood up to it remarkably well. Mine had already had enough. Mountaineering was not among Civil Service requirements.

The peak of the Grand Teton rose to 13,700 feet. The summit loomed very close. Patches of snow, half melted, exposed black-looking banks of scree. I came suddenly across a narrow trail winding past them like an eel: people had walked along there recently, scraping into the snow. I had, with some luck, come the right way. The cold bit down under my black jersey and through the thin shirt underneath, and I wished I had had the sense to bring gloves. But it couldn't be a great deal farther: through the short canyon pass, and out the other side. I looked at my watch. The climb had taken nearly three hours, and I was late.

It was darker in the canyon, but also invisible from the valley below. I took the small flashlight out of my jeans pocket, and shone it in front of my feet. Because of that, the whole expedition came unstuck.

A man suddenly rounded a corner a short way ahead and stood foursquare in the center of the trail. Startled even more than I was, the horse backed instantly away, tore the rope out of my hand, pulled me flat over as I tried to hang on, and skipped sharply away along a narrow ridge branching off to the left.

Sick and furious I got back on my feet and turned to go after him. The man took a tentative step down the trail and called out:

"Gene?"

It was Walt.

I bit my tongue literally to stop the rage in my mind from spilling over him. There wasn't time for it.

"I saw you coming. The light," he explained. "I

thought I'd come along to meet you. You're later than you said."

"Yes." I shut my mouth. There was half a million pounds loose in a death trap. My responsibility, and my fault.

The moon pushed out a feeble twenty watts. I couldn't see the horse. The path he had taken in panic was a ledge eighteen inches wide with sheer rock on the left and a fierce slope of scree on the right. A gradient so steep that it was as dangerous as a straight downdrop: and in its black invisible depths there would be the usual big slabs with upjutting edges.

"Stay here," I said to Walt. "And keep quiet."

He nodded without speaking, understanding that the situation was beyond apology. His instructions had been expressly to wait for me at one arranged spot.

The ledge was thirty feet long with a bend to the left. I walked along it slowly, not using the light, my left hand trailing along the rock wall, the gray light just enough to show the crumbly uneven outer edge.

After thirty feet the ledge widened into a saucer-shaped bowl three quarters surrounded by towering rocks. The sloping floor of the bowl led directly into the sharper slope of the scree. On the floor of the bowl were patchy snow and rough black pebble.

The horse was standing there, sweating. Quivering in every rigid limb. There was no way out except back along the ledge.

I stroked his muzzle and gave him four lumps of sugar, speaking gently to him in a voice much calmer than my feelings. It took ten minutes for the excessive tension to leave his body, and another five before he would move. Then I turned him carefully round until he was facing the way he had come.

Horses react instantly to human fear. The only chance I had of getting him safely back was to walk around there as if it were a broad concrete path across his own stable yard. If he smelled fear he wouldn't come.

Where the ledge began he balked. I gave him more sugar and more sweet talk. Then I turned my back on him and with the halter rope leading over my left shoulder, walked slowly away. There was the faintest of protesting backward tugs, then he came.

Thirty feet had never seemed so interminable. But an animal's sixth sense kept him from putting a foot over the edge, and the slithering clop of his hoofs on the broken ground came steadily after me all the way.

Walt, this time, made no sound at all. I came across him standing motionless several yards up the intended trail and he turned without speaking and went on ahead.

Less than half a mile farther the path descended and widened into a broad sweeping basin: and there, where Walt had been supposed to meet me, waited another man, stamping his feet to keep warm.

Sam Kitchens. Holding another horse.

With a powerful flashlight he inspected every inch of the one I'd brought, while I held his.

"Well?" I said.

He nodded. "It's Chrysalis, all right. See that tiny scar up here, under his shoulder? He cut himself on a metal gatepost one day when he was a two-year-old and a bit full of himself. And these black dots, sort of freckles, along that patch of his belly. And the way his hide grows in a whirl just there inside his hock. He always had clean legs. There's a mark or two on them now that wasn't there when I had him. But apart from knowing him from his general shape, like, I'd certainly swear to those other things in any court you'd like to mention."

"Was the cut from the gatepost bad enough to be treated by a vet?"

He nodded. "Five or six stitches."

"Good," I said. "Then off you go with him. And take good care."

Sam Kitchens grinned. "Who'd have thought I'd have seen him again up the Rocky Mountains in the middle of the night? Never you mind, I'll take care, all right."

He turned Chrysalis expertly round, clicking his tongue affectionately, and began the mile-long walk down to the

Teton camping ground, to where he and Walt and Sam Hengelman had come in a horse box.

Walt said, "It's too late for you to go back. Come with us."

I shook my head. "I'll meet you in Idaho Falls as we arranged."

Walt moved uncomfortably. "It's not safe to go back."

"I'll be fine. You just get the two Sams cracking. They've got to be well on their way before dawn. They've got that bill of sale?"

Walt nodded, looking at the big mountain pony beside me.

"He cost five hundred dollars. One bay horse, no markings, entire, aged seven or eight. As ordered. That's what the bill of sale says, and that's what we've got in the van, if anyone asks. Sam Kitchens chose it. Said it was as near as you would get, without actually paying thousands for a blood horse."

"This one looks fine. See you, then, Walt."

He stood in silence while I levered myself onto the new horse's bare back and gathered up the reins. I nodded to him, turned away, and started back up the trail to the canyon.

Late, I thought. Almost too late now. The wranglers would be high up in the hills by six, rounding up the horses. Dudes rode as usual on Sunday mornings. It was already five, and the first grayness of dawn had crept in as the moon faded. If they saw me out so early, I was in trouble.

At a jog trot, his sturdy legs absolutely at home on the terrain, the new horse took me back up into the canyon, past the fearful little ridge that Chrysalis had taken, and out onto the Clive valley side of the Tetons. From there down I looked out for a bunch of High Zee horses, but I was well below the snowline before I heard any of the bells.

There was a little group in a tree-filled hollow. They moved away at my approach, but slowly, and when I was among them and stopped, they stopped also. I slid off the horse I was riding, threaded my fingers through the mane of one of the High Zee group, and transferred the bridle from one to the other. Then, leaving Dave Teller's five-hundred-dollar purchase free on the hill, I pointed my new mount's nose homeward, and gave him a kick.

He knew the way, and he consequently could go much faster. The Wilkersons had told me the wranglers cantered down those steep rocky inclines, but until I did it I hadn't imagined what a hair-raising business it would be. The horse put his feet where I would have said no man could balance, let alone a quadruped, and when I turned him off the regular path he hardly slackened his pace. We went headlong down through pines and alders and groves of silver-trunked dead trees, back to the thicker woods with patches of grass underfoot, and more undergrowth of huckleberry and sapling. There was one sticky incline of black bog where a mountain stream had spilled out sideways onto a slope of earth, but my pony staggered across it, tacking downward, sinking in to his knees at every step. Farther on, he crossed the tumbling stream itself, picking his way through a mass of underwater rocks, and lower still he went straight down a bare pebbly slope where the normal path ran from side to side in easier zigzags. Whippy branches caught at us under the trees, but I laid my head flat beside his ear, and where he could go I went too.

The gentle dude rides had been no preparation for this reckless descent, and the one or two point-to-points I'd tried in my teens were distant memories and milksop stuff in comparison. But skills learned in childhood stay forever: balance still came instinctively. I didn't fall off.

We kept up the pace until there was less than a mile to go, then I veered the pony along to the right, up along the valley and away from the bridge to the ranch.

The wranglers would no doubt follow him up there to round him up, but I hadn't time to do the whole detour on foot. It was too light and too late to get back into the ranch across the bridge. It was going to have to cross the stream higher up and go down to my cabin through the woods on the far side.

I slid off the pony nearly half a mile upstream, and took off the bridle. The rough brown hide was streaked dark with sweat, and he didn't look at all like an animal who had spent a peaceful night grazing. I gave him a slap and he trotted away, wheeling around and upward, back onto the hill. With luck the wranglers wouldn't find him until he'd cooled down, especially as it wouldn't be him they'd be looking for.

I could hear the panic going on down by the ranch house as soon as I stepped cautiously out of the woods and began the freezing-cold traverse of the stream. The stones dug into my feet, and the water splashed my rolled-up trouser legs. But as from where I was I couldn't see any of the buildings, I trusted that no one there could see me. The shouts came up clearly, and then the thud of several horses cantering across the bridge. By the time I was across the stream and sitting down to put on my shoes again, they were going up toward the woods, and I could see them. Six wranglers, moving fast. If they looked back, they could see my head and shoulders sticking up out of the stretch of sagebrush.

A hundred yards of it between me and the safety of the trees on the ranch house side of the valley. I lay down flat on the ground for a few exhausted minutes, looking up at the dawn-filled sky: a high clear pale blue taking over from gray. The tracks of the mares and foals and both the stallions led straight uphill. I gave the wranglers time to go some way after them, and then quietly got to my feet and slipped unhurriedly across the sagebrush and down through the trees to my cabin.

It was ten past six. Broad daylight.

I pulled off my filthy sweaty clothes and ran a deep hot bath. Tiredness had gone down to the bone, and the water tingled like a friction rub on my skin. Relaxing, reviving, I stayed in it for half an hour.

The tape played back for me the heavy knocking on Yola's door and the head wrangler telling her that the mares and stallions were out.

"What do you mean, out?"

"The tracks lead down to the bridge. They're out on the hills."

"What?" Yola's voice screeched as the full meaning hit her. "They can't be."

"They sure are." The wrangler's voice was much calmer. He didn't know the size of the disaster: wasn't in the game. "But I can't understand it. The padlock was fastened like you said it must be, when I checked around yesterday evening."

"Get them back," said Yola sharply. "Get them back." Her voice rose hysterically. "That new stallion. Get him. Get him back."

There were sounds after that of drawers being pulled roughly open, and a door slamming, and silence. Yola was out looking for Chrysalis. And Chrysalis was on his way to Kentucky.

The ranch guests knew all about it at breakfast.

"What a fuss," Wilkie said. "You'd think they'd lost the deeds to a gold mine." They had.

"I'm glad they found the dear little foals anyway," Samantha said.

"They've found them?" I asked. The small paddock was still empty.

"They've put them in the barn," said Mickey, "with their mothers."

"Someone left the gate unlocked," Betty-Ann told me. "Isn't it a shame? Yola's obviously in a fearful state."

Yola had been in the dining room when I strolled in to breakfast, standing silent and rigid by the kitchen door, checking that all the guests were there, looking for signs of guilt.

Poise had deserted her. Her hair was roughly tied with a ribbon at the nape of her neck and the lipstick was missing. There had been no professional reassuring smiles. A muscle twitched in the strong jaw and she hadn't been in control of the wildness in her eyes.

I ate a double order of bacon and buckwheat cakes with maple syrup, and drank three cups of coffee.

Betty-Ann opposite me lit a cigarette and said did I

have to leave, couldn't I stay another few days. Wilkie gruffly said they shouldn't try to keep a feller. Wilkie had cottoned on, and was glad to see me go.

Strong footsteps came into the room from the door behind me, Betty-Ann looked over my head and her eyes widened.

"Why, hello there!" she exclaimed warmly, transferring her attentions. "How good to see you."

Wilkie, I thought in amusement, should be used to it by now. But the Wilkersons' problems blinked out of my mind forever when someone close called the new man by his name.

Matt.

Matt Clive spoke from behind my shoulder; a drawling bass voice under strict control.

"Listen, folks. I guess you know we've had a little trouble here this morning. Someone let out the mares and horses from their paddock over there. Now if it was any of you kids, we'd sure like to know about it."

There was a short silence. The various children looked uncomfortable and their parents' eyebrows peaked into question marks.

"Or if anyone knows that the gate wasn't properly fastened yesterday at any time?"

More silence.

Matt Clive walked tentatively round the long table, into my line of sight. About Yola's age, Yola's height. Same jawline. Same strong body, only more so. I remembered the two bedrooms in their cabin: the ringless fingers of Yola's hand. Yola's brother, Matt. I drank my coffee and avoided meeting his eyes.

One or two of the guests laughingly mentioned rustlers, and someone suggested calling in the police. Matt said they were seriously thinking of it. One of the stallions was quite valuable. But only, of course, if it was absolutely certain that none of the guests had left the gate open by accident.

Sympathetic murmurs were all he got. He might indeed be brave enough, or desperate enough, to call in the police. But if he did, they wouldn't recover Chrysalis, who should by now be hundreds of miles away on a roundabout route, accompanied by a strictly legal bill of sale.

Matt eventually went away, trailing a thunderous aura leaving the guests unsettled and embarrassed.

I asked the girl who waited at table if she could fetch my account for me, as I wanted to pay up before leaving, and after an interval she returned with it. I gave her cash, and waited while she wrote a receipt.

The Wilkerson family said their good-bys, as they were hoping to go riding if any of the wranglers had come back from searching for the missing horse, and I walked unhurriedly back to my cabin to finish packing. Up the two steps, across the porch, through the two doors, and into the room.

Yola came out of the bathroom carrying a rifle. The way she handled it showed she knew how to use it. Matt stepped from behind the curtained closet, between me and the way out. No rifle for him. A shotgun.

I put on the puzzled act, German accent stronger.

"Excuse me. I do not understand."

"It's the same man," Matt said. "Definitely."

"Where's our horse?" said Yola furiously.

"I do not know," I said truthfully, spreading my hands out in a heavy shrug. "Why do you ask such a question?"

Both the guns were pointing steadfastly my way.

"Excuse me," I said, "I have my packing to finish. I have paid the bill. I am leaving this morning."

"You're not going anywhere, friend," Matt said grimly.

"Why not?"

"You get that horse back here, and then you can go. Not before."

He was going to have a fine old time if he intended to keep a prisoner silent indefinitely on a ranch full of holiday guests.

"I can't get him back," I said. "I don't know where he is. Several friends of mine, however, do know where I am. They will be expecting me to be leaving here this morning."

They stared at me in silent fury. Children in crime, I thought, for all their ingenuity. They had walked straight in with their guns without thinking clearly through. They were, however, lethal children, ruled by impulse more than reason.

I said, "I am unlikely to go around saying 'I stole a horse from the Clives.' If you do nothing, and I now drive safely away, you may hear no more of it. That's the best I can offer. You will not, whatever you do, recover the horse."

The only sensible course open to them was to let me go. But Yola's finger tightened on the trigger, and I reluctantly decided it was time for the Luger. Watching her, I saw a split second too late in the looking-glass that Matt had taken a step behind me and was swinging his gun butt like a bludgeon.

He caught me solidly across the back of the skull and the patchwork quilt on the bed dazzled into kaleidoscopic fragments in my glazing eyes as I went down.

Chapter 10

WHEN I woke up it was pretty clear that I wasn't intended to be a hostage, but a corpse.

The cabin was full of smoke and small flames rose in a long uneven swath across the floor. I couldn't remember anything at first. I looked at the scene muzzily, half sitting up, my head dizzy and splitting with pain. The Clives, I thought. They'd emptied the whole tub of pep out into a straggling line, and set it alight. Sawdust and diesel oil burning slowly and billowing out unbreathable gases.

They'd laid me against the stove so that it would seem as if I'd fallen and hit my head on it. The empty pep tin rolled away from my foot as I tried to get up, and my hand brushed against a cigarette and a book of matches.

Most deaths in fires weren't caused by burns but by asphyxia. The cabin wouldn't burn down from fire on the floorboards: fire never burned downward, only up. The Clives were staging my exit for no better motive than revenge. And as an accident it was one of their poorer efforts.

Having staggered its way through those useless random thoughts, my brain cleared enough for me to decide it was high time to move if I was going to do anything about living. And I supposed I would have to.

I stumbled onto my feet, pulled the quilt off one of the beds, tottered into the bathroom with it and soaked it under the taps in the bath. Smoke was well down in my lungs, thick and choking. It's bloody stupid, I thought groggily, it's damn bloody stupid that boy-and-girl keep trying to shove me where I want to go, and I keep trying not to let them. Ridiculous. Ridiculous . . .

I found myself on my knees, half unconscious. The bath water still running. Pulled myself up a little, hauled out the dripping quilt, flung it over the worst of the fire. Silly, I thought. Much better to go out the door. Tried that. Damn thing was stuck.

Window, then. Stuck.

Wrapped my hand in the curtain and pushed it through one of the panes of glass. Some air came in. The screen stopped more.

Down on my knees again. Terribly dizzy. A black hell in my head. Smelled the quilt burning, lifted it off one lot of fire, and onto the next. Damped it all out into a smelly black faintly smoldering path and felt old and weak from too much scrambling up and down mountains and deeply ill from the crash on the brain and too much smoke.

Opened the front of the fat black stove. Shapleigh, it said. Gradually the smoke began to clear away up its pipe while I lay in a poor state beside the cabin door and breathed the fresh air trickling in underneath.

Several eras later I stopped feeling like morgue material and the hammer in my head died to a brutal aching throb. I began to wonder how long it would be before Matt and Yola returned to make their horrified discovery of my death, and wearily decided it was time for action.

I stood slowly and leaned against the door. They'd fastened it somehow from the outside, in spite of there being no lock: and it was simple enough to see when one's eyes weren't filled with smoke. The screen door opened outward, the wooden door inward. A small hook leading in through the latch was holding the two together. I pushed it up, and it slid away as the inner door opened.

My wallet lay on the table, not in my pocket. They'd been looking. Nothing for them to find, except their own photograph. They'd taken that. But they hadn't searched very far: the Luger was still in its holster at my back, under my outhanging shirt. I checked the magazine—still loaded—and put it back in place.

The only other thing I really wanted to take with me was my radio. I squashed down its extended antenna aerial and shoved it into my old suitcase on top of the things I'd packed before breakfast. Then, picking it up and fighting down the whirling chaos that resulted, I opened the screen door. Behind me the cabin lay in a singed shambles. Ahead, the comparatively short walk to the car seemed a marathon.

I might have made it in one if I hadn't felt any worse: but at the end of the woodland track, when all that was left to go was the open expanse of the car park, a wave of clammy sweating faintness seethed through me and I dropped the suitcase and leaned against a tree, waiting weakly for it to pass.

Yola came out the kitchen door and saw me. Her mouth fell open, then she turned on one heel and dived back into the ranch house. For the rifle. Or for Matt. My hands closed on the pistol at my back, but I was very loath to use it. Too many explanations to authority would be involved, and I preferred to avoid them at this stage.

"Hello," said a cheerful voice behind me. "We thought you'd gone ages ago."

I turned my wonky head and let my hand fall away

from the gun. Mickey and Samantha were coming down the track from the branch which led to the Wilkersons' cabin.

"And I thought," I said, "that you'd gone riding."

"The wranglers haven't brought in enough horses," Mickey explained sadly.

"Are you sick or something?" asked his sister, coming to a halt and staring up into my face.

"A bit," I admitted. "I'd be awfully glad if you'd carry my suitcase for me, across to that black car."

"Sure," said Mickey importantly, and Samantha took my hand in motherly solicitude. With one child on each side I completed the trip.

It was the rifle Yola fetched. She stood with it stiffly in her hands and watched the children put the suitcase in the car and stand close to my window while I started the engine. An accidental drowning, an accidental smothering she could manage: but three public murders by shooting were outside her range. Just as well. If she'd lifted that rifle toward the children, I would have shot her.

" 'Bye," they said, waving. Nice kids.

" 'Bye."

I released the brakes and rolled away down the drive in a plume of dust, accelerating fast as soon as I hit the paved road, and taking the main branch down to Jackson. If Yola thought of following in the pickup, she didn't do it fast enough. Repeated inspection in the mirror showed no Clives on my tail. The only things constantly before my eyes were bright dancing spots.

Through Jackson I turned north and west onto the winding road to Idaho Falls. Along there the Snake River and the Palisades Reservoir, sparkling blue against the dark pines, were stunningly beautiful. But my several stops weren't for appreciation: the cold sweating waves of dizziness kept recurring, like twenty-two over seven. I drove slowly, close to the side, never overtaking, ready to pull up. If I hadn't wanted to put a hundred miles or so between me and the Clives I wouldn't have started from Jackson. Most of the time I wished I hadn't.

Walt was pacing the motel lobby like a frenetic film

producer when I finally showed up at 5:30 in the afternoon.

"You are four and a half hours late," he began accusingly. "You said . . ."

"I know," I interrupted. "Book us some rooms. We're
staying here."

He opened his mouth and shut it tight.

"I'm sorry," I said, softening it, "but I feel ill."

"What's the matter?"

"Concussion."

Walt gave me a searching look, booked the rooms, and
even went so far as to carry my suitcase. I lay down on
the bed and he sat in an easy chair in my room and
rubbed his fingers.

"Do you need a doctor?" he said.

"I don't think so. It's not getting any worse."

"Well . . . what happened?"

"I'll give you some free advice," I said. "Don't ever let
Matt Clive come within bashing distance of your head."

The dizziness wasn't so bad lying down.

"Do you want a drink?" he asked.

"No. . . . Let's listen to a tape recording instead." I told
him how to open the back of the radio and to rewind the
reels.

"Neat little job," he commented. "Where did you get
it?"

"Had it specially made two or three years ago."

Walt grunted, and switched on. The head wrangler
banged on Yola's door and told her that the mares and
stallions were out. Walt's face lifted into a half-grin.

The recorder played twenty seconds of silence after
each take, and began again at the next sound. The next
piece was very short.

"Yola?" A man's voice, very loud. "Yola! Where the
hell is everybody?" A door slammed. Silence.

"That's Matt Clive," I told Walt. "He came back before breakfast."

The voices began again. Yola speaking, coming in-
doors. ". . . say the tracks go straight up the hill, but he

turned back at the high patch of scree and came down again."

That was a bit of luck.

"They'll just have to go on looking," Matt said. "Yola, for God's sake, we can't lose that horse." His voice was strained and furious. "I'll go over to the house and see if any of those kids had a hand in it."

"I don't think so. Not a darned one of them looks nervous."

"I'll try, anyway." His footsteps receded.

Yola picked up the telephone and made a call.

"That you, Jim? Have you seen any horse vans coming through Pikelet since last night?

"Well, no, I just wondered if you'd seen one. Not this morning, early? . . .

"No, it was just a chance. Sure. Yeah. Thanks anyway." She put down the receiver with a crash.

Walt raised his eyebrows. "Pikelet?"

"Couple of shops and a filling station where the Clives' own road joins the main road to Jackson."

"Just as well we didn't . . ." he began, and then changed it to, "Is that why you insisted on the long way around?"

"Partly," I agreed. "I wanted it to look as if Chrysalis had gone off by himself. I wanted to avoid them realizing he'd been deliberately stolen. Keep them guessing a bit, give us time to get well clear."

The tape began again. Matt came back running.

"Yola, that man. That damned man."

"What man?" She was bewildered.

"The man that pulled Teller out of the river. How long has he been here?"

Yola said almost in a whisper, "Here?"

Matt was shouting. "Here. Having breakfast. Staying here, you stupid bitch."

"I don't . . . I don't . . ."

"I saw him at Reading too," Matt said. "He called to see Teller in the hospital. They let him in past all the watchdogs. I saw him looking out the window. How the hell did he get here? Why, in God's name didn't you spot him, you stupid, stupid . . . He's the one that's taken the horse. And I'll damn well make him bring it back."

"How?" Yola said, wailing.

"Excuse me," said the voice of the girl who waited at table. "Excuse me Miss Clive. Mr. Hochner wants his bill."

"There on the desk," Yola said.

"Which is Hochner?" Matt, urgent.

"The German in cabin three."

"Where was he sitting at breakfast? What does he look like?"

"He had his back to the door from the hall," the girl said. "He's wearing a blue and white checked shirt, smoky glasses and he's quite tall and has dark-brown hair and a tired sort of face."

"Give him the bill then," Matt said, and waited until she had gone. "Hochner!" The voice was almost incoherent with rage. "How long has he been here?"

"Since . . . Tuesday." Yola's voice was faint.

"Get your rifle." Matt said. "If he won't give us that horse back . . . I'll kill him."

There were small moving-about sounds, and the tape went quiet. The time they had spent in my cabin telescoped into twenty seconds of silence; and the recording began again.

"He was right, Matt," Yola said. "We should have let him go." Her voice had gone quiet with despair, but Matt's still rode on anger.

"He had his chance. He should have told us what he'd done with Chrysalis."

After a pause Yola said, "He wasn't going to do that. He said so. Whatever you do, he said, you won't recover the horse."

"Shut up," Matt said violently.

"Matt." A wail in her voice. "He was right. We won't recover the horse, and his friends will come looking for him, like he said."

"They'll only find an accident."

"But they won't believe it."

"They won't be able to prove any different," Matt insisted.

After another pause Yola said almost without emotion, "If he got the horse clean away . . . if someone else has him now, and he's on his way back to Teller . . . they'll know we had Chrysalis here. We'll be arrested for that."

"Hochner wasn't going to say he'd stolen the horse from here."

"But you wouldn't listen." Yola suddenly flared into anger of her own. "He was right all the time. We should have let him go. We'd have lost Chrysalis . . . but this way we're in terrible trouble, they'll never believe he died by accident, we'll have the whole FBI here and we'll end up . . . we'll end up in . . ."

"Shut up," Matt said. "Shut up."

"He might not be dead yet . . . can't we go and stop it?" Her voice was urgent, beseeching.

"And have him accuse us of attempted murder? Don't be such a fool. No one can prove it isn't an accident, can they? Can they?"

"I suppose not . . ."

"So you leave him, Yola. You just leave him. He had his chance. I gave him his chance. . . . You just wait for some of the guests to see the smoke and come and tell you, like we said. Don't you try going up there. Just don't try it."

"No . . ."

"And I'm going back on the mountain with the wranglers. Chrysalis went across the bridge. His tracks are there. Well, I'm going tracking. Mr. Clever Hochner might be bluffing all along the line. He might have Chrysalis tied to some tree up there, and he might not have told anyone where he is, and no one will come asking." He convinced himself that this view of things was reasonable, and in the end Yola halfway agreed.

"We'll have to tell Uncle Bark," she said finally.

There was a blank pause while they considered this.

"He'll blow his top," Matt said gloomily. "After all that planning."

"He'll have to know," Yola said.

"I'll call him this evening, if we have to. But we might have found Chrysalis by then."

"I sure hope so . . ."

Matt went away then on his search, and presently, after Yola had left to go back to the ranch house, there was continued silence on the tape.

Walt switched the recorder off and looked across at me with a complete absence of expression.

"What did they do?"

I told him.

"Would it have passed as an accident?"

"I expect so. Neat little picture: man lighting cigarette, throws match absent-mindedly in tub of pep instead of wastebasket, panics, spills the stuff, steps wildly back from flames, trips over stove and knocks himself out. Bingo."

"Do you smoke, though?"

"Sometimes. They used my own pack, from the bedside table. And my own matches. It was impulsive, unpremeditated. They just looked around and used what came to hand. They're quite good at it."

"Lucky you woke up in time," Walt said.

"I suppose so." I shut my eyes and wondered how he would react if I asked him to go out for some codeine.

"I've worked with one or two people like you before," he said. "And I can't say I like it."

"Thanks," I said sardonically. No pills.

"With your kind," he said, "dying comes easy. It's living takes the guts."

I opened my eyes. He was watching me steadily, his sober face removing any possibility that he was intending to be funny.

"How are you on guts?" he asked.

"Fresh out."

He sighed deeply. "That figures."

"Walt . . ." I began.

"It struck me first last night, on the mountain. You were sure anxious about Chrysalis, but you didn't give a goddam about falling off the top yourself. It made me freeze just to watch you leading him along that ledge . . .

and you came back as calm as if it had been your own
back yard."

He was apologizing, in his indirect way, for his startling
appearance on the path.

"Walt," I said, half-smiling. "Will you go get me something for a headache?"

Chapter 11

EUNICE, Lynnie, Sam Kitchens, and stud groom Chub
Lodovski leaned in a row on the rail of the stallions'
paddock at Midway and watched Chrysalis eat Kentucky
grass, with opinions varying from Lodovski's enthusiasm
to Eunice's resignation.

The one and a half million dollars' worth looked none
the worse for his trip up the Tetons. Better than on the
ranch, as Sam Kitchens had removed all the Wyoming
dust from his coat on the journey back, and the bay hide
shone with glittering good health in the sunshine. There
wasn't, Lodovski assured me, the slightest chance of his
going missing again.

Batteries of photographers and newsmen had come and
gone: the stallion had been "found" straying on the land
of a friend of Dave Teller's about thirty miles from where
he had disappeared. All the excitement was over.

I walked back to Dave's house with Eunice and
Lynnie, and Eunice poured me a drink which was four
fifths whiskey and one fifth ice.

"Who put you through what meat grinder?" she said.
"You look like a honeymoon couple on the tenth
night."

Sam Hengelman had driven into Midway with Chrysalis at lunchtime (Tuesday). I had flown to New York with
Walt the day before, and had just backtracked to Lexington in time to catch the tail end of Eunice interviewing the
press. Several of that hard-bitten fraternity had tottered
out past me with pole-axed expressions and Lynnie had

been halfway through a fit of giggles. I made inroads into the hefty drink.

"I could do with a good long sleep," I admitted. "If you could give me a bed? Or there's the motel . . ."

"Stay here," Eunice said abruptly. "Of course you're staying here."

I looked from her to Lynnie. I couldn't stay in the house with one alone: perfectly proper with both. Silly.

"Thanks, then. And I must call Dave, in England."

Dave, still in the hospital, sounded incredulous.

"I heard it on a news flash not half an hour ago," he said. "Chrysalis just plain turned up."

"He sure did," I said dryly.

"Where had he been?"

"It's a long story," I said, "and wires have ears. But the expenses stand right now at somewhere near six thousand three hundred dollars. Is that enough for you, or do you want to go on for some answers?"

"To what questions, fella?" He sounded uncertain.

"To why Chrysalis was hijacked, and why you fell in the river. And another thing: do you want Allyx back?"

"For God's sake . . . do you know where he is?"

"No. But maybe I could find him. However, if I do, and we get as positive an identification as on Chrysalis, the insurance money on Allyx will have to be repaid to Buttress Life. That will be the equivalent of buying him all over again. He's three years older now, and you'll have lost three crops of foals. He may not be a good proposition for you or your syndicate any more. In which case you might prefer not to have him found. It's up to you."

"Jeez," he said.

"Will you think it over and call back?" I suggested. "Your wife and Lynnie are filling me up with food and drink, and I guess I'll be staying here tonight. But if you want me to go on, will you clear it with Keeble? I'm due back at my desk at nine next Monday morning, and I might not make it."

"Sure," he said, somewhat weakly, and I handed the receiver to Eunice.

"How's it going, honey?" she said, and I took a good swallow, put my head back on the chair, and listened to her long-married-wifely conversation with my eyes shut.

"Don't ask me how he did it, Dave, I don't know. All I know is he rang from New York yesterday afternoon and asked me for the name of any close friend of ours who was influential and respected, preferably high up in horse-breeding circles, and whose word would be taken as gospel by the press. So after a rake around I said I guessed Jeff Roots filled the bill; and lo and behold Chrysalis turned up on Jeff's land this morning. . . . Yup, the horse is as good as new; wherever he's been they've treated him right. . . . Look, Dave, surely enough's enough? I heard what Gene said about finding Allyx. Well, don't do it. We need Allyx like a dose of clap. And your boy here is no goddam Hercules, a puff of wind would knock him off, the way he's come back. . . . Lynnie's fine, sure. We're taking a trip tomorrow out to California, I'll measure up the curtains for the new place, things like that, and Lynnie can have some days on the beach and maybe try some surfing with those de Vesey boys. So look, why don't we take Gene with us, huh? . . . Sure, I've made reservations at The Vacationer in Santa Barbara . . . they're bound to have another room . . ."

I listened to her plans with disappointment. If I wanted to laze anywhere, it was right where I was, on the Midway Farm. By the peaceful pool in the quiet green garden, sleeping, drinking, and looking at Lynnie.

Eunice put down the receiver, and we had dinner, and late in the evening Dave rang through again.

"Gene?" he said, "Now listen, fella. Apart from curiosity, is there any good reason for finding those answers you talked about?"

"Forestalling repetition," I said promptly.

"No more stolen stallions and no more attacks on me?"

"That's right."

There was a pause.

"I'll buy the answers, then," he said, "if you can get them. And as for Allyx . . . if you think there's any chance of finding him alive and vigorous, then I guess I'm morally obliged to give you the go-ahead. I'd have to syndicate him all over again, of course. He'll be twelve now. That would give him only about six to eight more years of high potency . . . but his get from before his disappearance are winning all over Europe. Business-wise I'm not too happy about those three lost years. But blood-wise, it would be criminal not to try to get him back."

"All right," I said. "I'll see what I can do."

"What you spent on finding Chrysalis is less than his fee for covering a single mare. You've a free hand again for Allyx."

"Right," I said.

"Sim Keeble says you've got seven days' extension of leave. Something about it being due to you anyway, from a week you were entitled to at Christmas and didn't take."

"I'd forgotten about that."

"I guess I could fix it with him for more if the extra week isn't enough."

"If I haven't finished by then I'll have failed anyway, and might as well go home."

"Oh." He sounded disappointed. "Very well, we'll leave it like that for the present." He cleared his throat. "Eunice didn't seem to think you looked too well."

"The boy on the punt who knocked you out did the same thing for me."

"Gene!" His voice was shocked.

"Yeah. Don't tell my boss I'm that incompetent. Though come to think of it, he knows."

He laughed. "When you find that boy again give him a one-two from both of us."

"Sure," I said. But I'd been taught my job by cerebral people who didn't reckon a screener would ever have to fight for his life, and by the time I proved them wrong I was too old to become expert at boxing or judo, even if I'd liked the idea, which I didn't. I had learned instead to shoot straight, and the Luger had in the past three years extricated me unharmed from two sticky situations. But in a stand-up hand-to-hand affair with that young bull Mat Clive I would be a 500 to 1 loser, and "giving him a one-two from both of us" in any physical sense was a very dim possibility indeed.

"Keep in touch, fella," Dave said.

"Sure," I answered again, meaning it as little: and we rang off.

Curled opposite in a tomato armchair, Eunice said gloomily, "I gather we're stuck with that bloody Allyx."

"Only if we find him."

"Oh, you'll do that, blast you." Her bitterness was so marked that Lynnie stared at her. Too young to understand, I thought, that it wasn't me particularly that Eunice wanted to hurt, but life in general.

They went upstairs shortly afterward murmuring about California in the morning, and I switched off the light and sat in near darkness, finishing the fourth of Eunice's massive ideas on drink and working out the questions I would ask the next day. I could find Allyx on paper, if I was lucky: but he could hardly turn up loose after three years. Three weeks had been strictly the limit. The whole thing might have to be more orthodox, more public. And I wouldn't again, I decided mildly, put myself within accident reach of the murderous Clives.

After a while I deserted the last half of the drink and wandered upstairs to the spacious air-conditioned room Eunice had given me. With a tired hand I switched on the light inside the door, and yellow pools in frilly shades shone out on brown and gold and white furnishings.

One splash of jarring bright pink. Eunice herself in a fluffy trimmed wrapper, was lying on my bed.

I walked slowly across the thick white carpet and sat beside her on the white dotted muslin coverlet.

"What do you want?" I said gently.

"What do you think?"

I shook my head.

"Does that mean no?" Her voice was abruptly matter-of-fact.

"I'm afraid it does," I said.

"You said you weren't queer."

"Well, I'm not." I smiled at her. "But I do have one unbreakable rule."

"And that is?"

"Not to sleep with the wives—or daughters—of the men I work for."

She sat bolt upright so that her face was close to mine. Her eyes had the usual contracted pupils of the quarter drunk.

"That includes Lynnie," she said.

"Yes. It does."

"Well, I'll be damned. You mean that night you spent in New York with her you didn't even try . . ."

"It wouldn't have been much good if I had," I said, half laughing.

"Don't you believe it. She never takes her eyes off you, and when you were away she talked about nothing else."

I stared at her in real surprise. "You must be wrong."

"I wasn't born yesterday," she said gloomily. "She has two photographs of you as well."

"What photographs?" I was staggered.

"Some her brother took. That day on the river."

"But she shouldn't . . ."

"Maybe she shouldn't," Eunice said dryly, "but she does." She swung her legs carelessly around to sit on the edge of the bed beside me and I saw that for someone bent on seduction she had come well wrapped up.

"You expected me to say no," I said.

She made a face. "I thought you might. But it was worth a try."

"Eunice, you're nuts," I said.

"I'm bored," she said explosively, and with an undoubted depth of unbearable truth.

"That puts me into the golf and bridge category."

She was still playing games.

"At least you're goddam human," she said, her mouth

cracking into a smile. "More than you can say about most men."

"What do you like best about moving to California," I asked.

She stared. "Your mind's like a bloody grasshopper. What has that to do with sex?"

"You tell me and I'll tell you."

"For God's sake . . ." But she made some effort at concentrating, and in the end came up with the answer I had been most expecting.

"Fixing up the rooms, I guess."

"You did all these?" I waved my hand around, embracing the house.

"Yeah, I did. So what?"

"So why don't you start in business, doing it for other people?"

She half laughed, ridiculing the idea, and half clung to it; and I knew she'd thought of it in the past, because I hadn't surprised her.

"I'm no bloody genius."

"You have an eye for color. More than that: for mood. This is the most comforting house I've ever been in."

"Comforting?" she said, puzzled.

"Yeah. Laugh, clown, laugh. That sort of thing. You can fill other people even though you feel empty yourself."

Tears welled up in her gray-green eyes, and she shut the lids. Her voice remained normal.

"How do you know?"

"I know."

After a pause she said, "And I suppose what it has to do with sex is that interior decorating would be a suitable sublimation for a middle-aged woman whose physical attraction is fading faster than her appetite." The bitterness came from long acquaintance with the jargon and its point of view.

"No," I said mildly. "The opposite."

"Huh?" She opened her eyes. They were wet and shiny.

"Playing games is easier than working."

"Spell it out," she said. "You talk in goddam riddles."

"Sex . . . this sort of casual sex," I patted the bed where she'd lain, "can be a way of running away from real effort. A lover may be a sublimation of a deeper need. People who can't face the demands of one may opt for passing the time with the other."

"For Christ's sake, I don't understand a bloody word." She shut her eyes and lay flat back across the bed.

"Thousands of people never try anything serious because they're afraid of failing," I said.

She swallowed, and after a pause said, "And what if you do bloody fail? What then?"

I didn't answer her, and after a while she repeated the question insistently.

"Tell me what you do if you fail?"

"I haven't got that one licked myself yet."

"Oh." She laughed weakly. "Oh, God. The blind leading the blind. Just like the whole bloody human race."

"Yeah." I sighed and stood up. "We all stumble along in the dark, and that's a fact."

"I don't know if you'll believe it, but I've been utterly bloody faithful to Dave . . . except for this . . ."

"I'm sure of it," I said.

She got to her feet and stood swaying slightly.

"I guess I'm tight."

"Better than loose," I said, smiling.

"For God's sake, spare me goddam puns at one o'clock in the morning. I suppose if you're looking for that so-and-so Allyx there's no chance of your coming to California?"

"I wish there were."

"Goddam liar," she said vaguely. "Good night."

She made straight for the door and didn't look back.

I drove them to the airport in the morning. Eunice had lent me her car and the house for as long as I needed them, and had passed off her overnight visit with one sarcastic dig at breakfast. "Better undersexed than sorry."

"What?" said Lynnie.

"Eunice is offering a solution to the population explosion," I explained.

Lynnie giggled. Eunice showed me a double row of teeth and told me to pass the cream.

When I'd seen them off I followed a local road map and Eunice's inaccurate directions, and eventually arrived at the Perry Stud Farm, home of Jefferson L. Roots: chairman, among other things, of the Blood Horse Breeders Association. A houseboy in a spotless white coat showed me through the house and onto the patio: a house made of large cool concrete boxes, with rough-case white walls and bare golden wood floors. The patio was shaded by a vine trailed across a trellis. There was a glass and metal table, and low comfortable lounging chairs around it. From one of these Jeff Roots extricated himself and held out a welcoming hand.

He was a thick man with a paunch which had defied health farms, and he worried about his weight. His manner had the gentle, deprecating ease of the really tough American; the power was inside, discernible but purring, like the engine in a Rolls. He was dressed in a tropical-weight city suit, and while I was there an efficient girl secretary came to remind him that time and his connection to Miami would wait for no man.

"A drink?" he suggested. "It's a hot day already. What would you like?"

"Lime juice?" I asked. "Or lemon."

I got lime, squeezed fresh onto crushed ice. My host drank sugar-free tonic water and made a face over it.

"Just the smell of french fries and I'm a size larger in shirts," he complained.

"Why worry?" I said.

"Ever heard of hypertension?"

"Thin people can have it too."

"Tell that to the birds . . . or rather, tell it to my wife. She starves me." He swirled his glass gloomily, ice and lemon rising perilously to the rim. "So, anyway, Mr. Hawkins, how can I help you today?"

He pushed a folded newspaper across the table and pointed at it with an appreciative smile.

"Chrysalis Cocooned," the headlines said. And underneath, in smaller letters, "High-price stallion loses liberty, corralled at Perry, reshipped to Midway. And are the mares there glad, or are they? Our tip is syndicators breathe again." There was a picture of Chrysalis in his paddock, some mention of Dave's leg, and a few snide remarks about the police and the local horse folks who hadn't been able to spot a million dollars at ten paces.

"Where did you rustle him up from?" Roots asked. "Sam Hengelman wouldn't say. Most unlike him."

"Sam was an accessory to a conjuring trick. A little matter of substitution. We left a horse and took a horse. I guess he didn't want to talk himself into trouble."

"And naturally you paid him."

"Er, yes." I agreed. "So we did."

"But I gather from your call that it's not about Chrysalis that you want to see me now?"

"No. It's about Allyx."

"*Allyx?*"

"Yes, the other stallion which—"

"I know about all that," he interrupted. "They turned the whole state upside down looking for him and they found just as much trace as they did of Chrysalis."

"Do you by any chance remember, ten years ago, another horse called Showman?"

"Showman? Showman? He got loose from a groom who was supposed to be exercising him, or something like that, and was killed in the Appalachians."

"How certain was the identification?"

He put his tonic water down carefully on the table. "Are you suggesting he's still alive?"

"I just wondered," I said mildly. "From what I've been told, they found a dead horse two years after Showman vanished. But although he was in a high state of decomposition, he'd only been dead about three months. So it easily might *not* have been Showman, just somewhat like him in color and size."

"And if he wasn't?"

"We might just possibly turn him up with Allyx."

"Have you . . ." He cleared his throat. "Have you any idea where they . . . er . . . might be . . . turned up?"

"I'm afraid not. Not yet."

"They weren't . . . wherever you found Chrysalis?"

"No. That was only a shipping station, so to speak. Chrysalis was intended to go on somewhere else."

"And at that somewhere else, one might find . . . ?"

"There's a good chance, I think."

"They might have been shipped abroad again. Down to Mexico or South America."

"It's possible, but I'm inclined against it, on the whole." Uncle Bark, whoever he was, lived somewhere in the States. Yola had not needed to call the overseas operator to get through to him on the telephone. She hadn't even made it person to person.

"The whole thing seems so extraordinary," Roots said, shaking his head. "Some nut going around stealing stallions whose value at once drops to zero, because he can't admit he's got them. Do you think some fanatic somewhere is conducting experiments? Trying to produce a superhorse? Or how about a criminal syndicate all getting their mares covered by bluest blood stallions at donkey prices? . . . No, that wouldn't work, they'd never be able to sell the foals for stud, they wouldn't be able to cash in on the bloodlines . . ."

"I think it's a good deal simpler than either of those," I said, smiling. "Much more down to earth."

"Then what?"

I told him.

He chewed it over and I drank my lime juice.

"Anyway," I said, "I thought I'd try along those lines, and see if it leads anywhere."

"It's fantastic," Roots said. "And I hope to God you're wrong."

I laughed. "Yes, I can see that."

"It'll take you months to plow through all that work yourself . . . and I don't suppose you have too close a knowledge of the thoroughbred scene over here . . . so why don't I get you some help?"

"I'd be very grateful."

There was an outside extension telephone close to his chair. He lifted the receiver and pressed buttons. I listened to him arranging with the publishers of a leading horse journal for me to have the run of their files and the temporary services of two long-memoried assistants.

"That's fixed, then," he said, standing up. "The office is on North Broadway, along in Lexington. I guess you'll let me know how you make out?"

"I certainly will."

"Dave and Eunice . . . they're great guys."

"They are."

"Give her my best," he said, looking at his watch.

"She's gone to California."

"The new place?"

I nodded.

"Crazy idea of Dave's, moving to the Coast. The center of the bloodstock industry is right here in Lexington, and this is the place to be."

I made the sort of noncritical, noncommittal noise in my throat necessary on such occasions, and Jeff Roots thrust out a rounded hand.

"I have this stockholders' meeting in Miami," he said apologetically, and walked with me through the house to where his secretary waited in a Cadillac parked beside Eunice's Toronado Oldsmobile.

At the newspaper offices, I found, anything Jeff Roots wanted done was done wholeheartedly, and on the double. My two temporary assistants proved to be an elderly man who spent most of his time compiling an annual stallion register, and a maiden lady in her fifties whose horse face and crisp masculine voice were easy to take, as she had an unexpectedly sweet smile and a phenomenal memory.

When I explained what I was looking for they both stared at me in dumb-struck silence.

"Isn't it possible?" I asked.

Mr. Harris and Miss Britt recovered themselves and said they guessed so.

"And while we're at it we might make a list of people

whose name or nickname might be Bark. Or Bart, perhaps; though I think it's Bark."

Miss Britt promptly reeled off six names, all Barkleys,
living in and around Lexington.

"Maybe that's not such a good idea," I sighed.

"No harm in it," Miss Britt said briskly. "We can make
all the lists simultaneously."

She and Mr. Harris went into a huddle and from there
to the reference room, and were shortly up to their elbows
in papers and books. They told me to smoke and wait,
which I did all day.

At five o'clock they came across with the results.

"This is the best we can do," Miss Britt said doubtfully.
"There are well over three thousand stallions at stud in
the States, you see. You asked us to sort out any whose
fees had risen steadily over the past eight or nine years—
there are two hundred and nine of them." She put a
closely typed list in front of me.

"Next, you wanted the names of any stallions who had
been conspicuously more successful at stud than one
would have expected from their own breeding. There are
two hundred and eighty-two of those." She gave me a
second sheet.

"Next, you wanted to know if any of this year's two-
year-olds had proved conspicuously better at racing than
one would normally have expected from their breeding.
There are twenty-nine of those." She added the third
list.

"And, lastly, the people who could be called Bark . . .
thirty-two of them. From the Bar K Ranch to Barry
Kyle."

"You've done wonders," I said sincerely. "I suppose it's
too much to hope that any one farm is concerned on all
four lists?"

"Most of the stallions on the first list are the same as
those on the second. That stands to reason. But none of
the sires of the exceptional two-year-olds are on either of
the first two lists. And none of the two-year-olds were
bred by any of the Barks." Both of them looked downcast
at such negative results after all their work.

"Never mind," I said. "We'll try it another way tomorrow."

Miss Britt snorted, which I interpreted as agreement. "Rome wasn't built in a day," she said, nodding. Mr. Harris seemed to doubt that this particular Rome could be built at all with the materials available, but he turned up uncomplaining at nine the following morning, and they both dived in again, on new permutations.

By noon the first two lists had been reduced to twenty. We all adjourned for a sandwich. At two o'clock the searching began again. At 3:10 Miss Britt gasped sharply and her eyes went wide. She scribbled quickly on a fresh piece of paper, considered the result with her head on one side, and then looked across to me.

"Well," she said. "Well . . ." The words wouldn't come.

"You've found them," I said.

She nodded, only half believing it.

"Cross-checking them all by where they raced, their years of purchase, their markings and their approximate ages, as you asked . . . we came up with twelve possibles which appeared on the first two lists. And one of the sires of the two-year-olds fits your requirements and comes from the same farm as one of the first twelve. Er . . . do you follow me?"

"On your heels," I said smiling.

Mr. Harris and I both joined her and looked over her shoulder at what she had written:

Moviemaker, aged fourteen years; present stud fee $10,000.

Centigrade, aged twelve years; this year's stud fee $1,500; fee next year $2,500.

Both standing at Orpheus Farm, Los Caillos.

The property of Culham James Offen.

Moviemaker and Centigrade: Showman and Allyx. As clear as a frosty sky.

Stallions were normally booked for thirty to forty mares each breeding season. Forty mares at $10,000 a throw meant $400,000 every year, give or take a live foal or two. Moviemaker had coat $150,000 at public auction ten years ago, according to Miss Britt's researches. Since then Offen had been paid somewhere near $2.5 million in stud fees.

Centigrade had been bought for $100,000 at a Keeneland sale. At $2,500 a time he would earn that hundred thousand next year alone. And nothing was more likely than that he too would rise to a much higher fee.

"Culham James Offen is so well regarded," Miss Britt said in consternation. "I simply can't believe it. He's accepted as one of the top breeders."

"The only thing is, of course," said Mr. Harris regretfully, "that there's no connection with the name Bark."

Miss Britt looked at me and her smile shone out sweet and triumphant.

"But there is, isn't there? Mr. Harris, you're no musician. Haven't you ever heard of 'Orpheus in the Underworld' . . . by Offenbach?"

Chapter 12

WALT said, "For God's sake," four times and admitted Buttress Life might be willing to send him from coast to coast if Allyx was the pot of gold at the end of the rainbow.

"Los Caillos is a short distance northeast of Los Angeles," I said. "I thought of staying a bit farther north, on the coast."

"If you like."

"Come to the Vacationer, Grand Beach, Santa Barbara, then. I'll meet you there tomorrow."

He repeated the address. "Who's paying?" he said.

"Buttress Life and Dave Teller can fight it out between them. I'll put the motel on Teller's expenses. Can you wring the fare out of your office?"

"I guess so." His sigh came wearily over the wire. "My

wife and kids aren't going to like it. I was fixing to take them on a picnic this Sunday."

"Postpone it a week," I suggested.

"It's been postponed twice already, on your account."

"Oh."

After a short pause he said, "Around six tomorrow, local time. That do?"

"That would do very well."

"See you," he said briefly, and put down his receiver with a crash. I returned the Teller instrument more kindly to its cradle and surveyed the green and tomato room.

Nothing to do.

Mixed a drink with precision, and drank it. Wandered down to the pool, thought about a swim in the dusk, and couldn't be bothered to undress. Went back to the house, and ate a dinner cooked and served by Eva, who chattered so long in her pleasure at having someone to speak to in her own language that I heartily regretted I'd ever used it. Wished desperately she would stop and go away and when at last she did, that was no good either.

Tried to read and turned six pages without taking in a word. Wandered restlessly again into the black velvet-deep green garden and sat in one of the chairs by the pool, looking at darkness inside and out. Unreasonable, I thought drearily, that I shouldn't have recovered normally from losing Caroline, that I didn't value the freedom other men envied, that I couldn't be content with all I had; cruel that depression was no respecter of status or achievement and struck so deep that no worldly success could alleviate it.

Great fame, universal honor, droves of personal friends had demonstrably failed to save a whole string of geniuses from its clutches, and every year it bagged its thousands from unimportant people like me who would never see their name in print or lights, and didn't necessarily want to. Probably depression was an illness as definite as jaundice, and one day they would inoculate babies against it. I supposed I could count myself lucky not to have had it in its acute form, where its gray-black octopus tentacles reached out and sucked into every corner of the spirit until quite quickly life became literally unbearable, and the high jump suddenly presented itself with blinding clarity as the only logical, the only possible relief.

I wouldn't come to that day if I could help it. I would *not*.

The Vacationer was right down on the beach, with the sound of the bright blue Pacific creeping in a murmur under the transistors, the air conditioning, the civilized chatter, the squalling of children, and the revving of cars. There were no ocean rooms left. Walt and I, next door to each other, overlooked the parking lot.

Eunice and Lynnie were out when I arrived and still out when Walt checked in at six, but they were back when I went down with him for a drink before dinner. I had left a note at the desk for Eunice, but I hadn't told Walt she would be there. He stopped dead in his tracks when he saw her sitting with Lynnie, and turned on me a narrow-eyed composite glance of dislike and anger. If I'd told him she was to be with us, he wouldn't have come: he knew that I knew it. He was entitled to his rage.

Eunice was, however, the wife of a very good client of his firm. He swallowed his feelings like a pill, and chased them down in silence with a double bourbon. Eunice and Lynnie were on frosted-looking daiquiris and happy with it. They both looked marvelous, with honey-brown skin and a languorous sun-filled way of moving. Eunice wore fluorescent green with bits of gold at anatomical points like ears, wrists and feet. Lynnie had acquired a local-grown hot pink-orange tunic, and the few straps of her sandals seemed to be made of polished semiprecious stones. Even Walt, after a while, couldn't take his eyes away from them for long.

We had dinner outside, under a trellis lit by hundreds of tiny multicolored lights, on a shallow terrace which led directly out onto the sand. Eunice's language was for once as soft as the sea breeze, and consequently as a social evening it developed into a reasonable success.

Over the coffee I asked Eunice with a casualness which drew a piercing glance from Walt, "Have you by any chance heard of a race horse breeder called Culham James Offen?"

"Heard of him?" she said. "Of course I have. Everyone has."

"I haven't," Walt said flatly. One couldn't expect complete capitulation. He was doing very well.

"I mean, everyone in the bloodstock world would have heard of him," Eunice explained without obvious patience. "He has that terrifically successful stallion Moviemaker. And Dave says one ought to think of sending mares to another one of his, Centigrade . . . the first crop of foals are winning two-year-old races this season all over the place. But quite apart from that," she smiled broadly, "I guess we'll be seeing a good deal of him from now on."

"Er . . . why?" I asked diffidently.

"Our new place is right next to his."

Walt's mouth fell open and I stopped stirring my coffee.

"What did you say?" I said, feeling my eyes go blank, as I knew they always did under shock.

"Our new place, where we're moving to, is right across the road from Offen. We can see his paddocks from our bedroom windows." I gaped in fascination at Eunice while she outlined in such blissful ignorance the reason for the attempted murder of her husband. He himself had told me that the executors of the late David L. Davis had accepted his tender for the farm only recently, during the week before our momentous trip on the river. So the something "goddam stupid" which had happened to Yola and Matt Clive's scheme was that they had discovered that of all the people on earth it was to be Dave Teller who was to be Offen's new close neighbor. They had discovered it *after* they'd hijacked the horse, or they wouldn't have gone ahead with the plan.

"Why are you laughing?" Eunice asked, frowning. "What's so funny?"

"It's not funny," I agreed, straightening my face. "Far from it. Do you know Culham James personally?"

"Not yet. Does it matter?" She still looked puzzled.

"It could be wiser not to make close friends with him in too much of a hurry."

"Why not?"

"Might prove a prickly flower." I had a mental vision of Dave looking out of his bedroom window day after day, looking over to the paddocks where Chrysalis and Allyx were let out to graze. He might never have recognized them. But also he might. Culham James simply couldn't take the risk. Yola and Matt had flown immediately to England to dispose of Dave a long way from the real scene of danger.

While Allyx remained at Orpheus Farm and Dave continued making active plans to move alongside, the explosive situation would still exist. Though Matt Clive might have given up temporarily, I fervently hoped that Radnor-Halley wouldn't let their vigilance slide a millimeter. A call to Keeble would be wise . . . even at California-London rates.

"I'm going for a walk on the shore," said Lynnie, kicking off the pebbly sandals. "Who's coming?"

I beat Walt to it by quicker reflexes, and collected a grim look from him as I left him alone with Eunice. Lynnie remarked on it, grinning, as we ambled silently away on the trickling sand.

"He's put off by the bloodies," I explained. "That's all."

"She says it less often over here," Lynnie commented. "And she doesn't drink, except one or two before lunch, until after we've changed in the evening. Why is that, do you think?"

"She's escaped from the Lexington cage."

"That heavenly house . . . a cage?"

"Uh-huh."

"The new one isn't half so beautiful," she protested.

"It will be when Eunice has finished. And then the walls will close in again."

"Another cage, do you mean?" She sounded uncertain.

"Another cage," I agreed.

"Life can't be just escaping from one cage and ending

up in another," she said explosively, repudiating violently so bleak a vision.

"Everyone lives inside bars," I said. "The trick is not to want to get out."

"Stop it," she said in distress. "I don't want to hear that."

"They used to keep linnets as pets," I said. "But there aren't any linnets in cages any more. Budgerigars instead. You'll be all right, little linnet."

"I never know when you're being serious."

"Always."

"But half the time what you say is so—so crazy."

"Life is serious, life is crazy. Anything crazy is serious, and everything serious is crazy. . . . I'll race you along to the beach hut."

She beat me to it in her bare feet, and leaned against the rough wooden wall laughing and getting her breath back while I tipped half a ton of sand out of my shoes. We walked on a little farther, and then sat down in the warm night and looked out across the shadowy peaceful ocean. No land between us and Japan, half a world away.

"Did you come out here to be with us . . . or to find Allyx?" she said.

"Both."

She shook her head. "You brought Walt. That makes it to find Allyx."

"Walt would have chosen to stay somewhere else," I said, smiling. "So California for Allyx, Santa Barbara for you. Satisfied?"

She murmured something unintelligible, and we sat in silence while she scuffed sand into a heap with her toes.

"Will you find him, do you think?" she asked in the end.

"Allyx? We might do."

"When, roughly?"

"I don't know. Tomorrow, maybe."

"And then . . . you'll go home?"

"I guess."

"Back to an office . . ." She swept out an arm, embracing the wide sky. Back to an office, I thought coldly: and to the perpetual digging into people's privacy, to the occasional snaring of a bent applicant, to drizzle, to Putney, to the vacuum of the flat. To, in short, my normal life. The trick was not to want to slip through the bars.

"What are you going to do, now that you've left school?" I asked.

She sucked in a breath. "After this, all the old things seem horribly dreary."

"They'll soon give Dave a walking plaster."

"I *know*," she wailed. "Don't think I don't know. I was supposed to be starting a secretarial course in September. I utterly don't want to, any more. Why can't everyone just live on the beach and be warm all the time?" She rocked with her arms laced round her bent-up knees.

"Not enough beach."

She giggled. "You are just about the least romantic man alive. Comes of being a civil servant, I suppose. Like Daddy."

In time we walked back along by the edge of the sea and paused when we came level with the motel. She put her hand on my arm and simply stood there waiting. I kissed her forehead, and then her nose, and finally her mouth. It was all very gentle, and utterly unnerving.

"This is no good," I said, taking my hands from her shoulders, "no good at all."

"I've been kissed before," she said anxiously. "I really have."

"That isn't what I meant," I said, half laughing. "You'd qualify for a diploma. No, it's just, little Lynnie, that we're a long way from home . . . and I never kiss brunettes more than once on a Friday." I turned away toward the motel and jerked my head for her to follow. The best resolutions in the world would come a cropper faced with something like Lynnie, and immediate flight was the only course. It didn't seem to be popular with Lynnie herself, but I couldn't help that. I walked her briskly up the beach and made a joke about what Walt would be saying to Eunice, and we arrived back in reasonable order to find that it was nothing: they were sitting across the table from each other in a miles-apart silence. Eunice gave us a long cool look and Walt one of disillusion, and Lynnie quite unnecessarily blushed, confirming their obvious suspicion. The harmless little walk hadn't been a good idea from any one of four points of view.

Walt and I drove quietly into Orpheus Farm the following morning. He did the talking: a thoroughly professional piece of work, insurance patter at the double. A survey for new fire regulations, he glibly explained, necessitated us seeing over the entire establishment.

We saw. Every stall in every barn, every hayloft, every straw bale, every inch. We saw Moviemaker. We saw Centigrade. We made a great many notes.

Culham James Offen himself escorted us around the coolest barn containing his four prize stallions. A great deal of self-satisfaction sat on his shoulders like an impervious duck's-back mantle. I considered this with uneasy suspicion.

Uncle Bark was not only a man in his fifties with white hair, but he had a gray station wagon in a third of his large garage. I saw Walt giving it a sidelong glance. Undoubtedly it was Uncle Bark who had delivered the Snail Express trailer to old Hagstrom's boy at Rock Springs; and very likely Uncle Bark who had followed Sam Hengelman's van along the turnpike. Impossible to prove, though, at this distance.

The color of his hair was premature. Very few wrinkles marked the smooth suntanned face, from which white eyebrows stood out like a bracket of snow, nearly meeting over the nose. His eyelashes also were white, but the albino nonpigmentation stopped short of the eyes; not pink, but a clear pale blue.

He carried his head stiffly on a thick muscular neck, and the large body beneath the airy white shirt looked solid more than soft. Not a man to ignore in any company. A physique which teemed naturally with success: and success had given him an arrogance of expression where a decent humility would have been more fitting.

The whole farm had the high gloss of money-no-object.

Mathematically precise white-painted wood railings ringed the paddocks, and the approach to the Spanish-style house was landscaped with watered lawns and palms and an occasional bed of spiky red flowers with sharp purplish leaves. We didn't penetrate the house: Walt's fire insurance stretched only to the stabling.

After we'd seen the stallions Offen handed us over to his stud groom, a fair, surprisingly young man he called Kiddo, who had a drawling Western voice and an air of having been born without urgency. Every second word was "uh," and his walk was thirty-two frames a second; slow motion.

"Been here long?" I asked him, as he pointed out the spotless foaling stalls.

"Five or six months," he said, showing no resentment at a personal question: good-natured, unsuspicious, no sign of nerves.

"You must be good, to get a job like this so young," I congratulated him.

After a pause he said, "I got a feeling for horses, see? Mares, they foal down nearly always at night. Comes from having to give birth in the dark out in the wild, you understand?"

"Why in the dark?" asked Walt, puzzled.

Another pause. Not for a deliberate choice of what or what not to say, I realized, but just a moment of waiting while the instinctive knowledge coalesced into words.

"They drop 'em by day, some hungry hyena comes along and kills the foal in the first half hour. Foals, now, they're readier to run at birth than most other critturs, but you've got to give 'em a half hour to dry off."

"But they don't have to run, here," Walt protested.

"Nature don't know that," Kiddo pointed out reasonably. "Another thing, mares mostly drop their foals pretty quick. Don't take some of them no time at all. And then, see, I always know when a mare's ready, and most often I go out to the stall and make sure she's doing all right."

"How do you know?" I asked, fascinated.

A much longer pause. Then he said, "I don't know how I know. I got a feeling for it. I just wake up some nights and think that Rose is about ready, and I go on out to her, and maybe there she is, not needing a bit of help, or maybe with the cord round the foal's neck, strangling it. I bin with horses, see, all my life."

"Where were you before you came here?" I asked.

"Uh . . . all over. Had a job in Lexington a while back, but they said I didn't keep good time turning up at work." He grinned suddenly, a big mischievous lighting-up of the passive patient face. "Then . . . uh . . . I was with a feller in Maryland . . . he had a barn was falling down and honeysuckle breaking his fences and creeping into his windows, but he sure had some pretty mares and one of them was the dam of the horse who won the Preakness a year back. Though I don't go to the races myself."

"Where after Maryland?" I asked.

"Uh . . . here. I seen this ad in the *Blood Horse,* and I wrote. It was a joke, mostly. I never expected to hear a word, knowing this was a big place and everything. But Mr. Offen, it seems he didn't want no great businessman, just someone with a feeling for the mares . . . and he's keeping me on, he says, though there was two before me he let go after they'd been here a month."

It didn't seem to worry him. He had the God-will-provide nature which doesn't understand anxiety and never stores up winter nuts. Not that he had any need to. His "feeling for mares" was in fact priceless: he would probably never cash in on it as he could, but he'd never want for a job.

Kiddo watched us go in the same calm friendliness with which he'd shown us around. Walt and I agreed on the way back to Santa Barbara that he was only potentially an opponent. Loyalty might be given to Offen if he demanded it, but at present Kiddo had no idea what was going on.

"Unless," Walt said thoughtfully, "he's a brilliant actor."

I shook my head. "He wasn't acting. None of the signs."

Walt looked at me curiously, taking his eyes too long off the road. "Can you always tell?"

I smiled. "That's one of those unanswerable questions. I've a feeling for it, like Kiddo with his mares. But if he lets me down sometimes, how am I to know?"

"You'd know soon enough when secrets started leaking to the other side," Walt pointed out. "Have you ever passed as clear anyone who turned out to be a spy?"

"Yes."

"How often?"

"Once."

"In your first year, I suppose," Walt said with mild sarcasm.

"In my second year. He was the first serious spy I had to deal with, and I didn't spot him. The counterespionage chaps turned him up six months later when he'd done a good deal of damage, and the press made the usual scathing remarks about the feebleness of our screening system."

"Which you took to heart," Walt said dryly.

"I guess so."

He drove a mile and then said, "And now you're so good at it that they beat you up. What do you think about things when that happens?"

"That there's a big fish coming down the pipeline and they want me out of the way."

"So you look all the harder." A statement, not a question.

"You might say so. Yes."

"They'll kill you one of these days."

I didn't answer. Walt flicked a glance sideways and sighed. "I suppose you don't care."

"There are a lot of others in the department."

Walt drove into Santa Barbara without another word, where we joined Eunice and Lynnie in the terrace restaurant for lunch. They had, they said, bought that morning the big bright dangling earrings which swung with every turn of their heads. Lynnie's were scarlet, Eunice's acid green; otherwise identical. Still friends, I thought in some relief. Still in harmony. Whether Eunice would do a small chore for me was, however, another matter.

We had clam chowder with shrimp to follow, and Lynnie said with all this seafood she'd be growing fins. During coffee, when she stood up restlessly and said she was going down to the sea, it was Walt, after a pause, who said he would go with her. She looked at me questioningly, worriedly, and then turned and walked quickly off with him, talking a good deal too brightly.

"Don't you hurt that child," Eunice said fiercely.

"I don't want to."

"You're too bloody attractive."

"Yeah. Charm the birds off the trees," I agreed sardonically. "Little wives spill their husbands' secrets into my bloody attractive ears."

She looked shocked. Quite a change, I thought, from dishing it out.

"You mean you . . . *use* it?"

"Like a can opener. And as a catalyst. Who doesn't? Salesmen, politicians, actors, women, all using it like mad."

"For God's sake . . ." Her voice was faint, but she was also laughing.

"But not on Lynnie," I added wryly.

"You didn't need to, I guess. Dragging Dave out of the Thames was a lot more effective."

I watched Lynnie and Walt's backs as they reached the tide line.

"So that's why . . . ?" I said, almost to myself.

"Hero worship," Eunice said with barbs. "Does it give you a kick?"

"Like a mule's in the stomach."

She laughed. "It's not that you're so madly handsome in any obvious way."

"No," I agreed with truth, "I'm not."

She looked as if she was going to say more and then thought better of it. I jumped straight in while her mind was still half flirting, knowing, and despising the knowledge, that in that mood she was more likely to do what I asked.

"Has Lynnie still got those photographs of me?"

"Don't worry," she said sarcastically. "In a fire, she'd save them first."

"I'd like Culham James Offen to see them."

"You'd like *what?* What are you talking about?"

"About you and Lynnie driving over to pay a neighborly call on Culham James this afternoon. And easily, dearest Eunice, you could tell him about me pulling Dave out of the Thames, and Lynnie could show him my photograph. Especially the one of me sitting by a table outside a pub. That group of all of us."

She gaped and gasped, and then started thinking.

"You really can't be as pleased with yourself as all that . . . so, for God's sake, why?"

"An experiment."

"That's no answer."

"Earning my keep at the Vacationer."

A look of disgust turned down her mouth.

"Finding that bloody horse?"

"I'm afraid so."

"You don't mean . . . surely you can't mean that Offen has anything to do with it?"

"I'd like to make sure he hasn't."

"Oh, I see. Well, I guess that's not much to ask. Sure. I'll get Lynnie to come with me."

"And tell him I'm looking for Allyx."

She gave me a straight assessing stare, and said, "How about Chrysalis?"

"Whatever you like. Say that Dave employed me to get him back."

"I don't know why I'm doing it."

"More interesting than golf?" I suggested.

"Is it a game?" She was skeptical.

"Well, like hunting bears," I smiled.

"Oh, yes." She nodded sardonically. "A sport."

Chapter 13

I parked a rented car in some scrub off the road leading to Orpheus Farm, and smoked a rare cigarette. The fierce afternoon sun roasted through the metal roof and a water mirage hung in a streak over the dry road. A day for lizards to look for shade. They'd run out of air-conditioned heaps at the car rental place: I'd had to take one of those old-fashioned jobs where you breathed fresh air by opening the window. The air in question was as fresh as last week's news and as hot as tomorrow's.

At five past four Eunice and Lynnie passed unseeingly across my bows, heading back to Santa Barbara. I finished the cigarette and stubbed it out carefully in the flaked chromium ashtray. I looked at my fingernails for ten minutes. No special inspiration. At half past four I started the car, pointed its nose toward Orpheus, and went to call on Uncle Bark.

This time I drove straight up to the house and rang the ornate bell. A houseboy came: all on the same scale as at Jeff Roots'. When he went to find Culham James I followed quietly on his heels, so my host, even if he had meant to, had no chance to say he was out. The houseboy opened the door onto a square comfortable office-sitting room and Culham James was revealed sitting at his desk with a green telephone receiver at his ear.

He gave the houseboy and me a murderous glare between us which changed to reasonable affability once he'd got control of it. "I'll call you later," he said to the telephone. "A Mr. Hawkins has this minute arrived . . . that's right . . . later then." He put down the receiver and raised his eyebrows.

"Did you miss something this morning?" he asked.

"No; should we have done?"

He shook his head in mild annoyance. "I am merely asking the purpose of this return visit."

161

"My colleague and I wanted answers to one or two extra questions about the precautions you take against fire, especially as regards those two exceptionally valuable stallions . . . er . . . Moviemaker and Centigrade."

Under his suntanned face, behind the white bracket of eyebrows, Culham James Offen was beginning to enjoy a huge joke. It fizzed like soda water in his pale-blue eyes and bubbled in his throat. He was even having difficulty preventing himself from sharing it: but after a struggle he had it nailed down under hatches, and calm with a touch of severity took over. We went solemnly through the farce of fire precautions, me leaning on his desk and checking off Walt's solid-sounding inventions one by one. They mostly had to deal with the amount of supervision in the stallions' barn at night. Whether there were any regular patrols, any dogs loose on watch, any photoelectric apparatus for detecting opacity, such as heavy smoke?

Offen cleared his throat and answered no to the lot.

"We have the extremely expensive and reliable sprinkler system which you saw this morning," he pointed out. "It is thoroughly tested every three months, as I told you earlier."

"Yes. Thank you, then. I guess that's all." I shut my notebook. "You've been most helpful, Mr. Offen."

"You're welcome," he said. The joke rumbled in his voice, but was colored now with unmistakable malice. High time to go, I thought: and went.

When I got back to the Vacationer some while later I found Eunice and Lynnie and Walt sitting in a glum row behind empty glasses. I flopped into a chair opposite them and said, "Why the mass depression?"

"You're late," Walt said.

"I told you not to wait dinner." I caught a passing waiter on the wing and arranged refills all round.

"We were considering a search party," Eunice said.

I looked at all three of them more carefully. "You've been comparing notes," I said resignedly.

"I think it's terrible of you . . . *wicked*," Lynnie burst out, "to have made me go and deliberately . . . *deliberately* . . . put you in such frightful danger."

"Lynnie, stop it. I wasn't in any danger. Here I am, aren't I?"

"But Walt said . . ."

"Walt needs his brains seen to."

Walt glanced and compressed his mouth into a rigid line. "You didn't tell me you'd arranged for Offen to know you were the man who took Chrysalis. And you didn't tell me the Clives had tried to kill Mr. Teller."

"And you didn't tell *me*," Eunice added, "that the couple in the background of the photograph Lynnie showed Culham Offen had tried to kill you too."

"Or you'd never have let Lynnie show it to him?"

"No," she said slowly.

"Just as well I didn't."

"And you deliberately misled me by saying you wanted to clear Offen. It wasn't true."

"Er . . . no. But I did want you to behave naturally with him. And, anyway, why all the fuss?"

"We thought . . ." Lynnie said in a subdued voice, "we almost thought . . . as you were gone so long . . . that you . . . that they . . ."

"They didn't," I pointed out obviously, smiling.

"But won't you please explain why?" Lynnie said. "*Why* did you want me to give you away like that?"

"Several reasons. One was to make Dave safer."

"I don't see how," Eunice objected.

"By letting Offen know, and through him the Clives, that we could prove the Clives were in England and beside the Thames on the day of Dave's accident. Murder by accident is only a good idea as long as there's no apparent motive and the murderers have no apparent connection with the victim. We've shown them that we know their motive and their connection, and they must now be aware that if Dave was killed they would be the first suspects. This makes it less likely they will try again."

"Crikey," Lynnie said. "Go on."

"When Walt and I went to Orpheus Farm this morning saying we were making a survey for new fire precautions, Offen wasn't worried. He didn't know me from Adam then, of course. It was before you showed him my photograph. But he showed no anxiety at all about two strangers turning up on a pretext that he didn't even bother to check. None of the edginess one might have expected if he'd just had one stolen horse pinched back from him, and was in possession of two others standing in his barn. I didn't like it. It didn't feel right."

"He hasn't got them," Eunice said with relief. "I was sure it couldn't possibly be right that Culham Offen would steal horses. I mean, he's *respected*."

Walt and I exchanged a glance of barely perceptible amusement. To be respected was the best cover in the world for fraud. Fraud, in fact, could rarely exist without it.

"So," I said, "I thought it would be helpful if he knew for certain that I was especially interested in Moviemaker and Centigrade, and that I wasn't in fire insurance, but was the man he had to thank for losing Chrysalis. When I went back, after you two had left, he still wasn't worried. On the contrary, he was enjoying the situation. It amused him enormously to think that I believed I was fooling him. I asked him a lot of questions about the security precautions surrounding Moviemaker and Centigrade, and he was still completely untroubled. So," I paused, "it's now quite clear that the two horses standing in his barn called Moviemaker and Centigrade are in actual fact exactly what he says: Moviemaker and Centigrade. He isn't worried about snoopers, he isn't worried about me making clumsy peparations to steal them. He must therefore be confident that any legal proceedings will prove the horses to be the ones he says they are. He'd ambush me if I tried to steal them, and have me in real deep trouble, which would be to him some small compensation for losing Chrysalis."

Walt nodded briefly.

Eunice said obstinately, "I think it only proves that you're barking up the wrong damn tree. He isn't worried simply because he isn't guilty of anything."

"You liked him?"

"Yes," she said. "He was bloody sweet."

Lynnie nodded. "I thought so too."

"What did he say when you showed him the photographs?"

"He just glanced at them at first," Lynnie said. "And then he took them over to the window. And then he asked me who had taken them, and where, and when. So I told him about the day on the river, and about you and Dave going under the weir . . ."

At the side of my vision Eunice gave me an I-told-you-so smile.

". . . and he said one or two nice things about you," Lynnie finished. "So I told him you came over here to look for Chrysalis, and somehow or other you found him."

"He asked where you found him." Eunice nodded. "But we didn't know. I said you were now trying to find Allyx, and it certainly didn't worry him. I'm sure you must be wrong."

I smiled at her. She didn't want the horse found, and as an ally she was as reliable as thin ice on a sunny day. I didn't intend to tell her anything in future which I wasn't prepared to have passed on to Offen. Like most law-abiding citizens, she had not grasped that a criminal mind didn't show, that an endearing social manner could coexist with fraud and murder. "Such a *nice* man," the neighbors say in bewilderment, when Mr. Smith's garden is found to be clogged with throttled ladies. "Always so pleasant."

Eunice, propelled by a strong semiconscious wish for him not to have Allyx, might tell Offen anything, simply because she couldn't visualize a "sweet" man being deadly. She might also tell him anything propelled by the same impulse which had made her point a gun at me.

"Let's have dinner," I suggested; and Eunice and Lynnie went away to freshen up.

Walt looked at me thoughtfully, then raised his eyebrows.

I nodded. "I put a bug on the underside of his desk, two feet from the telephone. I was late back because I was listening. He called Yola and told her about my visit but there wasn't much else. I left the set hidden, and came back here."

"Do you mean it, that those two horses really are Moviemaker and Centigrade?"

"Sure. He bought them, remember. Openly. At bloodstock sales. And obviously he's kept them. I suppose he never could be certain that some ex-owner would turn up for a visit. Those horses will have been tattooed inside their mouths with an identity number when they first began to race. They have to be, over here, don't they? It'll be quite easy to establish that they're the right two."

"You don't think Mrs. Teller's right—that he never had Showman and Allyx after all?"

"I'll play you his call to Yola sometime. He had the foresight to whisk those horses away from Orpheus when we got Chrysalis. He was more or less waiting for something like our visit this morning. No flies on Culham James, I'm afraid. Er . . . Walt, did you give Eunice and Lynnie any details about our jaunt in the Tetons?"

He looked uncomfortable. "I was annoyed with you."

"What exactly did you tell them?"

"Not much. I was horrified at Lynnie's having shown Offen that picture of the Clives, and when Mrs. Teller said you'd planned it I said you must be mad, they'd tried to kill you once already."

"And you told them how?"

He nodded, not meeting my eyes.

"Did you tell them about the bugs and the wireless set?"

"No."

"It's important, Walt."

He looked up. "I didn't mention them."

I relaxed. "How about our mountain walk?"

"No details."

"Place?"

"I'm pretty sure I mentioned the Tetons."

Nothing there that would hurt.

"How much did you say about Showman and Allyx?"

"I told them that you'd worked out through the studbooks that Offen must have them."

"Did you say the words 'Uncle Bark'?"

He shook his head. "I'd forgotten about that."

I sighed. "Walt, Mrs. Teller doesn't want Allyx found any more than she wanted Chrysalis. Let's not entrust the state of the nation to the Indians."

He flushed a little and compressed his mouth. Eunice and Lynnie came back shortly after, and though we all four had dinner together it proved a taciturn and not overfriendly affair.

Walt came up to my room for a conference after the coffee.

"How do we find them?" he said, coming bluntly to the point and easing himself simultaneously into the only armchair.

"They've made us a gift of them, in one way," I said thoughtfully. "We can send a bunch of lawyers in to query Moviemaker and Centigrade's identity, and get it established beyond doubt that the two Offen showed us are in fact those two horses. He'll be keen for them to do it: and once he's done it, he'll be stuck with them. We will meanwhile do another little vanishing trick with the other two and start our own identification parade on our own ground. Once they are established as Allyx and Showman, Offen cannot possibly claim them back."

"Two objections," Walt said. "We don't know where Allyx and Showman are. And if we find them, why not get lawyers into the act right away? Why go to all the danger and trouble of taking them?"

"Same as Chrysalis," I pointed out. "The first sign of any real trouble, and they'd be shot. It's not illegal to kill a horse and whisk it smartly off to the dog food people. And vastly more difficult to identify a dead one. Impossible, I'd almost say, for the degree of certainty we need here."

"Even if we take them, and establish their identity, and

everything goes smoothly, Offen will still be raking in those colossal stud fees of half a million dollars a year, because we'd never be able to prove that for the past ten years Showman has been siring every foal that's down in the book as Moviemaker's."

I smiled. "We'll do something about that, once we've sorted out the rest."

"Which brings us back to square one," Walt said flatly. "Where the hell do we start?"

I perched on the window sill and looked down sideways into the brightly lit car park. Colored bulbs on the face of the motel raised rainbow shimmers on glossy hard tops and struck me as a deeply melancholy commentary on human achievement. Yet I wouldn't have wanted to live without cars or electricity . . . if I'd wanted to live. My room was only two floors up, with none above. Too near the ground. I'd known of a woman who'd jumped from five and bungled it. A gun was better.

"Well?" Walt said insistently.

"I'm sorry . . . ?" I said vaguely, turning my head back to him.

"Where do we look?"

"Oh . . . yes."

"On the ranch?"

"Very doubtful, don't you think? They must know that's the first place we'd think of."

"There's a lot of land there," he said. "And a lot of horses to lose them in."

I shook my head. "They'd have to keep them in a paddock close to the house. All the rest of the ranch is in the mountains, and they couldn't turn them loose for fear of their breaking a leg. We'd better check, though." I stared unseeingly at the carpet. "But I guess the horses are with Matt. Offen is at Orpheus Farm, and Yola is tied to the ranch seeing to about thirty guests, so where's Matt?"

"Where indeed," Walt said gloomily.

"He and Yola don't spend their winters on the ranch because the valley is blocked by snow. She told me that they go south. On one of those telephone calls she told

Offen they couldn't keep Chrysalis at a place called Pitts, because it wasn't suitable. But that was when they didn't know we were after them . . . when it wasn't an emergency."

"So somewhere south of the Tetons we find this Pitts, and Matt and the horses will be waiting for us?"

"Yeah." I smiled briefly. "Sounds too easy."....

"Easy!" Walt said.

"They must leave a forwarding address for mail," I pointed out. "They live a conventional law-abiding life with a long-standing business to give them obvious legal means of support. There must be dozens of people in Jackson who know their winter address."

"Our Buttress agent could get that, then. First thing in the morning."

"Fine."

Walt levered himself out of the armchair and hesitated.

"Come along to my room," he said. "I've got a bottle."

I wasn't sure that I wanted to, but he smiled suddenly, wiping out all resentments, and one didn't kick that sort of olive branch in the teeth.

"Be glad to," I said.

The smile went deeper and lasted along the passage to his room, which was almost identical to mine. The window looked out on the same cars from a slightly different angle, and he had two armchairs instead of one. There was a bottle of Old Grand-dad on a round tray with glasses and a water jug, and on his bedside table stood a leather-framed photograph. I picked it up idly while he went to fetch ice from the machine along the passage. Walt with his family. A good-looking woman, a plain girl in her early teens, a thin boy of about ten: all four of them smiling cheerfully into the lens. He came back as I was putting them down.

"I'm sorry about the picnic," I said.

"Next week will do just as well," he said. "We've got the whole of the summer, I guess."

We sat in the armchairs, drinking slowly, I didn't like

bourbon much; but that wasn't the point. He talked casually about the split-level ranch-type house they'd moved into the year before, and how his daughter got along just fine with the folks next door, and how they'd had trouble with the boy's health, he'd had rheumatic fever . . .

"How about your own future, with Buttress Life?" I asked.

"I've got about as high as I'll get," he said with surprising honesty. "There's only one more step up that I really want, and that's to chief investigator, claims division, and that'll come along next year when the present guy retires."

He poured more drinks, rubbed his thumb slowly over the round fingertips, and said Amy and the kids were asking him for a pool in their back yard, and that Amy's mother was a problem since Amy's father died last fall, and that he hadn't caught a single ball game last season, he'd been that busy . . .

We sat for more than an hour without mentioning the horses once. He yawned finally and I uncurled myself from the soft chair, putting down the third-time empty glass. He said good night sleepily with easy friendliness and, for the first time since I'd known him, without tension. Back in my own room, undressing, I wondered how long it would last. Until I made the next unpopular suggestion, I supposed. I didn't know whether to envy him his enclosing domesticity or to feel stifled by it. I did know that I liked him both as a man and as a working companion, moods and all.

The Buttress Life agent in Jackson came through with the Clives' winter address within twenty minutes of Walt's telephone call: 40159 Pittsville Boulevard, Las Vegas, Nevada.

I remembered Yola's smile at the thought of winter. Las Vegas explained it. Yola liked to gamble.

"What now?" Walt said.

"I'll go on out there and take a look."

"Alone?" There was a certain amount of anxiety in his

voice, which I interpreted as a desire not to be left in Santa Barbara with Eunice.

"We need you here," I said placatingly. "And don't tell her where I've gone."

He gave me a sharp glance. "I won't."

We drove in the rented car out to Orpheus Farm, where I showed him where I'd hidden the radio tape recorder between three rocks, with its aerial sticking up through the branches of a scrubby bush. The nearest neatly railed paddock was only feet away; the house, about four hundred yards. We picked up the radio and parked a short distance down the road.

"Supposing he sees us?" Walt said, watching me wind back the reel.

"He'll only think we're watching the farm routine, to know when to pinch Moviemaker. The radio will pick up the bug in his office from at least a quarter mile, but it gets fainter after that. It has to work on the air-vibration system. Not such good amplification as electricity. Do you ever use them?"

"Bugs?" He shook his head. "Not often. Cameras with telescopic lenses are better. Catch the claimants walking around on their paralyzed legs." Satisfaction echoed in his voice. Like me, a rogue hunter to the bone.

Smiling to myself, I switched on. Cutting in and out, Culham James's various conversations filled three quarters of an hour of tape time, but nothing he said was of any use to us. I rewound the reels again and we put the radio in among the rocks, Walt agreeing that he would come back after sunset and listen to the day's take.

He drove me then to the Los Angeles airport, where I hopped a plane to Las Vegas, arriving in midafternoon. The desert heat hit like a gust from an oven when the plane doors were opened, and from a nearby building the usual lighted numbers proclaimed to the populace that in the shade, if they could find any, it would be 108.

The air conditioning at the edge-of-town motel I booked into was turning itself inside out under the strain, and the Hertz man who presently took my money admitted that this was a little old heat wave, sure thing. Had to expect them in July. The inconspicuous Pontiac he rented me was this time, however, a cooled one. I drove around for a while to get my bearings, and then took a look at Pittsville Boulevard.

The high numbers ran two miles out of the town, expensive-looking homes along a paved road with the desert crowding in at their rear. The Clives' house was flanked by others on both sides: not near enough to touch, but too near for the invisible stabling of stallions. The place on Pitts wasn't suitable, as Yola had said.

It was low and white, with a flat roof and a frame of palms and orange trees. Blinds and screens blanked out the windows, and the grass on each side of the drive was a pale dry biscuit color, not green watered like its neighbors'. I stopped the car in the roadway opposite and looked it over. Not a leaf moved under the bleaching sun. Ten minutes ticked away. Nothing happened in the street. Inside the car, with the engine stopped, the temperature rose like Christmas prices. I started up again, sucked in the first cold blast from the air conditioner, and slid on along the way I was heading.

A mile past the Clives' house the paving ended, and the road ran out across the desert as a dusty streak of gravel. I turned the car and went back, thinking. The comparative dead-endedness of Pittsville Boulevard explained the almost total lack of traffic past the Clives', and also meant that I couldn't drive past there very often without becoming conspicuous to the neighbors. Keeping a check on an apparently empty house, however, wasn't going to get me much further.

About five houses along on the town side of the Clives' there was another with water-starved brownish grass. Taking a chance that these inhabitants too were away from home, I rolled the Pontiac purposefully into the palm-edged driveway and stopped outside the front door. Ready with some of Walt's insurance patter, I leaned on the bell and gave it a full twenty seconds. No one came. Everything was hot, quiet, and still.

Strolling, I walked down the drive and onto the road. Looking back one couldn't see the car for bushes. Satisfied I made the trip along to the Clives', trying to look as if walking were a normal occupation in a Nevada heat wave: and by the time I got there it was quite clear why it wasn't. The sweat burned dry on my skin before it had a chance to form into beads.

Reconnoitering the Clives' place took an hour. The house was shut up tight, obviously empty. The window screens were all securely fastened, and all the glass was covered on the inside with shades, so that one couldn't see in. The doors were securely fastened. The Clives had made casual breaking in by vagrants practically impossible.

With caution I eased round the acre of land behind the house. Palms and bushes screened a trefoil-shaped pool from behind overlooked too openly by the neighbors, but from several places it was possible to see the pools of the flanking houses some sixty yards away. Beside one of them, reminding me of Eunice, a woman in two scraps of yellow cloth lay motionless on a long chair, inviting heatstroke and adding to a depth of suntan which would have got her reclassified in South Africa. I moved even more quietly after I'd seen her, but she didn't stir.

The rear boundary of the Clives' land was marked by large stones painted white, with desert scrub on the far side and low-growing citrus bushes on the near. From their windows, brother and sister had a wide view of hills and wilderness; two miles down the road neon lights went twenty rounds with the midday sun, and the crash of fruit machines outdecibeled the traffic. I wondered idly how much of Uncle Bark's illicit proceeds found their way into Matt and Yola's pocket, and how much from there vanished into the greedy slot mouths in Vegas. The stud fees went around and around and only Buttress Life was the loser.

On the way back to the motel I stopped at every supermarket I came to, and bought two three-pound bags of flour from each.

From a hardware store I acquired a short ladder, white overalls, white-peaked cotton cap, brushes, and a half gallon can of bright yellow instant-drying paint.

Chapter 14

WALT listened to what I had to say in a silence which hummed down the telephone wires more eloquently than hysterics.

"You're crazy," he said at last, sounding as if he seriously meant it.

"Can you think of anything else?"

After a long pause he said grudgingly, "Nothing quicker."

"Right, then. I'll fix everything this end and give you a call in the morning. And let's hope it works."

"What if it doesn't?"

"Have to try something else."

Walt grunted gloomily and hung up.

I spent an hour at the airport, and then went back to the motel. The evening oozed away. I played some roulette without enthusiasm and lost backing black against a sequence of fourteen reds; and I ate a good steak listening to a girl singer whose voice was secondary to her frontage. After that I lay on my bed for a while and smoked, and kept the blues from crowding in too close by thinking exclusively of the job in hand.

At two I dressed in a dark-green cotton shirt and black jeans, went downstairs, stepped into the car, and drove along Pittsville Boulevard to 40159. The town itself was wide awake and rocking: the houses along Pitts were dark and silent. With dimmed lights I rolled quietly into the Clives' driveway and stacked the bags of flour close to the front door. Then, holding the car door but not shutting it, I eased the Pontiac back along the road and parked it in the driveway of the same empty house that I had used in the afternoon. Again, not wanting any neighbors to remember hearing a car door slam, I left it ajar and walked back to the Clives'.

The night was warm and gentle with a deep navy-blue

174

sky and stars like fluorescent polka dots. Two miles away
the blazing lights of Vegas raised a bell-shaped orange
glow, but among the palms and orange trees the shadows
were thick and black and comfortably concealing.

The Clives' was only the latest of a great many houses
I had broken into. My short cuts to truth were scandalous
by all public and private standards, and Keeble rarely
asked how I got my information: and as I would have
had the press, the police and public opinion all balefully
against me if I'd ever been caught, Agag on eggs would
have been clumsy in comparison. Law-abiding citizens
never knew I'd been their guest. For the Clives, however,
I had alternative plans.

Wearing surgeons' rubber gloves, and with my shoes
stuck through my belt to the left of the Luger, I worked
on the lock on the back door, and after not too bad a
time, considering its complexity, the two sets of tumblers
fell sweetly over, and the house was mine.

Inside, the air was stale and still, and dust sheets
draped the furniture, looking like pale boulders in the dim
light of my flashlight. The rear door opened into a
spacious hall which led straight through to the front. I
walked across, unbolted and unfastened the front door,
brought in the bags of flour, and left the door ajar, as I'd
left the one I'd come in by: the value of always being
prepared for instant flight had been drummed into me by
an ex-burglar who had once neglected it.

I went into the bedroom. Large separate single-bedded
rooms again for Yola and Matt, and a guest bedroom,
with a bathroom to each. I pulled all the covers off the
furniture and flung onto the floor everything they had left
in the chests and closets. Over the resulting mess in each
room I shook six pounds of self-rising flour.

In the kitchen I emptied onto the floor a packet of soap
flakes, a packet of rice, some cereal, and four pounds of
brown sugar, which were all lying handy in the pantry. I
unlocked the pantry window and unfastened its outer
screen, leaving both open: and as an afterthought tumbled some canned fruit off the shelf beneath it, to show
that the intruder had come in that way.

In the spacious living room I again removed all the covers, put every ornament and small loose object in a heap on the floor, and flung flour over them and around the whole place. A smaller cozier room, facing the road, contained a desk full of papers, two large bookshelves, and a well-filled sewing box. Together the jumbled contents made a splendid ankle-deep mess on the floor. Pounds of flour fell over everything like snow.

It was while I was tearing open the last bag, ready for a final scatter around the hall, that I heard the distant police siren. Frozen, I doubted for a second that it was for me: then considered that either a too-watchful neighbor had seen my flashlight in chinks through the blinds or else that the Clives' complicated locks weren't their only protection, and that they had a direct burglar alarm line to the police.

Without wasting much time I shut the front door and heard the lock engage. Emptied the last bag of flour over a plastic flower arrangement on a table in the hall. Flitted through the rear door and clicked it shut behind me. And thrust the flashlight into my pocket.

The siren wailed and stopped at the front of the house. Doors slammed, men shouted, boots ran. Someone with a megaphone urged me to come out with my hands on my head. The edges of the house were outlined by a spotlight shining on its front.

With bare seconds to spare before the first uniform appeared in silhouette around the corner I reached the nearest of the bushes flanking the trefoil pool and dived behind it. Being quiet enough was no problem, as the law was making an intimidating clatter all around the house, but staying invisible was more difficult. They brought another spotlight round to the rear and shone it full on the house. The shuttered windows stared blindly and unhelpfully back, reflecting the glare almost as far as my cover.

Lights appeared in neighboring houses, and heads stuck like black knobs out the windows. I eased gently away past a few more bushes and thought I was still a great deal too close to a spell in the zoo.

A shout from the side of the house indicated that they had found the open pantry window. Four troopers, I judged. All armed to the teeth. I grimaced in the darkness and moved another few yards with less caution. I wasn't going to give them any forefinger exercise if I could help it, but time was running out.

They were brave enough. One or more climbed in through the window and switched on the lights. I more rapidly crossed the last stretch of garden, stepped over the white-painted stones, and headed straight out into the desert.

Five steps convinced me I needed to put my shoes on. Ten steps had me certain that the only vegetation was prickly pear, and close-ranked at that. I should imagine I impaled myself on every one in the neighborhood.

Back at the Clives' they had temporarily stopped oohing and ahing over the mess, and were searching the grounds. Lights moved round the next-door houses as well. If they went five along and found the car, things would get very awkward indeed.

I had meant to be safely back in my motel long before I called the police early in the morning to say I was a civic-minded neighbor who had just seen a prowler coming out of the Clives' . . .

When they showed signs of shining the light out toward where I was stumbling along I lay down flat on the ground and listened to the thud of my heart. The spotlight beam flickered palely over the low scrubby bushes and outlined the flat spiky plates of the prickly pears, but in the shifting uneven shadows that they threw, I reckoned I must be just another clump. There was a good deal of shouted discussion about whether it was necessary to take a look-see in the desert, but to my relief no one came farther out than the boundary stones. Gradually, frustrated, the dazzle and commotion retreated and died away.

The lights inside the Clives' house went out. The police car drove off. The neighbors went back to bed. I got to my feet and brushed off the surplus of dry sandy earth. What with that and flour dust even the blindest cop would have little difficulty in buttoning me onto the crime.

With more care than on the outward trip I headed back toward the houses, but at an angle I hoped would bring me near the car. The sooner I beat it from that little neck of the woods, the better.

I stopped dead.

How might one catch a prowler? Just pretend to go away, and wait somewhere down the road, and when he thought everything was safe, he'd come carelessly along and fall into your waiting hands like a ripe plum.

I decided not to drive back toward Las Vegas from that quiet cul-de-sac. Just in case.

At the fifth house along everything was quiet. I cat-footed through the grounds, around the house, and took a distant look at the car. Still there. No trooper beside it. I stood in the shadows for longer than was probably necessary, then took a deep breath and risked it. I completed the steps to the car and peered in through the window. Empty. Made a quick cautious tour of the row of spiky low-growing palms hiding it from the road.

Nothing. No irate shouts. All quiet. Car undiscovered. Sighing with relief, the vision of the malicious Clives dancing at my trial fading a little, I pulled wide the already open door and folded like an understuffed rag doll into the driving seat. For five minutes I did nothing more energetic than to breathe freely, and enjoy it.

There remained, however, the problem of telephoning to Walt: and I chewed it over thoughtfully while absent-mindedly pulling prickly pear needles out of my legs.

I was a fair hand at wiretapping when I had the kit: but it was in Putney. No doubt there would be a telephone in the empty house alongside. But I wasn't sure that I wanted to risk this house too being directly connected to the police, if that was what had happened at the Clives'. On the other hand, I had been in the Clives' house twenty minutes before the police showed up. Yet they might be quicker on a second call.

After half an hour I pulled on the rubber gloves, climbed out of the car and picked the front door lock. It turned all right, but unfortunately the prudent householders had also used bolts. Always a tossup which door of the house people bolted. I walked round to the rear, and let myself in. There was a telephone on a table in the hall. I walked over to it, then turned, retraced my steps, left the door ajar, went round to the car, started up, and drove quietly away in the dead-end direction, not stopping until I was off the paved road onto the gravel, and round a couple of bends. I switched off the lights and smoked a cigarette.

Another half hour passed. No lights went on along the houses; no police sirens, no disturbances at all. I drove gently back, parked in the same spot as before, went round into the house, and called up Walt.

He wasn't amused at being woken at five A.M.

"A slight change of timing," I said apologetically. "The police have already seen the mess."

He drew in a sharp breath. "They didn't catch you!"

"No." No point in telling him how close it had been: he hadn't approved of my going in at all.

"I suppose you want me to come now, then?" he said with resignation.

"Yes, please. As soon as you can. Leave the car keys at the inquiry desk at Los Angeles airport, and I'll pick them up. The helicopter pilot I've engaged at Las Vegas is Michael King. He's expecting you. Just ask for him. The helicopter radio will pick up the frequency of the bug I've got with me, so you won't need to bring my recorder. Was there anything on the tape today?"

"Yesterday," Walt corrected. "Not much. I went over after dinner last night and ran it through. Offen had a friend over. There was two hours of just ordinary yapping. I didn't get back here to bed until one."

"When this is over you can sleep for a week."

"Yeah?" He said sarcastically. "Tell it to the Marines."

He put down his receiver with less of a crash than usual. Smiling, I took out a five-dollar bill and left it stuck half under the telephone. Then I let myself out, relocked the door behind me, and went back to the car.

Three hours went by uneventfully. Night changed to

day. The air temperature began its morning climb. A few energetic birds sang; and I smoked another cigarette.

Soon after eight a patrol car went up the road, siren fortissimo. Pittsville Boulevard woke up. I eased out of the car, walked carefully down toward the road, and tucked myself invisibly between a palm and a bush, from where I had a clear view of everyone driving up toward the Clives'.

From along the road I could hear several excited voices, most of them children's: and a small boy and a girl came past close to me doing an Indianapolis on their tricycles.

Several cars drove down from the houses, all with men alone, going in to Las Vegas. One woman followed. Three women came the other way, all looking eager. At 9:30 two men drove in from Vegas, one of them adjusting a large folding camera: the local press.

An hour later a quiet-engined helicopter drifted over and landed out of sight behind a fold of hill.

At 10:50 the hawk came to the lure.

A sky-blue convertible Ford, with the hood down. Matt, driving fast, hunched with anger. Youth, strength, and fury knotted into one callous, reckless personality. Even in a speeding car the impression came across with the solidity of a shock wave. Standing on his brakes flamboyantly late, he screeched down from sixty to nil outside his own house, scattering children like pigeons.

Satisfied, I got stiffly to my feet and went back up the drive to the car. There I removed from the trunk the white overalls, white cotton gloves and cap, and put them on, along with a new and darker pair of sunglasses. With a screwdriver from the tool kit I opened the tin of paint and gave the oily yellow contents an encouraging stir; cleaned and replaced the screwdriver, and rested the paint lid gently back on the tin. Then, picking it up by its handle with my right hand, and carrying brushes and ladder with my left, I strolled out onto the road, and along to the Clives'.

Matt's Ford stood at the door at a crooked angle to the patrol car. Many people were still standing around, staring and gossiping in the sun. I meandered slowly through them and took a closer look at the blue convertible, and then withdrew discreetly to the edge of the proceedings.

Taking the bug out of my pocket, I talked to Walt, hoping he could hear. He couldn't answer: it was strictly one way traffic on the midget transmitter.

"Do you read me, Walt? This is Gene. Our young friend came in his own car, not a rented one or a taxi. His name is on the registration. Pale-blue new Ford convertible, at present with the top down. Gray upholstery. Nevada plates, number 3711-42. I'll do the paint if I possibly can, though he may deal with it, of course; and I'll put this bug in the car. When he starts up, you'll hear him. Good luck. And for God's sake don't lose him."

Indirectly, vaguely, I again approached the car. No one took any notice. I was merely one of the time-passing onlookers, a workman who wasn't working. Several of the children and some of their mothers had seen the state of the well-floured rooms and thought it a dreadful shame. I leaned my ladder against the rear of the blue convertible, put the brushes and paint pot down casually on the flat surface of the trunk, and mopped not too imaginary sweat off my face and neck.

Some of the blinds in the Clives' house had been raised, so that in places one could see into the house. No one was looking out. I stretched a hand in over the side of the car with the bug in my palm, and felt its sucker cling snugly under the glove compartment.

Still no faces at the windows.

I said to the nearest little boy, "Someone told me the intruder got in through the pantry window, round that corner."

"No kidding!" he said, his eyes wide.

"Sure thing."

He told his mother. They went to look. Nearly everyone followed them, especially as someone nudged the press photographer, who said he would take a picture.

I took a last comprehensive look at the windows, turned to walk away, and with a quick backward flip of a gloved hand, tipped over the can of paint. The lid came off. The can rolled slowly across the flat top of the trunk and clanked heavily to the ground. The result was a bright broad spreading pool of yellow on blue, and a proper lake on the gravel.

I was out on the road when the first child saw it and ran after me.

"Your paint's tipped over, mister."

"Yeah, I know. Don't touch it. Don't let anyone touch it, huh? I'm just going to fetch the stuff to get it off."

He nodded importantly and ran back, and I made it safely along to the car, and drove away in peace toward Las Vegas, taking off the useful cap and gloves as I went. Back at the hotel I showered, changed, packed, and paid my account; drove to the airport and returned the car to the Hertz agent; kept a very wary eye open in case Matt Clive had decided to travel by air; ate a much-needed sandwich, and caught the first plane out to Los Angeles.

When I collected the car keys at the inquiry desk, there was a note from Walt as well.

You're one great crazy guy. And don't think I don't realize what you risked. If you're reading this, I guess you've made it, and aren't behind bars. My pal in the CIA told me you could be relied on to do mad things and, boy, was he right. What do you use for nerves? Count me strictly out next time.

                                                    Walt

Surprised, and not ungrateful that he should have bothered, I slipped his letter into my pocket and drove into the city to look for a good place for tape recorders. I managed in the end to rent for one week an elaborate recorder which would play at the ultraslow 15/16 of an inch per second, the speed of my own, and with it sitting on the passenger seat beside me, pointed my nose toward Orpheus Farm, Los Caillos. There I removed the full reel from the radio recorder and fixed it up with another: no one appeared to have disturbed it in its bush and boulder hiding place, and as far as I could tell, no one saw me come and go.

Lynnie and Eunice were just walking up from the beach when I got back to the Vacationer: but they both greeted me with ten degrees of frost and went straight on past, murmuring that they guessed they would see me at dinner.

Slightly puzzled, shrugging, I carried my bag and the recorder up to my room, rewound the tape I had collected, and started it to run through while I took off my city suit and turned the air conditioning to high.

Yola rang up, in great agitation. The houseboy answered, and went to tell Offen, who was still in bed. By great good fortune the houseboy neglected to go back to replace the downstairs receiver when Offen lifted the bedroom extension, and the bug in consequence had picked up the whole conversation.

"I've had a call from the cops in Vegas . . ."

"Don't shout, Yola. I'm not deaf."

She didn't listen. "Some vandals have wrecked the house at Pitts." She really minded: there was grief as well as anger in her voice.

"How do you mean, wrecked?"

"They say everything in the house has been thrown on the floor, and flour and sugar and stuff have been tipped over everything. They want to know what's been stolen, they want me or, better, Matt to go down there and deal with it . . . and I can't, Uncle Bark, I simple can't. We've got thirty-two people in, and I can't possibly get away. Matt will have to go."

"But Matt . . ."

"Sure," she wailed. "Do you think I don't *know?* But he'll have to. Those horses won't die if he leaves them for a few hours. It's much further for me, I'd be away at least two days. It's *hopeless.* Everything's gone wrong since we took that damn Chrysalis."

"And if you remember," Culham James said tartly, "that was your and Matt's idea. I always said it was too soon after the last one. You and Matt have been too greedy ever since you found out."

"Relatives ought to share their good luck, not keep it to themselves."

"So you're always saying."

Nothing like a little blackmail to cement a family together, I thought in amusement. Offen had been happy with his half million a year, it seemed; but Matt and Yola, stumbling on the honey pot, had been in a hurry for more. Impulsive, ingenious, greedy Clives; if they had only been content with a share from Showman and Allyx, Offen would never have been found out.

Yola glossed over the long-standing squabble and returned to the current disaster. "I didn't get Matt's number. What is it?"

"I haven't got it here, it's in my book downstairs . . ."

"Well, look, will you call him? Tell him to get right on over, the cops will be there waiting. Tell him to call me from there and tell me what gives. I can't bear it if those bastards have stolen my mink wrap . . . and there's all that money in the safe . . ."

"Better face up to it that it's gone," Offen said, with the tiniest trace of malice.

"They might not have had time," Yola said. "The alarms go off when anyone goes into the den, and there isn't supposed to be time for anyone to find the safe and open it before the cops get there. We paid enough for it . . ."

It had been their bad luck that by the merest chance I had left the den until last.

Yola disconnected, and after the twenty seconds gap on the tape, Uncle Bark called up Matt from the downstairs telephone. Matt's comments were mostly inaudible though detectably explosive. He agreed to go to the house, but nothing Offen said gave any clue as to where Matt was at that moment. It appeared only that he was somewhere within a reasonable radius of Las Vegas, as he was going to be able to drive there, see to things at the house, and get back in time to feed the horses in the evening: which narrowed it down to somewhere in an area of roughly 150,000 square miles. A pocket handkerchief.

A brief telephone conversation of no interest followed

and then, presumably in the afternoon, Often had switched on his television set to watch a racing program. As far as I could tell from spot checks, it had used up the whole of the rest of the four-hour playing time.

Sighing, I switched off, and went downstairs. Lynnie and Eunice, dressed in dazzling colors, were drinking daiquiris and watching the Pacific sunset. I got another cool welcome and monosyllabic replies to my inquiries about their day.

Finally Eunice said distantly, "Did you have a good time in San Francisco?"

I blinked. "Yes, thank you."

They relapsed into a longer silence, which was broken only by a waiter coming to tell me I was wanted on the telephone.

It was Walt.

"Where are you?" I said.

"Las Vegas airport."

"And how did it go?"

"You can relax," he said comfortably. "The horses are on a small farm in a valley in Arizona, out beyond Kingman. We landed there and I asked around some. Seems the couple who own the farm don't make much of a living, but last week they said a friend was giving them a trip to Miami, and a young fellow would be looking after the place while they were away."

"That's great," I said with emphasis.

"The paint made it easy. We heard him yelling blue murder when he saw it, but I guess it had dried on by then and he couldn't get it off, because it was way past midday, and I'd begun to worry that he'd gone already and we hadn't heard him or that they'd picked you up planting the bug. Anyway, we took off when his engine started, and the yellow splash was easy to see from a height, just as you said. He went right through Las Vegas and out on the Hoover Dam road and across into Arizona. I kept the binoculars on him and we never flew near enough for him to notice us, I'm certain of that. He went up a winding graded road into the hills southeast of Kingman, and that was it."

"You've done marvels."

"Oh, sure. It was simpler than we were prepared for, though. You could hear the bug pretty clearly through the helicopter's headsets as high as two thousand feet, and we could have followed him in the dark if we'd had to, especially as he had his radio on for most of the way. We could hear music and news broadcasts now and then."

"Are you coming back tonight?"

"Yeah, there's a plane a half hour from now. But it'll be better than midnight when I get in."

"I'll be awake," I said. "And just by the way, Walt, what did you tell Eunice and Lynnie I was doing in San Francisco?"

He cleared his throat. "I said you had some unfinished business there."

"What sort of business?"

"Uh . . . like . . . er . . . female."

"Thanks," I said sarcastically. "You're a right pal."

Something very like a laugh lingered in my ear as I disconnected.

Chapter 15

LYNNIE and Eunice talked brightly to each other over dinner and I sat making plans for the next day and didn't listen. Politely after coffee we parted for the night, and at eleven I drove out to Orpheus with a fresh reel for the receiver in the rocks, and brought back the one I had fitted earlier.

Walt came back into my room as I was running it through, and we both listened to Culham James Offen talking first to Matt and then to Yola.

Yola was a better bet from our point of view, because her angry feminine voice scattered higher sound waves out of the receiver, and one could imagine Uncle Bark holding it inches away out of deference to his eardrums.

He was doing his best to soothe her. "Matt says it could have been worse; some of these vandals have thrown molasses and preserves and even sewage around in people's houses . . ."

"He says the whole place is *covered* in flour . . . it'll take weeks to clean up."

"It'll vacuum quite easily, won't it? It's not sticky and it doesn't stain."

But she couldn't be consoled, not even when he reminded her that the money was safe and that her mink wrap hadn't been stolen.

"But Matt says," she wailed, "that it was *white.*"

"Flour will shake out . . . and might even clean it."

"You don't understand."

"Sure I do, Yola," he said patiently. "You feel like it was you who was assaulted, not your house. You feel dirty and furious and you'd like to kick the bastards who did it. Sure, I know. We had thieves in here once, when your aunt Ellen was alive. They stole all her rings, and she said it was like being raped."

They talked about the break-in for a good while longer, and Walt raised an eyebrow and remarked that I seemed to have gotten reasonable revenge for that clap on the head.

We were both yawning by the time Offen was through for the evening. The last half hour consisted of his telling his houseboy his plans and requirements, and none of these betrayed any anxiety or uncertainty. Culham James was confident, and I was glad of it. Worried men patrol their defenses.

Walt went off to bed, and although I hadn't slept at all the previous night I woke again after only three hours. The colored lights on the outside of the motel threw prismatic reflections on the ceiling. I stared up at them, trying to make patterns and shapes, trying any silly ruse to stop my mind from nose-diving into the pit. The tug of the unfinished chase was very faint, and whether Allyx and Showman ever sired another foal seemed a matter of supreme unimportance. Fraud, theft, attempted murder . . . who cared?

I had left the Luger in its belt holster across the room on a chair. Neither the Clives nor Offen were likely to come creeping through the night to do me in, and my usual enemies were 6,000 miles to the east. The only danger lay in myself, the deadliest enemy of the lot. The theory that going to bed with the gun out of reach would lessen its magnetic temptation was proving a dreary flop.

One more day, I thought in the end. Anyone could manage just one more day. If one said that firmly enough every night, one might even finish the course.

Dawn crept up on the colored bulbs and washed them out. I took a shower and shaved, and admitted that I had seen healthier-looking men than the one in my reflection.

Walt came along to my room when I was midway through orange juice and coffee at 8:30. "What you need," he said, eying this, "is some good solid food."

"I don't feel hungry."

His eyes slid to my face and away. "Come on down and eat with me."

I shook my head. "I'll wait for you."

He wouldn't go alone. He ordered griddle cakes and eggs and coffee from room service, and we got straight down to business while he demolished them.

"It'll take two and a half days for Sam Hengelman to get to Kingman," I said.

He nodded with his mouth full.

"He was starting early this morning," I went on. "I called him last night, after you'd been through from Las Vegas. He's driving the van himself, and he's coming alone. That means his journey time will be longer, but it seemed better that way from the secrecy point of view."

"Did you tell him it was another snatch?" Walt said doubtfully.

I smiled. "I engaged him to come and collect a horse belonging to Dave Teller. He asked if we were likely to be collecting this one in a lonely place at night, and I said yes we probably would."

"And he didn't back out?"

"He merely remarked that he had no great objection to an easy buck if I would assure him he couldn't go to jail for it."

Walt wiped errant egg off his chin. "And could he?"

"I couldn't tell him it was impossible. Odds of a thousand to one, I said. He said a thousand bucks against one chance of going to jail wasn't enough."

Walt laughed. "So how much is he coming for?"

"Fifteen hundred, plus the normal renting fee, plus expenses."

"Not bad for one week's work." He paused, stirring sugar, then said tentatively, "What do you get out of this yourself?"

"Me?" I said in surprise. "I've no idea. Three weeks' heat wave instead of the English summer . . ."

"Didn't you negotiate a fee?"

"No."

"How come?"

"It didn't occur to me."

His face crinkled into a mixture of emotions with what appeared to be amazement and pity coming out on top.

"How about you?" I said.

"I'm not on vacation," he pointed out. "I get a pretty good salary, and also a cut of everything I save the company."

"So Chrysalis has been worth the extra work?"

"At a million and a half, are you kidding?" Walt looked at me earnestly. "Look, Gene, I'm going to give you one half of that cut—"

"No," I said interrupting. "I don't want it."

"You know darned well I wouldn't have found that horse, not in a million years. Nor got him back alive so quickly. And as for these other two . . ."

"You keep it for your kids," I said. "But thanks, anyway."

He would have gone on insisting, but I wouldn't listen, and after two attempts he gave it up. In the back of my mind, as I outlined what I suggested we should do next, there lingered a bitter suspicion that I hadn't accepted his gift because it would be a selfish waste if I didn't stick around to spend it. I had rejected any strings of conscience tying me to life. The death-seeking force was up to another of its tricks.

"A pincer movement, I think," I said. "Or, rather, a simultaneous attack on two fronts."

"Huh?"

"Keep Culham James Offen's attention riveted on the Moviemaker and Centigrade he has on his farm while we spirit away the others."

"Er, quite," Walt agreed.

"You can take Offen," I said.

"And you take the horses?"

I nodded. Walt considered what might happen if we exchanged roles, and didn't argue.

"What are the chances of finding out which company Matt insures the Las Vegas house with?"

Walt thought about it. "Our agent there might be able to. But why?"

"I . . . er . . . would rather take those horses when I know Matt is safely away."

Walt smiled.

"So," I went on, "it shouldn't be too difficult to get him to go back to the house on Pitts. Say, for instance, his insurance company required him to make an inspection of his security arrangements and sign some document or other, before they would renew full cover? We know from the telephone calls to Offen that Matt and Yola have a safe in the den with a lot of money in it. Matt won't want to be uninsured for more than a minute, after having one break-in already."

"We couldn't ask his company to do that." Walt paused and looked at me with suspicion.

"Quite right," I nodded. "You can. You know all the jargon. As soon as we hear from Sam Hengelman that he has reached the Arizona border, you can start the spiel on Matt."

"From here?"

"Yes. Ask him what time would be convenient for him, but try to maneuver him into coming late in the afternoon or early evening, say six or seven. Then it would be dark when he got home, and late, which should hamper him a bit when he finds the horses are gone. . . . He might even stop off in Las Vegas for a couple of hours at the tables."

Walt said thoughtfully, "I suppose I'd better go to the house at Pittsville and meet him."

"No," I said abruptly.

He looked at me. "You'd thought of it?"

"You are not going anywhere near Matt Clive."

"And why not?"

"You want a split skull or something?"

"Like webbed feet." The smile hovered. "All the same, what is Matt going to do when he arrives at his house and no insurance man turns up? What would you do? Call the company, I guess. And then what? He discovers no one in the company knows anything about his having to come back to the house, and he starts thinking like crazy. And if I were him I'd call the local cops and get them whizzing out to the farm for a look-see. You didn't see the road there from Kingman. But I did. There are no turnings off it for the last ten miles to the farm. What if you met the cops head on, you and Sam Hengelman and two stolen horses?"

"He wouldn't risk calling in cops."

"He might reckon that if he was losing everything anyway, he'd make sure you went down as well. And I mean down."

Every instinct told me not to let Walt meet Matt Clive.

"Suppose he won't make a late appointment?" he said. "When, I grant, most of the company would have gone home and it would be more difficult to check. Suppose he insists on three in the afternoon, or even the next morning? Do you want to snatch those horses by day?"

"Not much. But it would take him at least two hours each way. Add an hour for waiting and checking. Even if he called the police, it wouldn't be for three hours after he left home. We'd have been gone with the horses for two of those."

Walt obstinately shook his head. "The limits are too narrow. A horse van won't be able to do better than thirty miles an hour on the farm road, if that much. You have to go into Kingman, which is in the opposite direction from Kentucky, and then round and across Arizona. There aren't too many roads in that state, it's mostly desert. The police could find you too easily."

"Down through Phoenix . . ."

"The road to Phoenix twists through mountains, with hairpin curves most of the way."

"I don't want you walking into an empty house with Matt Clive."

He looked at me without expression. "But you would go. If he didn't know you, I mean."

"That's different."

"How?" he said, half insulted, half challenging.

I looked at him sideways. "I bet I can run faster than you."

His forehead relaxed. "You're in pretty good shape, I'll give you that. All the same, I'm going to Las Vegas."

He'd maneuvered me into not being able to persuade him against it on the grounds of safety; and from all other points of view it was a good idea. Against my instinct I agreed in the end that he should go.

"I'll drift on out tomorrow and look at the farm beyond Kingman," I said. "I suppose you couldn't see whether there were any other horses there besides the two we're after?"

He looked startled. "You mean there might be another identification problem?"

"Perhaps. Though I'd say it's certain our two have Moviemaker and Centigrade's studbook numbers tattooed inside their mouths. They would have to, to satisfy visiting grooms, for instance, that their mares were being mated with the right stallion. But I've never seen them . . . Showman and Allyx. If there are other horses there, it'll simply mean going round peering into all their mouths until I find the right ones."

Walt raised his eyes to heaven. "You make everything sound so darned easy. Like it's only five miles to the top of Everest, and everyone can walk five miles, can't they?"

Smiling, I asked him for precise directions to the farm, and he told me.

"And now this end," I said. "How many strings can you pull with the Los Angeles fraud squad?"

"Not many," he said. "I don't know anyone out there."

"But with Buttress Life behind you?"

He sighed. "I suppose you want me to go and dip my toes in the water?"

"Jump right in," I agreed. "Talk your way to the top chap, and tell him Buttress Life suspect that Moviemaker and Centigrade are Showman and Allyx. Get everything nicely stirred up. Make Offen prove beyond any doubt that the two horses at Orpheus literally are Moviemaker and Centigrade."

He nodded. "O.K. I'll start this morning. Have to go a little carefully, though, or Offen will come up so fast with a libel suit that we'll wonder what hit us."

"You must be used to ducking."

"Yeah."

I gave him the page Miss Britt had written out for me in Lexington.

"Here are the figures. No one can question these, not even Offen. You might find them useful in getting the law moving."

He tucked the paper into his pocket and nodded, and shortly after, with the habitual martyred sigh, levered himself out of his chair and ambled on his way.

I sat and thought for a while but got nowhere new. There was going to be little else for me to do but wait and watch for the next few days while Sam Hengelman rolled his way 2,000 miles across the continent.

When I went down to lunch I found Eunice and Lynnie sitting in cool bright dresses under the dappled shade of the sea-facing terrace. Their hair was glossy and neat, their big earrings gently swinging, their legs smooth and tanned, the whites of their eyes a detergent white.

They didn't get the lingering scrutiny they deserved.

With them, equally crisp, equally at ease, sat Culham James Offen, Uncle Bark.

All three seemed a trifle disconcerted when I folded myself gently onto the fourth chair round the low table on which stood their long frosted drinks.

Offen and I nodded to each other. There was still in his manner the superior, self-satisfied amusement he had treated me with at his house. Reassuring. Lynnie smiled, but with a quick sidelong glance at Eunice to make sure such treachery hadn't been noticed. Eunice had on an "I-am-your-employer's-wife" face, which didn't wipe from my mind, nor hers, I imagine, the memory of the fluffy pink wrapper.

"We thought you'd gone to L.A. with Walt," Lynnie said.

Eunice gave her a sharp glance which she didn't see. "We ran into Mr. Offen in the lobby here, wasn't that extraordinary?"

"Extraordinary," I agreed.

Offen's white eyebrows went up and down in an embarrassment he couldn't entirely smother.

"It sure has been a pleasure," he said, "to get to know you folks better." He spoke exclusively to Eunice, however.

She had warmed again to the charm he had switched on for her, and gave me the tag end of a scornful glance. How could I, she implied, imagine this nice influential citizen could be a crook?

"How are Matt and Yola these days?" I said conversationally.

Offen visibly jumped, and a blight fell on the party. "Such charming young people," I said benignly, and watched Eunice remembering what had happened to Dave, and also perhaps what Walt had told her about their attack on me. "Your nephew and niece, I believe?"

Offen's pale-blue eyes were the least impressive feature in his tanned face with its snow-white frame. I read in them a touch of wariness, and wondered whether in prodding Eunice to face reality I had disturbed his complacency too far.

"They would sure like to meet you again," he said slowly, and the heavy ill-feeling behind the words curdled finally for Eunice his milk-of-human-kindness image.

"Are you expecting them within the next few days?" I asked, dropping in the merest touch of anxiety.

He said he wasn't, and his inner amusement abruptly returned. I had succeeded in convincing him I would be trying to remove his horses from Orpheus pretty soon now; and shortly afterwards he got purposefully to his feet, bent a beaming smile on Eunice, a smaller one on Lynnie, and a smug one on me, and made an important exit through the motel.

After a long pause Eunice said flatly, "I guess I was wrong about that guy being sweet."

We ate an amicable lunch and spent the afternoon on the beach under a fringed umbrella, with the bright green-blue Pacific hissing gently on the sand. Out on the rollers the golden boys rode their surfboards, and flat by my side little Lynnie sighed to the bottom of her lungs with contentment.

"I wish this could go on forever," she said.

"So do I."

Eunice, on the other side of Lynnie, propped herself up on one elbow. "I'm going to take a dip," she said. "Coming?"

"In a minute," Lynnie said lazily, and Eunice went alone. We watched her tight, well-shaped figure walk unwaveringly down to the water, and Lynnie said what I was thinking. "She hardly drinks at all now."

"You're good for her."

"Oh, sure." She laughed gently, stretching like a cat. "Isn't this heat just gorgeous?"

"Mm."

"What are all those scars on you?"

"Lions and tigers and appendicitis."

She snorted. "Shall we go in and swim?"

"In a minute. What did you and Eunice and Offen say to each other before I arrived?"

"Oh . . ." She sounded bored. "He wanted to know what you were doing. Eunice told him you and Walt were cooking something up but she didn't know what. And . . . er . . . yes . . . he asked if Walt was really an insurance man, and Eunice said he was . . . and he asked other things about you, what your job was and so on, and why you were out here with us . . ."

"Did Eunice tell him I got her to show him that photograph on purpose? Did she tell him that I was certain the horses that he has at Orpheus Farm are Moviemaker and Centigrade?"

Lynnie shook her head.

"You're quite sure?"

"Yes, absolutely. Would it have been a nuisance if we had?"

"A fair way to being disastrous."

"Don't worry then. He was only here about a quarter of an hour before you came down, and all Eunice said was that you were er . . . er . . . well, her actual words were, some dim bloody little office worker on vacation." Lynnie laughed. "She said her husband had been grateful to you for saving his life and was paying your bill here, and that all you seemed to be interested in at present was a girl up in San Francisco."

I looked down to where Eunice's head bobbed in the surf and wondered whether she'd given him perfect answers from design or bitchiness.

"What's she like?" Lynnie said.

"Who?"

"The girl in San Francisco."

"You'd better ask Walt," I said, turning my head to look at her. "He invented her."

She gasped and laughed in one. "Oh, good! I mean . . . er . . . then what were you really doing?"

"Ah, well," I said, "now that's something I'd hate Eunice to have told Culham Offen."

She lay looking back at me steadily for several seconds. So much more assurance, I thought idly, than on that day on the river, when she had still been a child.

"Is that why you've told us practically nothing? Don't you trust her?"

"She's never wanted the horses back."

Lynnie blinked. "But she wouldn't . . . she wouldn't have ruined on purpose what you're trying to do. After all, you're doing it for her husband."

I smiled, and she sat up abruptly, and put her arms round her knees.

"You make me feel so . . . *naive.*"

"You," I said, "are adorable."

"And now you're laughing at me."

I wanted impulsively to say that I loved her, but I wasn't sure that it was true. Maybe all I wanted was an antidote to depression. She was certainly the best I'd found.

"I'm going away again in the morning," I said.

"To San Francisco?"

"Somewhere like that."

"How long for?"

"Two nights."

"This is your last week," she said, looking out to sea.

The thought leapt involuntarily, *if only it were.* I shook my head abruptly, as if one could empty the brain by force, and climbed slowly onto my feet.

"There's today, anyway," I said smiling. "Let's go and get wet."

Walt came back at seven with dragging feet and a raging thirst.

"Those detectives from the D.A.'s office will scalp me if they find out we're only using them," he said gloomily, up in my room. "Two of them have agreed to go out to Orpheus Farm tomorrow, and I'm meeting them on the L.A. road to show them the way. Day after tomorrow, some guy from the bloodstock registry office is going out. I got the D.A.'s office to call him and fix it."

"Couldn't be better."

Walt recharged his batteries with Old Grand-dad and said, "So what's new with you?"

"Offen came here on a fact-finding mission."

"He did *what?*"

"Came looking for answers. Got some real beauties from Eunice, which won't help him any, and went away believing we'd be back on his doorstep pretty soon."

"I guess," Walt said, "that he wanted to know if we'd called it off and gone home, and whether it was safe to bring those horses back again. It's days since he saw any sign of us. Must have been like sitting on an H bomb with a tricky firing pin." He swallowed appreciatively and rolled his tongue over his gums. "He'll get all the action he wants tomorrow."

When he plodded tiredly off to shower before dinner, I telephoned to Jeff Roots.

"How was Miami?" I said.

"Hot and horrible, and I gained four pounds."

Commiserating, I thanked him for his help with the newspaper files and told him that owing to Miss Britt we had found the two stallions.

"I wish I didn't believe it. Are you certain?"

"Yes."

His sigh was heartfelt. "We'd better start proceedings . . ."

"I've . . . er . . . already started them. We may in a day or two have two horses on our hands which will need to be stabled somewhere eminently respectable while their identity is being investigated. Owing to the length of time they've been lost, it may take a couple of months to re-establish them. Where would you think it would be best to put them?"

After a pause he said, "I suppose you're asking me to have them here?"

"Not really," I explained. "Too much of a coincidence after Chrysalis, perhaps. I'd thought rather of a more official place. . . . I don't know what you have."

"I'll think of something." He coughed slightly. "There won't be anything illegal about their recovery?"

"No more than for Chrysalis."

"That's no answer."

"There shouldn't be any trouble with the police," I said.

"I guess that'll have to do." He sighed. "When do I expect them?"

"If all goes well, they should reach Lexington on Sunday."

"And if all doesn't go well?"

"You'll have no problem."

He laughed. "And you?"

"One more won't matter."

Chapter 16

FOR most of thirty hours I sat in the mountainous Arizona desert and looked down at Matt Clive leading a boring life.

Like his sister, he was capable, quick, efficient. He watered the stock and mended a fence, swept out the house, and fed the hens; and spent a good deal of time in the largest barn on the place.

I had found myself a perch among the rocks on the east-facing side of the valley, half a mile off the dusty road to the farm. At nearly three thousand above sea level the heat was bearable, though the midday sun blazed down from nearly straight overhead, and eggs would have fried on the sidewalks if there had been any. Desert plants were designed to save themselves and no one else: at my back grew a large agave, its central stem rising six feet high with flat outspreading flowers turning from red to brilliant yellow. For leaves it had razor-sharp spikes springing outward from the ground in one large clump. Stiff; angular; not a vestige of shade. The spindly buckhorn and the flat devil's-fingers would have been pretty useless to a midget. I folded myself under the overhang of a jagged boulder and inched round with the meager shade patch until the sun cried quits behind the hill.

Showman and Allyx had to be in the big barn: though I saw no sign of them, nor of any other horses, on the first

afternoon. By air to Las Vegas and rented car to Kingman had taken me all morning, and at the last fork on the
way to the farm I'd had to decide whether to risk meeting
Matt head on on the road or to walk ten miles instead. I'd
risked it. Ten miles there was also ten miles back. The car
had bumped protestingly off the road two miles short of
his farm, and was now out of sight in a gully.

Binoculars brought every detail of the meager spread
up clear and sharp. The small dilapidated house lay to the
left, with the big barn on the right across a large dusty
yard. Along most of a third side of the rough quadrangle
stretched an uneven jumble of simple stone buildings, and
behind those the rusting guts of two abandoned cars lay
exposed to the sky.

Maintenance was at a minimum: no endemic prosperity
here. The owners scratched for a living in a tiny valley
among the Arizona hills, existing there only by courtesy of
the quirk of rock formation which had brought under-
ground water to the surface in a spring. The small river
bed was easy to follow from where I sat. Grass and trees
circled its origin, sparse paddocks stretched away to sagging fences on each side of its upper reaches, a corn patch
grew beside it near the farm buildings, and lower down it
ran off into the desert in a dry wide shallow sandy trough.
Heavy rain would turn it every time into a raging torrent,
as destructive as it was vital. High behind the house,
dominating the whole place, a huge onion-shaped water
storage tank sat squatly on top of a spindly looking
tower.

Mile after mile of plain dark poles stretched along the
road to the farm, carrying an electric cable and a telephone wire, but civilization had fallen short of refuse
collection. A sprawling dump at one side of the big barn
seemed to consist of a brass bedstead, half a tractor, a
bottomless tin bath, the bones of an old wagon, a tangled
heap of unidentifiable rusting metal, and roughly fifty
treadless tires of varying sizes. Filling every crevice
among this lot were bottles and empty food cans with
labels peeling and jagged lids mutely open like mouths.
Over the top the air shimmered with reflected heat.

Matt had already spent at least a week in this ugly oasis. Walt shouldn't find it too hard to persuade him to make an evening visit to Las Vegas.

I watched until long after dark. Lights went on and off in the house, and Matt moved about, visible through the screens because he didn't draw any curtains. If, indeed, there were any.

Cautiously, at some time after one o'clock, when all the lights on my side of the house had been out for more than two hours, I picked my way down to the farm. The night was still warm, but as the only light came from the stars it was black dark on the ground, and with agave clumps in mind I reckoned my flashlight held lesser risk.

I reached the farmyard. Nothing stirred. Quietly, slowly, I made the crossing to the barn. Matt in the house slept on.

No padlocks: not even bolts. There weren't any. The wide door of the barn stood open; and with this invitation, I went in. Inside, the barn was divided into six stalls along one side, with feed bins and saddlery storage racks along the other. Here and everywhere else dilapidation and decay were winning hands down: everything my light flicked over looked in need of help.

Four of the stalls were empty, but in the two central ones, side by side, stood two horses. Gently, so as not to frighten them, I went over, talking soothingly in a murmur and shining the beam on the wall in front of their heads. Their eyes in the dim light rolled round inquiringly, but neither gave more than a single stamp of alarm.

The first one tried to back away when I shone the torch into his mouth: but an exceedingly strong-looking head collar and a remarkably new chain kept him from going more than a few feet. I ran my hand down his neck and talked to him, and in the end got my inspection done. The tattooed mark, as often, was none too clear: but discernibly it was 75207. The registration number of Moviemaker.

The tattoo on the second horse was more recent and also clearer: the registration number of Centigrade.

Satisfied, I gave them each a friendly slap, and with

great care left the barn. Matt still slept. I hesitated, thinking that enough was enough, but in the end went down to
the end of the farmyard to take a quick look through the
other buildings. In one only, a deep narrow garage, was
there anything of interest: a car.

It was not Matt's pale-blue convertible, but a tinny
black sedan three or four years old. My flashlight picked
out a piece of paper lying on the passenger seat, and I
opened the door and took a look at it. A copy of a work
sheet from a garage in Kingman. Customer's name:
Clive. Work required: Remove yellow paint from Ford
convertible. Further instructions: Complete as soon as
possible.

I put the paper back on the seat and shone the light
over the dashboard. A small metal plate screwed onto it
bore the name of the garage in Kingman: Matt had
rented this car while his own was being cleaned.

Outside, everything was still, and feeling like a shadow
among shadows I went quietly out of the farmyard and
along the dusty road toward Kingman. It seemed a lot
farther than two miles to the flat stones I had left one
on top of the other as a marker, and even after I had
reached them it took me quite a while to find the hidden
car and get it back on the road.

It was well after three when I called Walt. He sounded
resigned, but he'd known it would be sometime in the
night.

"Are they there?" he said.

"They are. They're quite unguarded, and there's only
Matt on the place. How about things your end?"

"Oh." Amusement crept in. "Offen was full of offended
dignity. Didn't know how anyone could suggest he was
engaged in fraud; that sort of thing. It didn't impress the
D.A.'s squad at all, because they get that sort of bluster
every time. Made them all the keener, if anything. They
had quite a long session with him, all fairly polite but
definitely needling. Artists, they are. From our point of
view Offen said nothing significant except for one little
gem. The D.A.'s guys asked to see the stud groom. That's

Kiddo, remember? The one who told us about the mares foaling at night?"

"I remember," I said.

"Well, it seems it's a slow time around studs just now, and Kiddo went off on a vacation the day after our first visit."

"He didn't say anything about that when we were there."

"He sure didn't. Offen says Kiddo will be back in three weeks. By then, I guess, he expects to have had Moviemaker and Centigrade identified as themselves, and then when the dust has settled he can bring Showman and Allyx quietly back, and it'll be safe for Kiddo to return. I guess Offen didn't know which way he'd jump, and booted him off out of trouble."

"I'm sure you're right," I said. "Anything interesting on the tape?"

"I've been listening to that damned machine until I'm bored to death with it," he said wearily. "Today's run was mostly the D.A.'s men talking to Offen, so I heard all that twice over. He then called both Yola and Matt and told them about it, and he sounded pretty pleased with the way things were going. I'd say Matt was a mite annoyed at having to stay where he is: Offen was telling him not to be stupid, what was a week or two with so much at stake. Also Yola must be wanting Matt back, because Offen smoothed her down with the same spiel." Walt paused and cleared his throat. "What would you say is the relationship between Matt and Yola?"

Smiling into the receiver I said, "Such thoughts, Walt, from you!"

"It's possible . . ." he said uncomfortably.

"It sure is. But there's nothing to indicate it except for their not being married."

"Then you don't think . . . ?"

"I'd say they're certainly centered on each other, but how far it goes I couldn't guess. The only times I've seen them together they've had their hands full of punts and guns."

"Yeah. . . . Well, maybe crime is how it takes them."

I agreed that it probably was, and asked him if he'd got Matt set up for the insurance meeting.

"I sure have," he said, with satisfaction. "I called him this afternoon. It must have been soon after he'd been talking to Offen, I guess, because he seemed to be glad enough to be given a reason for going to Las Vegas. I suggested six P.M. which sounded all right, but he himself asked if I could make it later."

"He'll probably want to feed the horses about then, when the day gets cooler," I said. "And those horses would come first."

"Yeah. At three million for the two, they sure would. It beats me why he doesn't guard them every minute."

"Against what?" I said.

"You've got a point," he conceded. "Only us. And we're obviously concentrating on the two at Orpheus. Right?"

"Right."

"Anyway, Matt said could I make it later than six, and we agreed in the end on nine. That should mean he'll take that gander at the roulette tables on his way home, and maybe give us most of the night to get the horses clear."

"Good," I said. "That's fine. But, Walt . . ."

"Yes?"

"Take care."

"Go teach your grandmother," he said, and I smiled wryly and asked him if he'd heard from Sam Hengelman.

"Sure, he called this evening, like you asked. He'd reached Santa Rosa in New Mexico and he was going on to Albuquerque before stopping for the night. He said he'd be in Kingman by four or five tomorrow afternoon—today, I suppose, technically—and he'll meet you at the Mojave Motel. I told him the return trip wouldn't be starting before eight, so he's going to take a room there and catch a couple of hours' sleep."

"Thanks, Walt, that's great," I said.

"We're all set, then?" There was a hint of unease in his

voice, and it raised prickles again in my early-warning mechanism.

"You don't have to go to Las Vegas," I said reasonably. "We've time enough without it."

"I'm going," he said. "And that's that."

"Well . . . all right. I think we could do with a checkpoint, though, in case anything goes wrong. Let's say you wait in the lobby of the Angel Inn from eight to eight-thirty tomorrow evening. That's where I stayed. It's right on the edge of Las Vegas, but it's an easy trip to Pittsville Boulevard. I'll call you there sometime during that half hour; and if I don't, you stay put, and don't go out to Matt's house."

"O.K.," he said, and although he tried there was distinct relief in his voice.

We disconnected, and I ate a sandwich and drank coffee at an all-night lunch counter at the bus station before returning to my rented car and pointing its nose again toward the farm and the hills. The two flat stones came up again in the headlights, and restowing the car in its former hiding place, I finished the journey on foot.

Back in the shelter of the same jagged rock I tried for a time to sleep. There was still an hour or more before dawn, and the sun wouldn't be too hot for a while after that, but in spite of knowing that I'd get no rest at all during the following night my brain stayed obstinately awake. I supposed an inability to sleep on open ground surrounded by cacti and within yelling distance of a man who'd kill me if he had a chance could hardly be classed as insomnia in the ordinary way; but I had no illusions. That was precisely what it was. The restless, racing thoughts, the electrical awareness, the feeling that everything in one's body was working full steam ahead and wouldn't slow down; I knew all the symptoms much too well. One could lie with eyes shut and relax every muscle until one couldn't tell where one's arms and legs were, and still sleep wouldn't come. Breathe deeply, count all the sheep of Canterbury, repeat once-learned verses; nothing worked.

The sun came up and shone in my eyes. Inching out of

its revealing spotlight I retreated round the side of the rock and looked down to the farm through the binoculars. No movement. At five-thirty Matt was still in bed.

I put down the glasses and thought about a cigarette. There were only four left in the packet. Sighing, I reflected that I could easily have bought some in Kingman if I'd given it a thought. It was going to be a long day. All I'd brought with me besides the binoculars was a bottle of water, a pair of sunglasses, and the Luger in my belt.

At 7:30 Matt came out through the rickety screen door of the house, and stood in the yard stretching and looking around at the cloudless cobalt-blue sky. Then he went across to the barn and poked his head briefly inside.

Satisfied that the gold was still in the bank, he fetched buckets of water and joined it for long enough to muck out the stalls and see to the feed. After a time he came out with a barrowful of droppings and wheeled it away to empty on the far side of the barn, out of my sight.

The hens got their grits, and the calves in a near compound their ration of water, and Matt retired for his breakfast. The morning wore on. The temperature rose. Nothing else happened.

At noon I stood up for a while behind the rock to stretch my legs and restore some feeling to the bits that were numb from sitting. I drank some water and smoked a cigarette, and put on the sunglasses to circumvent a hovering glare headache: and having exhausted my repertoire except for a few shots from the Luger, folded myself back into the wedge of slowly moving shade, and took another look at the farm.

Status quo entirely unchanged. Maybe Matt was asleep, or telephoning, or watching television, or inventing systems for his trip to Las Vegas. He certainly was not doing much farming. Nor did he apparently propose to exercise the horses. They stayed in their stalls from dawn to dusk.

By two I knew intimately every spiny plant growing within a radius of ten feet of my rock, and found my eyes going far oftener to the broad sweep of desert on my left than to the dirty little farm below. The desert was clean in its way, and fierce, and starkly beautiful. All hills and endless sky. Parched sandy gray dust and scratchy cactus. Killing heat. A wild, uncompromising, lonely place.

When I first felt the urge just to get up and walk away into it I dragged my eyes dutifully back to the farm and smoked the second cigarette and thought firmly about Matt and the horses. That worked for a while, but the barren country pulled like a magnet.

I had only to walk out there, I thought, and keep on going until I was filled with its emptiness, and then sit down somewhere and put the barrel of the Luger against my head, and simply squeeze. So childishly easy; so appallingly tempting.

Walt, I thought desperately. I couldn't do it because of Walt and the unfinished business we were embarked on. The horses were there in front of me, and Walt and Sam Hengelman were on their way. It was impossible just to abandon them. I hit my hand against the rock and dragged my mind back to the farm and the night ahead. And when I'd gone through that piece by piece I concentrated one at a time on Yola and Offen, and Eunice and Dave Teller, and Keeble and Lynnie, trying to use them as pegs to keep me believing that what I did mattered to them. That anything I did mattered to anybody. That I cared whether anything I did mattered to anybody.

My hand had been bleeding. I hadn't even felt it. I looked dispassionately at the scraped skin, and loathed myself. I shut my eyes, and the desolation went so deep that for an unmeasurable age I felt dizzy with it, as if I were in some fearful pitch-black limbo, with no help, no hope, and no escape. Spinning slowly down an endless shaft in solitary despair. Lost.

The spinning stopped after a while. The internal darkness stayed.

I opened my eyes and looked down at the farm, only half seeing it, feeling myself trembling and knowing that there wasn't much further to go.

Matt came out of the house, walked across the yard, took a look into the barn, and retraced his steps. I watched him in a disoriented haze. Those horses in the barn, what did they matter? What did anything matter? Who cared a sixpenny damn about bloodlines, it would all be the same in a hundred years.

Dave Teller cared.

Let him.

Dave Teller cared a $10,000 damn what happened to them.

Crystal clear, like distilled-water logic, it occurred to me that I could give us both what we wanted if I postponed my walk into the desert until later that night. I would pack the horses off with Hengelman and, instead of driving back to Kingman after him, I would set off on foot, and when it was nearly dawn, and everything looked gray and shadowy, and the step would be small . . . then . . .

Then.

Immediately after making this firm decision, which seemed to me extremely sensible, I felt a great invasion of peace. No more struggle, no more fuss. My body felt relaxed and full of well-being and my mind was calm. I couldn't think why such an obvious solution hadn't occurred to me before. All the sweat and sleeplessness had dissolved into a cool, inner, steady light.

This stage lasted until I remembered that I had once been determined not to reach it.

After that, creeping in little by little, came the racking conviction that I had merely surrendered, and was not only despicable but probably insane.

I sat for a while with my head in my hands, fearfully expecting that with the false peace broken up and gone, back would come the shattering vertigo.

It didn't. There was only so great a tiredness that what I'd called tiredness before was like a pinhead on a continent. The dreary fight was on again; but at least I'd survived the bloodiest battle yet. Touched bottom and come back. I felt as if I'd passed some obscure crisis, and that after this I really could climb right out if I went on trying.

A long way to go. But, then, I'd have all the time I needed.

Chapter 17

I had cramps right down both legs. Matt came out of the house and I woke up to the fact that the shade patch had moved round while I hadn't. When he went into the barn I started to shift the necessary two yards and found my muscles in knots.

The shade wasn't much cooler, but much better cover. I sat in it waiting for Matt to come out of the barn and for my legs to unlock. What they needed was for me to get to my feet and stamp about: but if Matt caught sight of anyone moving so close to him the whole project would lie in ruins.

He fetched water for the horses, for the calves, and for the hens. I looked at my watch, and was horribly startled to see it was nearly six. It couldn't be, I thought; but it was. Four hours since I had last checked. Four hours. I shivered in the roasting air.

Matt brought the empty muck barrel around and into the barn, and came out with it filled. For the whole afternoon I'd fallen down on the surveillance, but looking back I was fairly sure nothing had changed at the farm. Certainly at this point things were as they had been: Matt had no helpers and no visitors, and when he left for Las Vegas the horses would be alone. For that piece of certainty I had been prepared to watch all day, and a poor job I'd made of it.

Matt shut the barn door and went into the house. Half an hour later he came out in a cream-colored jacket and dark trousers, a transformation from his habitual jeans and checked shirt. He opened the doors of the shed containing the car, went inside, started up, and drove out across the yard, round the bend onto the road, and away over the desert toward Kingman.

Satisfied, I finally got to my feet. The cramps had gone. I plodded tiredly off to the two-mile-distant hidden car,

and wished the night was over, not beginning. I hadn't
enough energy to lick a stamp.

Matt's dust had settled when I followed him along the
empty road, but when I got into Kingman he was still
there. With shock I saw him standing outside a garage I
was passing, and I pulled over to the curb fifty yards on
and looked back. The black sedan he had rented and his
own blue Ford were both standing there in the forecourt.
An overalled girl attendant was filling the Ford's tank
from the pump, and Matt was looking in snatches at his
watch and exhibiting impatience: 7:20, and a hundred
miles to Las Vegas. He would be a few minutes late for
his appointment with Walt.

Slumping down in my seat I fixed the driving mirror so
that I could watch him. He paid the girl for the gas and
hopped into his car over the top, without opening the
door. Then he pulled out onto the road, turned in my
direction, and went past me with his foot impressively on
the accelerator. I gently followed for a while at a respectable distance, content to keep him only just in sight, and
turned back to the town once he was conclusively topping
the speed limit on Route 93 to Las Vegas.

Outside the unprosperous-looking Mojave Motel Sam
Hengelman's horse van took up a sixth of the parking
space. Inside, they told me that he had arrived at 4:30
and was along in Room 6, sleeping. I left him to it,
because we couldn't move anyway until I'd phoned Walt
at eight, and went into the bus station for some coffee. It
came in a plastic carton out of an automat, black but
weak. I drank it without tasting and thought about some
food, but I wasn't really hungry enough to bother, and I
was too dirty and unshaven for anywhere good. Until
after eight I sat on the bus station bench staring into
space, and then used the bus station telephone to get
through to Walt.

He came on the line with little delay.

"How's things?" he said.

"Matt left Kingman for Las Vegas at seven-thirty, so
he will be a little late.

"Left Kingman?" Walt sounded surprised.

I explained about Matt changing cars.

"I suppose his Ford wasn't quite ready when he got there. Anyway, he's coming in that, not the rented one."

"Are you all right?" Walt said hesitantly.

"Of course."

"You don't sound it."

"Sam Hengelman's here," I said, ignoring him. "He's asleep along at the Mojave Motel. We'll start as soon as I get back there and wake him up."

"It's all safe at the farm?" He seemed anxious.

"Deserted," I assured him. "Has been all yesterday, all last night, and all today. No one around but Matt. Stop worrying. You just see Matt and put on your act, and then head straight back to Santa Barbara. As soon as Sam's clear of the area I'll follow you. See you for breakfast about twelve hours from now."

"Right," he said. "Well, keep your nose clean."

"You too."

"Sure thing. It's not me that's nuts."

The line clicked clear before I found an answer, and it left me with a vague feeling that there was more I should have said, though I didn't know what.

I knocked on Sam's door at the motel, and he came sleepily stretching to switch on the light and let me in.

"With you in a minute," he said, reaching for his shoes and looking round for his tie.

"Sam, you don't have to come."

"Eh?"

"Go back to sleep. I'll go and fetch the horses. That way you won't be so involved."

He sat on the edge of the bed looking down at the floor. "I'm still driving them to Lexington?"

"Unless you want out. Leave the van and fly home."

"Nope." He shook his head. "A bargain's a bargain. And I may as well come all the way. That van's none too easy in reverse . . . don't know that you could handle it."

I half smiled and didn't argue. I'd wanted him with me, but only willingly, and I'd got that. He knotted his tie and brushed his hair and then took a sidelong glance at my own appearance, which fell a ton short of his. He was a fleshy man of about fifty, bald, pale skinned, and unexcitable. His nerves, I thought, were going to be at least equal to the evening's requirements.

"Let's go, then," he said cheerfully. "I paid in advance."

I followed him across to the van and climbed into the cab. Sam started the engine, told me he'd filled up with gas when he'd first reached Kingman, and rolled out southeast on the road to the farm. His broad face looked perfectly calm in the glow from the dashboard, and he handled his six-stall horsebox like a kiddycar. We went eight miles in silence, and then all he said was "I'd sure hate to live this far from town, with nowhere to get a beer."

We passed the third of the three side roads and started on the last ten uninhabited miles to the farm. Three miles farther Sam gave an alarmed exclamation and braked from his cautious thirty to a full stop. "What is it?" I asked.

"That gauge." He pointed, and I looked. The needle on the temperature gauge was quivering on red.

"Have to look-see," he grunted, and switched off the engine. My thoughts as he disappeared out of the cab were one enormous curse. Of all hopeless, dangerous places for his van to break down.

He came back and opened the door on my side. I jumped down beside him and he took me round to show me the exhaust.

"Look," he said unnecessarily. "Water."

Several drops slid out, glistening in the beam of his flashlight.

"Gasket," he said, putting into one word the enormity of the disaster, and what he thought of fate for trapping us in it.

"No water in the radiator," I said.

"Right."

"And if we go on, the engine will seize up."

"Right again."

"I suppose you don't carry any extra water in the van?"

"We sure do," he said. "Never travel without it."

"Can't we pour some in the radiator?"

"Yeah," he said. "We can. There's two gallons. We can pour in a quart, and go three miles maybe before it's all leaked out, and then another quart, another three miles. Four quarts, twelve miles. And that's it."

Thirteen miles out from Kingman. We could just about get back. Seven to the farm. We could refill the radiator at the farm, but Sam couldn't set out on his 3000-mile journey with a stolen cargo in a van emptying like a dry dock.

"There's an extra gasket, of course," he said.

"A spare one?"

"Sure. Always carry a full set of spares. Never know where you're going to need them. Universal joints, big ends, carburetors—I carry them all. Anyone with any sense does that."

"Well," I said in relief, "how long will it take you to fit the spare?"

He laid the engine bare and considered it.

"Cylinder head gasket. Say three hours."

"Three hours!"

"Won't take much less," he said. "What do you want to do?"

I looked at my watch. 8:50. Three hours made 11:50; and if we then went on to the farm and picked up the horses we couldn't be back through Kingman until 1:15.

Matt would reach Pittsville Boulevard by 9:30, and finish his insurance business long before ten. If he drove straight home again he would be on the farm road at midnight. If Sam changed the gasket, so would we.

If Matt stopped to play the tables, he would be at least an hour later. His clothes had suggested he would stop. But whether for one hour or six, there was no way of telling.

"Change the gasket," I said abruptly. "Then we'll see."

Sam nodded philosophically. It was what he would have done in any case if the van had broken down anywhere else, and without more ado he sorted out what he wanted and started unscrewing.

"Can I help?" I said.

He shook his head and clipped his flashlight onto a convenient spar to give a steady working light. There seemed to be little haste in his manner, but also no hesitation and a good deal of expertise. The heap of unplugged parts grew steadily on a square of canvas at his feet.

I walked away a few steps and felt for the cigarettes. Two left. I'd still forgotten to buy more. The smoke didn't help much toward making the next decision: to go on or to go back.

I'd already gambled on Matt's staying to play. If it had been Yola, I would have felt surer that it would be for most of the night: but her brother might not have the fever, might only want a short break in his boring stint with the horses. How short? How long?

The decision I came to, if you could call it that, was to wait and see at what time Sam restarted the engine.

The night, outside the bright pool by the van, was as dark as the one before. The stars glittered remotely, and the immensity of the American continent marked their indifference to the human race. Against such size, what did one man matter? A walk into the desert . . .

Carefully I pinched out the end of my cigarette and put the stub in my pocket. A good criminal, I thought wryly: I'd always been that. I had a job to do, and even when I'd finished it I was going for no walks into the desert. I was going back to Santa Barbara, to have breakfast with Walt and Eunice and Lynnie. The prospect at that moment seemed totally unreal, so far were the Arizona hills from the lush coast, so far had I been into the wasteland inside me.

I went back to Sam and asked how it was going. He had the cylinder head off and was removing the cracked gasket.

"So-so," he said calmly, "I'm breaking the record."

I did my best at a smile. He grunted, and said he could do with a cup of coffee, and I said so could I. We hadn't brought any.

He worked on. The air was still warmer than an English summer and he wiped sweat off his bald forehead with the back of a greasy hand. The light shone on his thick stubby fingers, and the click of his wrench echoed across the empty land. The hands on my watch went round in slow fractions. The gasket was wasting the night. And where was Matt?

After two hours Sam's spanner slipped on a nut and he cursed. In spite of his calm, the tension wasn't far from the surface. He stopped what he was doing, stretched upright, took three deep breaths and a look at the night sky, and waited for me to say something.

"You're doing fine," I said.

He sniffed. "What'll happen if they catch us here?"

"We won't get the horses."

He grimaced at my nonanswer and went back to his task. "What have you been doing all day?"

"Nothing. Sitting still."

"You look half dead," he commented. "Pass me those two washers, will you?"

I gave him the washers. "How much longer?"

"Can't say."

I stifled the urge to tell him to hurry. He was going as fast as he could. But time was ticking away, and the postponed decision had got to be made. Turning my back on the tugging desert I climbed up to sit in the cab. 11:20. Matt could be a bare quarter of an hour out from Kingman. Or glued to the green baize and the tricky numbers in Las Vegas.

Which?

For a long half hour I looked out the back windows while no helpful telepathic messages flowed through them. A straightforward gamble, I thought. Just decide if the winnings were worth the risk.

An easier decision if I'd come alone: but if I'd come alone I couldn't have mended the gasket.

At 11:40 Sam said gloomily that he was having to fix
the water pump as well. It was sticking.

"How long?"

"Another twenty minutes."

We stared at each other in dismay.

"Go on then," I said in the end. There was nothing
else to do.

I left the cab and walked restlessly a short way back
along the road, fearing every second to see Matt's headlights and wondering how best to deal with him if we had
to. I was all for stealing from him what wasn't his, but not
for damaging his skin. He, however, would have no such
inhibitions. There would certainly be blood. Not fair to
make it Sam's.

At two minutes past midnight he called out that he had
finished, and I walked quickly back to join him. He was
pouring water into the radiator, and screwed on the cap as
I came up.

"It should be O.K. now," he said. His hands were
covered in grease and his big body hung tiredly from the
shoulders. "Which way do we go?"

"On."

He nodded with a wide slicing grin.

"I figured you'd say that. Well, I guess that's O.K. by
me."

He swung up into the cab and I climbed in beside him.
The engine started sweetly at first try, and switching on
his headlights, he released the brake and eased away along
the road.

"If anyone catches us here from now on," I said,
"duck."

"Yeah?"

"Yeah."

"Tell you something," he said comfortably. "I swing a
mean left hook."

"The chap we'd be taking on goes for the head. But
with a club of some sort in his fist."

"Nice guys you play with," he said. "I'll remember
that."

We covered the remaining distance at a good speed and

in silence. The horsebox crept round the last corner and its headlights flickered over the farm ahead. I put my hand on Sam's arm, and he braked to a halt a short way from the yard.

"Switch off, would you? Lights too," I said, and jumped quickly down from the cab to wait a few precious seconds until my eyes and ears got used to silence and dark.

No lights in the house. No sound anywhere except the ultra-faint ringing vibration of limitless air. The calves and hens were asleep. The horses were quiet. I banged on the cab door and Sam switched his headlights on again before climbing down to join me. The bright shafts lit up the back of the house and wouldn't shine straight into the horses' eyes when I led them from the barn. Over on the shadowy side of the yard the open doors of the shed where Matt had kept his car yawned in a deep black square. The jumbled rubbish dump just in front of us threw surrealist shadows across the dusty ground, and its smell of decay brushed past our noses.

Sam swept it all with a practiced glance. "Not much of a place." His voice was as low as a whisper.

"No. . . . If you'll unclip the ramp, I'll go fetch the horses. One at a time, I think."

"O.K." He was breathing faster and his big hands were clenched. Not used to it, after all.

I hurried down toward the barn. It wasn't far; about forty yards. Now that we were totally committed my mind raced with urgency to be done, to be away, to be safely through Kingman before Matt came back. He could have been on the road behind us, be rushing at this moment across the desert to the farm. . . .

What happened next happened very fast, in one terrifying cataclysmic blur.

There was an urgent shout behind me.

"Gene!"

I turned, whirling. There were two sets of headlights where there should have been one.

Matt.

The voice again, yelling. "Gene! Look out." And a figure running down the yard toward me.

Then there was a roar behind me and I turned again and was met full in the eyes by the blinding glare of two more headlights, much closer. Much closer.

Moving.

I was dazzled and off balance and I'd never have got clear. The running figure threw itself at me in a football tackle with outstretched arms and knocked me over out of the way, and the roaring car crashed solidly into the flying body and left it crumpled and smashed and lying on top of my legs.

The car which had hit him turned in a wide sweep at the end of the yard and started back. The headlights lined themselves up like twin suns on their target and with a fraction of my mind I thought it ironic that now, when I'd decided not to, I was going to die.

Half sitting, half kneeling, I jerked out the Luger and pumped all of its eight bullets toward the windshield. I couldn't see to aim straight . . . my eyes were hurting from the glare . . . Not that bullets would do any good . . . the angle was wrong . . . they'd miss the driver. . . . By the time I fired the last one the left headlight was six feet away. I uselessly set my teeth against the mangling, tearing, pulping collision . . . and in the last tenth of a second the straight line wavered . . . the smooth side of the car hit the back of my shoulder, the front wheel ran over a fold of my shirt, and the rear wheel gave me a clear inch.

Almost before I realized it had missed me, the car crashed head on into one of the buildings at my back with a jolting screech of wood and metal. The bodywork crumpled and cracked. The stabbing lights went black. The engine stopped. Air hissed fiercely out of a punctured tire.

Gasping, dreading what I would find, I leaned over the heavy figure lying on my legs. There were more running footsteps in the yard, and I looked up hopelessly, unable to do any more. I'd used all the bullets . . . none left.

"You're alive!" The voice came from the level of my ear, the man kneeling. Sam Hengelman. I looked at him in a daze.

"I thought . . ." I said, with no breath, "this was you."

He shook his head. "No . . ."

He helped me raise and turn the man who'd saved me; and with sickness and unbearable regret I saw his face.

It was Walt.

We laid him on his back, in the dust.

"Look in the car," I said.

Sam lumbered silently to his feet and went away. I heard his footsteps stop and then start back.

Walt opened his eyes. I leaned over him, lifting his hand, feeling with surging hope for his pulse.

"Gene?" his voice mumbled.

"Yes."

"He didn't come."

"Didn't . . .?"

"Came to help you . . ."

"Yes," I said. "Thanks, Walt."

His eyes slid aimlessly away from my face.

"Christ," he said distinctly, "this is it. This is . . . really . . . it."

"Walt . . ." His hand was warm in mine, but it didn't move.

"Sod it," he said. "I wanted . . . I wanted . . ."

His voice stopped. There was no pulse. No heartbeat. Nothing. Nothing at all.

I put down gently on the ground the warm hand with the rounded fingertips, and stretched out my own, and shut his eyes. It should have been me lying there, not Walt. I shook with sudden impotent fury that it wasn't me, that Walt had taken what I'd wanted, stolen my death. . . . It would have mattered so little if it had been me. It wouldn't have mattered at all.

Walt . . . Walt . . .

Sam Hengelman said, "Is he dead?"

I nodded without looking up.

"There's a young guy in the car," he said. "He's dead too."

I got slowly, achingly, to my feet and went to look. The

car was the blue Ford convertible and the young guy was Matt.

Without caring, automatically, I took in that the car had smashed the right-hand door of the garage shed and plowed into the wall behind it. Most of the windshield was scattered in splintered fragments all over the inside of the car, but in one corner, where some still clung to the frame, there was a finger-sized hole.

Matt was lying over the steering wheel, his arms dangling, his eyes open. The skull above the left eyebrow was pierced and crumpled inward, and there was blood and hair on the chromium upright which had held the windshield. I didn't touch him. After a while I went back to Walt.

"What do we do?" Sam Hengelman said.

"Give me a moment . . ."

He waited without speaking until eventually I looked up and down the yard. Two sets of headlights still blazed at the way in.

"That's Walt's car up there?"

"Yeah. He drove up with the devil on his tail and jumped out and ran down after you . . ."

I turned the other way and looked at the dark garage.

"The young guy must have been in there all the time, waiting for us," Sam said. "He came roaring out and drove straight at you. I couldn't have stopped him . . . too far away. Walt was halfway down the yard . . ."

I nodded. Matt had been there all the time. Not in Las Vegas. Not on the road. Lying in ambush, waiting.

He hadn't passed us on the road, and there was no other way to the farm. He must have gone back ahead of us. Turned round on the road to Las Vegas and driven back through Kingman while I was sitting in the bus station waiting to telephone to Walt.

But why? *Why* should he have gone back? He hadn't seen me following him, I'd been much too far behind, and in any case I'd left him once he was safely on the highway.

It didn't matter why. It only mattered that he had. Sam

Hengelman looked down at Walt and summed up the mess we were entangled in.

"Well, what the heck do we do now?"

I took a deep breath.

"Will you fetch that flashlight of yours?" I asked, and he nodded and brought it from his van. I went with it over to the Ford, and took a longer, closer look. There wasn't much to see that I hadn't seen before, except for a bottle of bourbon that had been smashed in the impact. The neck and jagged top half lay on the floor to Matt's right, along with several smaller pieces and an uneven damp patch.

I walked into the garage and looked at the Ford from the front. It wouldn't be driving anywhere any more.

The big torch lit up clearly the interior of the deep shadowy garage. Quite empty now, except for a scatter of cigarette stubs against the left-hand wall. Matt had been smoking and drinking while he waited. And he'd waited a very long time.

The bullet hole faced me in the windshield and left me with the worst question unanswered.

I'd have to know.

I stood beside Matt and went over every inch of his body down to the waist. He'd taken off the cream-colored jacket and was wearing the checked shirt he'd worked in. There were no holes in it: no punctures underneath. His head was heavy. I laid it gently on the steering wheel and stepped away.

None of the bullets had hit him. They'd only smashed the windshield and blinded him, and he'd slewed a foot off course and run into the wall instead of me, and his head had gone forward hard against the slim metal post.

Slowly I returned to where Sam Hengelman stood beside Walt. He drooped with the utmost dejection and looked at me without hope.

"Did you unclip the ramp?" I asked abruptly.

He shook his head. "Didn't have time."

"Go and do it now. We're taking the horses."

He was aghast. "We can't!"

"We've got to. For Walt's sake, and your sake, and Dave Teller's sake. And mine. What do you propose? That we call the police and explain what we were all doing here?"

"We'll have to," he said despairingly.

"No. Definitely not. Go and let down the ramp."

He hesitated unbelievingly for a few seconds, and then went and did as I asked. The horses stood peacefully in the barn, apparently undisturbed by the racket, the shots and the crash. I untied the nearest, Showman, and led him quietly up the yard and into the van.

Sam watched me in silence while I tied him into one of the stalls.

"We'll never get away with it."

"Yes, we will," I said. "As long as you take these horses safely back to Lexington and never tell anyone, anyone at all, what happened here tonight. Blot it out of your mind. I'll let you know, when you get back, that you've nothing to worry about. And as long as you tell no one, you won't have."

The broad fleshy face was set in lines of anxiety.

"You've collected two horses," I said matter-of-factly. "An everyday job, collecting two horses. Forget the rest."

I returned to the barn, fetched Allyx, and loaded him up. Sam still hadn't moved.

"Look," I said, "I've . . . arranged . . . things before. There's a rule where I come from—you take a risk, you get into a mess, you get out." He blinked. "Walt threw himself in the way of that car," I said. "Matt didn't intend to kill *him*. . . . You didn't see a murder. Matt drove straight into the wall himself . . . and that too was an accident. Only two automobile accidents. You must have seen dozens. Forget it." He didn't answer, and I added brusquely, "The water can's empty. You can fill it over there."

With something like a shudder he picked up the container and went where I pointed. Sighing, I checked that he had brought three days' fodder for the stallions, which he had, and with his help, on his return, shut the precious cargo up snugly for their long haul.

"You don't happen to have any gloves around?" I asked.

"Only an old cotton pair in the tool kit."

He rooted about and finally produced them, two filthy objects covered with oil and grease which would leave marks on everything they touched, as tablebearing as fingerprints. I turned them inside out and found they were thick enough to be clean on the inside. Sam watched wordlessly while I put them on, clean side out.

"O.K.," I said. "Will you turn the van, ready to go?"

He did it cautiously as far away from Walt as he could; and when he'd finished I stepped with equal care into the car Walt had come in, touching it as little and as lightly as possible, and drove it down into the yard, stopping a little short of the screen door to the house. There I switched off the engine and lights, put on the brake, and walked back to talk to Sam where he sat in his cab.

"I've three jobs to do," I said. "I'll be back as quick as I can. Why don't you just shut your eyes for a couple of minutes and catch a nap."

"You're kidding."

I concocted a replica of a smile, and a fraction of the tension in his face unwound.

"I won't be long," I said, and he nodded, swallowing.

With his flashlight I surveyed the yard. The Luger was an automatic pistol, which meant it threw out the cartridge after each shot. No one would find the spent bullets, but eight shiny metal shells scattered near Walt's body were something else. Seven of them winked in the light as I inched the light carefully around, and I collected them into my pocket. The eighth remained obstinately invisible.

The ejection slot had been on the side of the gun away from Walt, but the cases sometimes shot out straight upward instead of sideways, and I began to wonder if the eighth could possibly have traveled far enough over to be underneath him. I didn't want to disturb him: but I had to find the little brass thimble.

Then, when I'd decided I had no choice, I saw it. Bent and dusty, partly flattened, no longer shining. I picked it up from the spot where I had been half lying in the path of Matt's car. He had run over it.

After that I attended to the ground itself. Tire marks didn't show on the rough dusty surface, but the hoofprints did to some extent. I fetched a broom of twigs from the barn and swept them out.

The garage was next. I punched through into the car the remaining corner of the windshield with its significant bullet hole, and I picked up every one of the cigarette stubs which told where and how long Matt had waited. They went into a trash can standing a few yards away from the house door.

Matt hadn't locked the house when he went out. I went in to look for one essential piece of information; the address of the place, and the name of its owner. The flashlight swept over the threadbare covers and elderly furniture, and in one drawer of a large dresser I found what the farmer used for an office. The jumble of bills and letters gave me what I wanted. Wilbur Bellman, Far Valley Farm, Kingman. On the scratch pad beside the telephone Matt had written a bonus. In heavy black ballpoint were the simple words: "Insurance. 9 P.M."

Before leaving I gave the big dilapidated living room a final circuit and the beam flickered over a photograph in a cardboard folder standing on a shelf. Something about the face in it struck me as familiar, and I swung the light back for a second and closer look.

The patient passive face of Kiddo smiled out, as untroubled as it had been when he told Walt and me about Offen's mares. Loopy unformed writing straggled over the lower half of the picture. "To Ma and Pa, from your loving son."

If Offen had sent his stud groom to Miami to join his parents, Kiddo's loyalty to his employer was a certainty. I almost admired Offen's technique in furnishing himself in one throw with an obscure hideout for the horses and a nontalking employee.

After the house there remained only Walt. Nothing to do but to say good-by.

I went down on my knees beside him in the dust, but the silent form was already subtly not Walt. Death showed. I took off one glove and touched his hand: still warm in the warm air, but without the firmness of life.

There was no point in saying to him what I felt. If his spirit was still hovering somewhere around, he would know.

I left him lying there in the dark, and went back to Sam.

He took one slow look at my face and said in an appalled voice, "You're not leaving him there?"

I nodded, and climbed up beside him.

"But you *can't* . . ."

I simply nodded again, and gestured to him to start up and drive away. He did it with a viciousness that must have rocked the stallions on their feet, and we went back to Kingman without speaking. His revulsion at what I had done reached me in almost tangible waves.

I didn't care. I felt only one grim engulfing ache for the man I'd left behind.

Chapter 18

LYNNIE put her brown hand tentatively on mine and said, "Gene, what's the matter?"

"Nothing," I said.

"You look worse than you did when you came back with Chrysalis. Much worse."

"The food doesn't agree with me."

She snorted and took her hand away. We were sitting on the sea terrace, waiting for Eunice to come down for dinner, with the sun galloping the last lap to dusk and the daiquiris tinkling with civilized ice.

"Is Walt back yet?" Lynnie said.

"No."

"He's a funny man, isn't he?" she said. "All moods and glum looks, and then suddenly he smiles, and you realize how nice he is. I like him."

After a pause I said, "So do I."

"How was San Francisco?" she asked.

"Foggy."

"What's the matter?"

"Nothing."

She sighed and shook her head.

Eunice arrived in a cloud of yellow chiffon and clanked her gold bracelet as she stretched for her drink. She was cheerful and glowing; almost too much to bear.

"Well, you son of a bitch, when did you crawl in?"

"This afternoon," I said.

"So what's new?"

"I've given up trying to find the horses."

Eunice sat up straight with a jerk. "For crying out loud!"

"I'll be starting home soon. Tomorrow evening, I expect."

"Oh, no," Lynnie said.

"Oh, yes, I'm afraid so. The holidays are over."

"You don't look as if they've done you much good," Eunice observed. "So now how do you deal with it?"

"With what?"

"With flopping. With not making out."

I said wryly, "Look it smack in the eye and dare it to bite you."

"It probably will," said Eunice sardonically. "It'll chew me to bloody bits." She drank the second quarter of her drink and looked me thoughtfully over. "Come to think of it, it seems to have done that to you already."

"Maybe I'll take up golf."

She laughed, more internally relaxed than I'd ever seen her. "Games," she said, "are a bore."

When they went in to eat I couldn't face it, and drove off instead to fetch the tape recorder from the rocks at Orpheus Farm. The short journey seemed tiresomely long. It had been nearly 450 miles back to Santa Barbara from Kingman, and neither bath, shave, nor two hours flat on the bed seemed to have had any effect.

Back in my room at the Vacationer I listened to the whole of the tape's four-hour playing time. The first conversations, two or three business calls, were from the previous morning, after Walt had put in a new reel. Then there was almost an hour and a half of an interview between Offen and a man from the bloodstock registry office. They had already been out to see the horses, and Offen was piling proof on proof that the horses in his barn were veritably Moviemaker and Centigrade. A groom who had cared for Centigrade during his racing days was asked in to sign a statement he'd made that he recognized the horse and would if necessary swear to its identity in any inquiry.

The bloodstock man apologized constantly that anyone should have doubted Offen. Offen enjoyed the scene, the joke rumbling like an undertone. After they'd gone he laughed aloud. I hoped he'd enjoyed it. He wouldn't be laughing much for a long time to come.

Next on the tape was a piece of Offen giving his houseman instructions for replenishing the drink stocks, then an hour's television program. And after that Matt telephoned.

I couldn't hear his voice at all, only Offen's replies: but they were enough.

"Hello—Matt."

"Slow down, I'm not taking this in. Where did you say you were?"

"What are you doing on the road to Las Vegas?"

"Well, I can see the house must be insured."

"You found *what* under the glove compartment?"

"How do you know it's a homer?"

"All these minute transmitters are a mystery to me."

"Who could have put it there?"

"I don't follow you. What was that about yellow paint?"

"But the police said it was vandals!"

"All right, Matt, don't shout. I'm doing my best. Now, let's get this clear. You were fumbling for a pack of cigarettes and you dislodged this . . . thing. Bug, whatever you said. And you're worried now that Hawkins and Prensela put it in your car, and that they used that and the yellow paint to follow you, so that they know where you've been staying, or maybe. Is that right?"

"Matt, I think you're blowing this thing up too big."

"But did you actually *see* a plane following you?"

"Well, yes, sure, if you think you should go back, go back. The horses are far more important than the insurance on the house. But I think you're wrong. Hawkins and Prensela have been concentrating on Moviemaker and Centigrade here, they've stirred up the D.A.'s office from L.A. and the bloodstock registry, and it's been a three-ringed circus here for the last couple of days. They wouldn't have been trying to find any horses anywhere else, because they're sure they're here in the barn."

"Well, I don't *know* who could have planted the bug."

"Yeah. All right. Go on back, then."

"Call me in the morning."

"Good night, Matt."

The receiver went down, and for a few seconds there were the indistinct noises of Offen going over the conversation again in his mind, punctuating it with "umphs" and small doubtful grunts.

I switched the tape off temporarily and thought bitterly about Matt finding the bug. I hadn't had a chance to remove it: on my first night visit to the farm the car in the garage had been the one he'd rented while his own was being cleaned of paint. But neither had I looked upon it as a very great hazard, because the little capsules were light and clung tightly. It had been long odds against him groping for cigarettes while driving in the dark, and dislodging it. I hadn't taken it into account.

Some time on his way back to the farm it must have struck him that the insurance appointment might be phony; that if we had tricked him into going to Las Vegas once already, we might be tricking him again. If we'd got him out of the way, it could only be to take the horses. So he'd wait; in the dark, ready to spring.

He must have begun to think, when he'd sat out the three hours it took to mend the gasket, that Uncle Bark was right and he was wrong: but all the same he'd gone on waiting. And, in the end, we had come.

I switched the tape on again for the rest. The whole night had been telescoped into the few seconds' silence, because when Offen made his next call it was clearly morning.

"Yola, is that you?"

A faint clacking reached the bug. Yola's higher-pitched voice disturbed more air.

"Have you heard from Matt?"

"_____."

"No, he said he'd call me this morning, and he hasn't. I can't get any answer from the farm."

"_____."

"I'd forgotten the hens and the calves."

"_____."

"Well, not really. He called me last night because he had some crazy idea Hawkins had traced the horses . . ."

A loud squawk from Yola.

"Something about a listening bug and yellow paint."

Yola talked for some time and when Offen answered he sounded anxious.

"Yeah, I know he found the first one when we thought that was impossible. . . . Do you really think Matt may be right?"

"_____."

"Yola, that's right out. Why don't you go yourself?"

"_____."

"Close the ranch then. Send them all home."

"_____."

"Look, if you're right, if Matt's right . . . Say when he went back last night the D.A.'s men were sitting there waiting for him? Say they're sitting there right now, waiting for me to turn up and see why Matt doesn't answer his calls? No, Yola, I'm not walking into that farm and find I have to answer questions like what I am doing there, and what are those two horses in the barn, with Moviemaker and Centigrade's registrations tattooed inside their lips? I'm not going."

"_____."

"Matt may be off on some plan of his own."

"_____."

"No. I'll give him today. If I haven't heard from him by morning I'll . . . well, I'll think of something."

Yola's final remark was loud, and I heard it clearly. Full of anxiety, full of anguish.

"If anything's happened to Matt . . ."

The end of the tape ran off the reel, and I switched off the recorder. For Yola, as for Walt's wife, life would never be the same again.

I went to bed and lay awake, feeling feverish from lack of sleep. Relaxed every limb, but my mind would have none of it. It was filled too full, as it had been all day, of a picture of Walt still lying on his back in the farmyard. The sun had risen and blazed on him, and set again. He would have no shelter until tomorrow. I couldn't sleep until he had. I tried to, but I couldn't.

On my way back to Santa Barbara I'd stopped for coffee and a handful of change, and I'd telephoned to Paul M. Zeissen in the Buttress Life office on Thirty-third Street. It had been nearly 6 P.M. New York time. Zeissen was preparing to go home for the weekend. I was a little worried, I told him, about Walt. He had gone to do some life insurance business on a farm in Arizona, and I hadn't heard from him since. Zeissen and I talked it over for a few minutes in unurgent civilized tones, and arranged finally that if I hadn't heard from Walt by morning, Buttress Life would ring the Arizona State Police in Kingman, and ask them as a favor to go out to the farm, just to check.

In the morning I would ring Zeissen at his home. By noon, perhaps, the Kingman police would reach the farm. They would read the story: insurance salesman arrives for appointment, gets out of car. Matt Clive, hurrying back to meet him, swings into the yard, sees a dark figure too late, hits him, runs straight on into wall because judgment suspended by horror at collision. Matt, with whiskey inside him and a bottle in the car. Inside the house, the 9 P.M. insurance appointment written in Matt's hand. And nothing else. No horses. No suggestion of visitors. No sign that it could have been anything but a tragically unlucky accident.

Matt had been good at accidents.

So was I.

I lay on my stomach on the beach all morning while Lynnie sat beside me and trickled sand through her fingers. Eunice had gone to Santa Monica, down the coast.

"Are you really going home this evening?" Lynnie said.

"First hop, yes."

"Would you mind . . . if I came with you?"

I stirred in surprise.

"I thought you wanted to stay here forever."

"Mm. But that was with you . . . and Eunice. Now you're going . . . and Eunice hasn't been here much this week, you know. I've spent ages all on my own, and there isn't that much to do on a beach, when you do it every day."

"Where has Eunice been?"

"Santa Monica, like now. There's some place there she spends all her time in, where they import vases and bits of sculpture and expensive light fittings, and things like that. She took me there the day before yesterday . . . I must say it's pretty gorgeous. Marvelous fabrics, too."

"She might feel hurt if you just pack up and leave her."

"Well, no. I mentioned it to her before she went this morning, and honestly I think if anything she was relieved. She just said if I really wanted to go, O.K., and she would probably be moving down to Santa Monica in a day or two anyway."

"If you really want to, then. I'm catching the night flight to Washington. . . . I've a visit to make in Lexington tomorrow morning. After that, back to New York, and home."

"You don't mind if I tag along?" She sounded a bit uncertain.

"Come to think of it," I said, "you can wake me at the stops."

We had a sandwich for lunch which I couldn't eat, and at two the girl from the reception desk came to say I was wanted on the telephone. Paul M. Zeissen told me in a suitably hushed voice that the Arizona police had been most cooperative and had gone to Bellman's farm as asked, and had found Walt dead. I made shocked noises. Zeissen said would I pack Walt's things and send them back? I said I would.

"I suppose," he suggested diffidently, "that you and he had not completed your other business?"

"The horses?"

"One horse. Allyx," he said reprovingly. "Showman was insured with another company."

"Oh . . . yes. Allyx should be in circulation, safe and authenticated, within a month or so. I expect the Blood Horse Breeders Association will be getting in touch with you. Walt worked very hard at this, and it was entirely owing to his efforts that Buttress Life will be recovering most of the million and a half it paid out."

"Where did he find the horse?"

"I can't tell you. Does it matter?"

"No . . ." he said thoughtfully. "Goods back, no questions asked . . . we work on that principle, the same as any other company."

"Right then," I said. "And you'll of course pay his commission to his widow?"

"Uh . . . of course. And naturally Walt had insured his life with us. . . . Mrs. Prensela will be well provided for, I feel sure."

Provided for. Money. But no Walt. No picnic.

I said good-by to Zeissen and went slowly back to Lynnie. When I told her Walt was dead, she cried for him.

Upstairs, when I packed his clothes, I lingered a good while over the framed photograph of him with Amy and the kids, and in the end put it in my suitcase, not his. It could hardly be the only photograph his wife would have of him, and I didn't think she'd worry much if it didn't return with his baggage.

Eunice came back tired and abstracted from Santa Monica, and after absorbing the shock of Walt's death was unaffected when Lynnie told her over early dinner that she was going home with me.

"Much better to travel with a man to look after you, honey," she agreed absent-mindedly: and then, giving me a more characteristic sharp glance, added, "Don't let him get up to any tricks."

Lynnie sighed. "He wouldn't."

"Huh," she said, but without conviction, and then asked me, "Will you be seeing Dave when you get back?"

I nodded. "Very soon after."

"Tell him then, will you, that I've found a darling little business in Santa Monica. They're looking for a partner with some capital, to open another branch, and if the accounts are right I'd like to do it. I'll write him, of course, but you could explain. . . . I guess you could explain better than anyone."

"I'll explain."

She said she was too tired to come all the way back to Los Angeles to see us off, and we said good-by to her in the lobby, where she kissed Lynnie and then me on the cheek with a quite surprising strength of feeling.

Lynnie said, as we drove away, "I'll miss her. Isn't that extraordinary. I'll really miss her."

"You'll come back."

"It won't be the same."

I returned the rented car to the Hertz agent at the airport, we caught the plane to Washington, and I made up on parts of the way for the three nights without sleep. Lynnie said at Lexington that she could quite see why I needed someone to wake me at the stops.

We went in a taxi to Jeff Roots's house and his teen-age daughters took Lynnie off for a swim in the pool while I sat with him under his vine-covered trellis and thought how cool and substantial he looked in his bright open-necked Sunday shirt.

"Sam Hengelman should reach Lexington sometime this afternoon or early evening," I said. "He'll call you to know where to take the horses."

"That's all fixed," Roots nodded.

"Would you give him a message from me?"

"Sure."

"Just tell him everything's O.K.; that I said so."

"Sure. You are, aren't you, one hundred percent certain that these two definitely are Showman and Allyx?"

"One hundred percent. There isn't the slightest doubt."

He sighed. "I'll get the identification started. Though who is to know Showman after ten years? A bay with no markings . . . and only a four-year-old when he came from England." He paused, then said, "Have you any suggestions as to how we can start prosecuting Offen for fraud and theft?"

I shook my head. "I'm not a policeman. Not interested in punishment, only prevention." I smiled briefly. "I came to get the horses back. Nothing else. Well, they're back. I've done what I was engaged for, and that's as far as I go."

He eyed me assessingly. "Do you want Offen to go on collecting huge stud fees, then?"

"He won't," I said. "Not if someone starts a quick rumor immediately that both Moviemaker and Centigrade have been suffering from an obscure virus which will certainly have affected their virility. Owners of mares can be quietly advised to insist they don't pay any stud fees until the foals have shown their quality. After that . . . Well, Offen does legally own Moviemaker and Centigrade, and he's entitled to the fees they earn on their own merits."

"You're extraordinary," he said. "Don't you want to see Offen behind bars?"

"Not passionately," I said. Offen had enjoyed his prestige almost more than his income. He would be losing both. And Yola . . . She was going to have to work hard without Matt, and probably without the expensive house on Pitts. Bars seemed superfluous.

He shook his head, giving me up as a bad job. "We'll have to prosecute, I'm sure of it. I'll have to get lawyers to see about it."

He called the houseman to bring out drinks, and merely sighed when I said I'd as soon share his sugar-free tonic.

We sipped the well-iced innocuous stuff and he said again that Offen would have to be prosecuted, if only to provide a reason for Allyx and Showman having disappeared for so long a time and to account for the tattoo marks inside their mouths.

"I can see you would think that," I said. "I also think you'll have a terrible job proving that any of the mares booked to Moviemaker and Centigrade were actually covered by Showman or Allyx. I didn't find Showman and Allyx on Offen's farm. I doubt if anyone would testify that they were ever there. Certainly Offen would deny it, and go on denying it to the bitter end. It's his only hope." I paused. "I did manage to get some tape recordings, but unfortunately, even if they could be used as evidence, they are inconclusive. Offen never mentioned Showman or Allyx by name."

Roots stared gloomily into space.

"This makes it difficult," he said. "What you are in fact saying is that we know Offen switched the stallions, because of the tattoo marks, but no one will be able to prove it?"

I looked down to where Lynnie was jumping into the pool in a big-splash contest with Roots's daughters. Her lighthearted laughter floated up, carefree and very young.

"I wouldn't try," I said. "Rightly or wrongly I decided to repossess the stolen goods by stealing them back. First, so that Offen would have no chance of destroying them. Second, so that there shouldn't be years of delay while lawyers argued the case, years of the stallions standing idle, with their value diminishing day by day and their bloodlines wasting. Third, and most important, that there should be no chance of Offen getting them back once the dust had settled. Because if he had any sense he would swear, and provide witnesses to swear, that the horses in dispute were two unraced half-bred animals of no account, and he'd explain the tattoos on their lips by saying he'd used them to try out some new type of ink. What more likely, he would say, than that he should repeat the numbers of his two best horses? He could make it sound a lot more reasonable than that he should have stolen two world-famous stallions and conducted a large-scale fraud. He has great personal charm."

Roots nodded. "I've met him."

"Showman and Allyx were being looked after by Offen's nephew," I said. "Offen can say he'd lent him two old nags to hack around on, and he can't imagine why anyone would want to steal them."

"He could put up an excellent defense, I see that," he admitted.

"His present stud groom is innocent," I added. "And would convince anyone of it. If you leave things as they are, Offen won't get Allyx and Showman back. If you prosecute him, he may."

He looked shattered, staring into his glass but seeing with experienced eyes every side of the sticky problem.

"We could try blood tests," he said at last.

"Blood tests?"

"For paternity," he nodded. "If there is any doubt about which horse has sired a certain foal, we take blood tests. If one disputed sire's blood is of a similar group to the foal's, and the other disputed sire's is different, we conclude that the foal was sired by the similar sire."

"And like in human beings," I asked, "you can tell which horse could *not* have sired which foal, but you couldn't say which, of a similar blood group, actually did?"

"That's right."

We thought it over. Then he said cheerfully, "If we can prove that none of the so-called Moviemaker foals could in fact have been sired by Moviemaker, but could all have been sired by Showman, we'll have Offen sewed up tight."

"Couldn't he possibly have made sure, before he ever bought Moviemaker, that his and Showman's blood groups were similar? I mean, if he's a breeder, he'd know about blood tests."

Roots's gloom returned. "I suppose it's possible. And possible that Centigrade and Allyx are similar too." He looked up suddenly and caught me smiling. "It's all right for you to think it's funny," he said wryly, matching my expression. "You don't have to sort out the mess. What in God's name are we going to do about the Studbook? Moviemaker's—that is, Showman's—get are already siring foals, in some cases. The mix-up is in the second generation. How are we ever going to put it straight?"

"Even if," I pointed out, trying hard to keep the humor out of my voice and face, "even if you prove Moviemaker couldn't have sired the foals he's supposed to have done, you can't prove Showman *did*."

He gave me a comically pained look. "What other sire could have got such brilliant stock?" He shook his head. "We'll pin it on Offen in the end, even if we have to wait until after Showman and Allyx have been resyndicated and their first official crops have won as much stake money as all the others. Offen wouldn't be able to say then that they were two half-bred nags he'd given his nephew to hack around on. We'll get him in the end."

"The racing scandal of the year," I said, smiling.

"Of the year? Are you kidding? Of the century."

Lynnie and I flew from Kennedy that night on a Super VC 10, with dinner over Canada at midnight and breakfast over Ireland three hours later. I spent the interval looking at her while she slept beside me in her sloped-back chair. Her skin was close-textured like a baby's and her face was that of a child. The woman inside was still a bud, with a long way to grow.

Keeble met us at Heathrow, and as usual it was raining. Lynnie kissed him affectionately. He went so far as to shake my hand. There was a patch of stubble on his left cheek, and the eyes blinked quickly behind the mild glasses. Santa Barbara was 6,000 miles away. We were home.

Keeble suggested a cup of coffee before we left the airport and asked his daughter how she'd enjoyed herself. She told him nonstop for twenty minutes, her suntan glowing in the gray summer morning and her brown eyes alight.

He looked finally from her to me, and his face subtly contracted.

"And what have you been doing?" he said.

Lynnie answered when I didn't. "He's been with us on the beach a good deal of the time," she said doubtfully.

Keeble stroked her arm. "Did you find the horses?" he asked.

I nodded.

"All three?"

"With help."

"I told Dave I'd drop you off at the hospital when we leave here," he said. "He's still strung up, but he hopes to be out next week."

"I've a lot to tell him, and there's a lot he'll have to decide." The worst being, I thought, whether to carry on with his move alongside Orpheus Farm, or to disappoint Eunice in her newfound business. Nothing was ever simple. Nothing was easy.

"You don't look well," Keeble said abruptly.

"I'll live," I said, and his eyes flickered with a mixture of surprise and speculation. I smiled lopsidedly and said it again, "I'll live."

We stood up to go. Instead of shaking hands Lynnie suddenly put her arms round my waist and her head on my chest.

"I don't want to say good-by," she said indistinctly. "I want to see you again."

"Well," I said reasonably, "you will."

"I mean . . . often."

I met Keeble's eyes over her head. He was watching her gravely, but without disquiet.

"She's too young," I said to him, and he knew exactly

what I meant. Not that I was too old for her, but that she was too young for me. Too young in experience, understanding, and wickedness.

"I'll get older," she said. "Will twenty-one do?"

Her father laughed, but she gripped my arm. "Will it?"

"Yes," I said recklessly, and found one second later that I really meant it.

"She'll change her mind," Keeble said with casual certainty.

I said, "Of course," to him, but Lynnie looked up into my eyes and shook her head.

It was late afternoon when I got back to the flat. The tidy, dull, unwelcoming rooms hadn't changed a bit. When I looked at the kitchen I remembered Lynnie making burned scrambled eggs, and I felt a fierce disturbing wish that she would soon make some more.

I unpacked. The evening stretched grayly ahead.

I sat and stared vacantly at the bare walls.

If was a grinding word, I thought. If Sam Hengelman had taken longer to mend that gasket, Walt would have found us on the road and would have stopped us from going to the farm. If Sam had mended it faster, we'd have reached the farm well before Walt, and Matt would have killed me, as he'd meant.

If I hadn't decided to recover the horses by stealing them, Walt would be alive. They might collectively be worth nearly $5 million, but they weren't worth Walt's life.

I wished I'd never started.

The gray day turned to gray dusk. I got up and switched on the light, and fetched two objects to put on the low table beside my chair.

The Luger, and the photograph of Walt with his wife and kids.

The trouble with being given a gift you don't really want is that you feel so mean if you throw it away. Especially if it cost more than the giver could afford.

I won't throw away Walt's gift. Even if Lynnie changes her mind, I'll survive.

Tired beyond feeling, I went to bed at ten. I put the Luger under the pillow, and hung the photograph on the wall.

And slept.